Mark
of the
Breenan

Emma Shelford

Enjoy the magic!
- Emma Shelford

This is a work of fiction. Names, characters, places, and incidents either are the product of the author's imagination or are used factitiously, and any resemblance to any persons, living or dead, business establishments, events, or locales is entirely coincidental.

MARK OF THE BREENAN

Copyright © 2014 Emma Shelford
Cover design by Melissa Bowles
Editing by Precision Editing Group

www.emmashelford.com

First edition: October 2014
ISBN: 978-1502318329

For Mum

Prologue

Gwen screamed, as loud and high as only a four-year old can.

"No! No, I don't want to go!" Her breathing came quickly, in and out and in again. She wouldn't go. She didn't want to leave their house, her room with the pink hippos painted on the wall, the rope swing dangling from the apple tree in the backyard.

Her father sighed and knelt down to look into her tear-filled eyes.

"I'm sorry Gwennie, but we have to move. If we don't, Daddy won't have a job." His voice became lighter, more joking. "If Daddy doesn't have a job, all we'll be able to eat is broccoli and brussels sprouts. That wouldn't be very nice, would it?"

Gwen glared at him through narrowed eyes, her hands balled into fists and her body stiff. He couldn't make her go. She squeezed out a few more words to make him understand.

"No. No. No. I won't go." She shut her eyes tight against the unfairness of it all. Her whole body started to shudder and something deep inside her belly began to get hot and wriggly.

"I know it's hard, Gwennie, but sometimes life is mean like that." Her father put his hand on her shoulder. "You'll like Vancouver, I promise."

Gwen's body was tight and hot. The warmth in her middle was spreading, the heat flowing into her legs and arms and up her neck. Her cheeks were hot and flushed like she'd just run back from the corner store. Something began to rattle noisily behind her father, but she ignored it. Nothing mattered except making her father understand that they couldn't leave.

"What the…" her father said incredulously.

Gwen couldn't contain herself any longer. She opened her mouth and a huge release of a scream ripped out of her chest. The heat flowed out and away from her body in a great wave.

There was a shattering explosion behind her father. Gwen's eyes popped open in shock as her father turned back to face her. His face dripped with black ink, but between dark streaks his skin was bloodless white. His wide eyes looked at her with a wariness tinged by fear.

Gwen's lip trembled. What had just happened? Had she made her artist father's ink bottle explode? She had. It was her fault. She was just so angry. She didn't feel that way anymore. Her body was cool and calm now, the extraordinary heat of the previous moment extinguished.

She hadn't meant to hurt her daddy. Her eyes filled

with tears and she blinked quickly as her lip quivered. She stepped forward.

"I'm sorry, Daddy," she sobbed. Her father quickly dropped to his knees and put his arms around her. She shook in his embrace and he kissed the top of her head.

She pulled back, sniffing.

"We can go to Vancouver. I don't mind." She bit her bottom lip as she looked around the room at the destruction, ink splatters covering the walls and ceiling in a mockery of wallpaper. "I don't mind anymore."

Chapter 1

Bzzzzt.

Eighteen year-old Gwen Cooper twitched out of a daydream from the vibration of her phone. She glanced around at her university classmates, all either staring vacantly toward the front or scribbling notes. The professor had her back to the class, focused on keeping her laser pointer steady on the screen above. Gwen slid her hand into her jeans pocket and wiggled the phone free. A text waited from her best friend Ellie Brown.

I have an adventure for us. You ARE coming.

Gwen smiled wryly. Ellie was always hatching up crazy plans, like the time she wanted Gwen to join her in a hot yoga-polar bear swim combo class. She texted back.

What is it THIS time? ;)

We're going to ENGLAND. To live in a CASTLE.

For a whole MONTH.

***

"We are *absolutely* going." Ellie slurped her pop with enthusiasm, her blond braid quivering as she wriggled in her chair.

"I'm not signing up for anything without more info." Gwen took a resolute bite of her tuna sandwich. The cafeteria buzzed around them with the hungry hum of undergrads. Gwen and Ellie had managed to snag a table as another group was leaving, Ellie swooping in front of some unfortunate dawdlers as Gwen bent her head and slipped into a chair, avoiding the eyes of the slow students.

"It's a proper university, we take courses and get credits and everything," Ellie said. "So we can just use the credits as electives. It's all focused on British stuff. Art history, English lit, as long as it has a British theme." She waved her hand in the air. "And did I mention it's in a castle? In England?" She put her hands flat on the table, imitating the voice of a pompous psychology professor they often mocked. "This is an incredible opportunity to immerse ourselves in our studies, Gwendolyn."

Gwen laughed and took another bite of her sandwich.

"You just want to go because you're into everything medieval. How old is the castle?"

"It was built in fourteen fifty-three," Ellie said in an awestruck tone. "But seriously, it'd be so cool. Check out the website later." She tugged a pamphlet out of her

9

backpack and shoved it across the table. "What do you think?"

Gwen was tempted. The classes did look interesting, and she hadn't started looking for a summer job yet. Her stomach gave a little twinge of excitement as she skimmed the pamphlet—it was filled with glossy photos of green pastures and crumbling castles. She'd never done much traveling. The thought of a trip abroad both excited her and made her nervous. Her stomach lurched again as she thought of another reason to go to England, one she didn't bring up with Ellie. She took her time over the pamphlet, sensing Ellie wriggling with impatience across the table. She hid a smile.

"One last, very important point." Ellie leaned forward toward Gwen, her index finger tapping the point home on the table. "British boys." She leaned back as if she'd given irrefutable evidence at a trial.

Gwen couldn't help laughing aloud at this.

"Oh, Ellie. You're such a sucker for an accent." Ellie stuck her tongue out at her. Gwen grinned and looked down at the pamphlet again. "Wait a minute—it's all of May. You're going to miss the Renaissance fair. You love the Renaissance fair. How will you deal?" She raised an eyebrow.

"But this is like all Renaissance fairs at once!" Ellie bounced in her seat.

"But wasn't your medieval dance troupe giving a demonstration this year?" Gwen raised an incredulous eyebrow at Ellie. "You've been practicing like crazy, on top of all your other dance classes."

As she always did, Ellie said, "You should totally join one my classes. It's so much fun." Gwen bit her apple without looking at Ellie, and Ellie sighed dramatically. "Fine, miss out on all the action. One day you'll stop caring about looking silly and just have a good time. I know it." She looked out the window for a moment, and said tentatively, "You know, it might be nice to see where you were born. Maybe you could find some relatives there or something."

Gwen swallowed the last of her apple, avoiding Ellie's eyes.

"Yeah, I thought of that."

***

The elevator wheezed and trundled up to the eleventh floor apartment Gwen shared with her artist father, Alan Cooper. The mirrored wall across from Gwen reflected mid-length black hair whose soft waves contrasted with the sharp planes of her face. Gwen wasn't conventionally attractive. But her face was so distinctive, all angles and high cheekbones and sharp lines, that it warranted a second look. Hazel-green eyes, usually lively and quizzical, gazed vaguely as Gwen's thoughts strayed to Ellie's castle abroad.

Gwen snapped to attention as the elevator creaked open. She shifted her backpack to one shoulder as she dug for keys in her raincoat pocket. She fitted the key into the lock, brushing her left hand over the doorframe's peeling paint as she entered the apartment. Throwing her keys on the carpeted floor in the entryway, she shrugged out of her coat and backpack, calling out a greeting.

"Hello?"

"In the studio," a voice replied a few beats later. Gwen smiled. Her father was in the middle of a project and his concentration was legendary. She walked through the kitchen, grabbing a banana on the way, and leaned against the doorway of her father's 'studio.' The apartment they shared had only two bedrooms, so the studio did double duty. The wall to the left of the window housed a narrow bed and was plastered with sketches and watercolors depicting scenes of nature and landscapes, although these were liberally interspersed with images of Gwen. The right-hand wall was a pure, unblemished white. Gwen's father said he was inspired by both walls, "One for ideas, one for peace. Chaos and calm in equal measure. That's what creates magic."

Gwen watched her father smear a mossy green over a canvas with sure strokes.

"Do you think the landlord will ever paint our hallway?" she asked casually. "He said he'd do it three months ago."

"Oh, maybe someday. But putting up with him is how we get such low rent, right downtown. And can you beat the view?" He swept his paintbrush majestically toward the wall of windows. The setting sun glinted off a nearby skyscraper, highlighting the deep green of Stanley Park and glittering off the ocean beyond which was uncommonly still for January.

Gwen laughed and took a bite of her banana.

"Fair enough,' she said between chews.

"So, what'd you learn today?" Her father peered at her over his glasses. His kind, cheerful face tried to look stern and professorial, but laughing brown eyes softened the expression.

12

Gwen was ready for his question.

"There's a castle, in England."

"Indeed, there are many." Her father raised an eyebrow.

"Let me finish!" She reached forward and swatted his arm. "Ellie wants to go. It's a one month program where you go live in a castle and take classes for credit. It's affiliated with the university here." She bit her lip. "I think there are scholarships if you're accepted in."

"So, back to the old country. I never took you, did I?" He swiveled side to side on his stool. "I think it's high time. So Ellie wants to go. Do you want to?" He gazed at her searchingly.

Gwen looked out the window, considering.

"Actually, yes. The courses sound good, and I'd like to see the country where I was born. And of course Ellie needs someone to look after her." Gwen didn't add the final reason, the most important of all.

Her father laughed, a nice deep one from the belly.

"She sure does." He swiveled again. "Well, if it's what you want, I'm all for it. Try for the scholarship, but we'll make it work no matter what." He raised an arm, and Gwen hugged him close.

"Your paint's drying," she said.

"Darn. Oh well. Pizza tonight?"

"I'll go call it in," she said, kissing the top of his head.

***

Gwen's father was still painting when the pizza arrived, so Gwen delivered a few pieces to the studio, grabbed her own, and flopped onto the couch on her stomach. She flipped her laptop open and booted up, glancing at the studio door. There was no sign of her father, except for the occasional squeak of his swivel stool. She typed in the web address of the British census from memory. In the box labelled *Given Name* she typed 'Isolde,' and '1960-1975' in the date of birth. She hit enter. A long list of hyperlinked names appeared on the screen, half of the links on the first page already purple with previous clicks. She selected the next on the list, an 'Isolde Smith.' Results flashed onto the screen.

Isolde Smith

Born August 25th, 1961

Emigrated to United States of America 1976

This one had moved out of the country at age fifteen. Gwen tried the next name.

Isolde O'Connor

Born May 13th, 1968

This one looked promising. Isolde O'Connor was the same age as her father and had lived in Cambridgeshire the year Gwen was born, eighteen years ago. She still lived there now. Gwen opened a search engine and typed 'Isolde O'Connor Cambridgeshire.' She reached into the backpack at her side and carefully pulled out a folded piece of paper, opening it gingerly and smoothing out the well-worn creases. A woman's face appeared, sketched in pencil. She was exotically beautiful, with wavy dark hair cascading past the edge of the image. Her large eyes gazed out of the page, sultry and confident. Her pointed chin was raised in pride and self-awareness of her beauty. In her father's loopy hand on the bottom right was written 'Isolde.'

Gwen propped the paper up beside her laptop screen and pulled up image results for her search. Twelve pictures of the same woman appeared, grinning and apple cheeked, blond but greying hair piled on top of her head in a loose bun. The rest were unrelated photos. Gwen's shoulders slumped resignedly.

"Oh, love. Are you still trying to find your mother?"

Gwen jumped and turned to see her father behind her. She realized belatedly that the squeaking of his chair had ceased minutes ago.

"I just thought—if I actually go to England…" Her voice faltered. She turned back and stared into the eyes of the portrait. Her father sighed and sat down on the couch beside her.

"Scooch a little. We've looked before and found nothing. I doubt she would have appeared since."

"I know." Gwen leaned her head into her arms. "I just thought I'd try."

Her father rubbed her back in slow comforting circles.

"I'm sorry I don't know more. She wasn't very forthcoming, and I didn't know you'd be arriving on my doorstep nine months later, needing answers."

"Tell me again how you two met," she said into the couch.

"Well now," he said, leaning back. She wriggled to accommodate him. "I was doing a 'grand tour' of Europe, as I liked to call it, off traveling while more diligent and responsible friends worked. It was just me, my backpack, and an entire continent's worth of art at my fingertips. England was on the list, of course, because I had my Aunty Ada to visit. I'd run out of

15

money by the time I hit Cambridge, so I got a job sweeping out a bakery that Aunty Ada's friend owned.

"One day, when it was actually clear for once instead of all the endless rain, I snuck away from my sweeping and took my sketchpad for a walk. I wanted to capture the lush greenery and rolling fields that folk in the town seemed to take for granted."

"Enough about art, Dad. When did you meet my mother?" Gwen nudged her father with her knee.

"I'm telling the story, impatient one. Well, as I tried to figure out the best way to capture the mist and fog, I heard a voice behind me.

"'You have a talent for art,' it said. I whirled around and saw the most beautiful woman I'd ever seen. Her face and form were flawless, pale skin against perfect red lips. She had on a green swirling cloud of a dress. Even now I've never seen fabric like it. It was an old-fashioned dress that fell to the ground, with ribbons and laces and huge floating sleeves. She had spring flowers entwined in her hair, and somehow the petals floated down, even though the flowers stayed whole. I was young and didn't know what to say, although I imagine I'd still be speechless now. My first thought was, 'If I could capture her likeness on canvas, I'd consider myself a true artist.'

"She asked me to come with her, and it would have been a stronger and more foolish man than me to say no. She led me to a clearing in the woods where there was a pavilion, with food and drink, velvet pillows, the whole works. I stayed with her for seven days, not thinking even once about Aunty Ada worrying, just blissfully happy and falling deeply in love. On the eighth morning

I awoke shivering, alone and naked in the middle of the clearing. Everything had vanished—plates, pillows, everything. And *she* was gone, taking a piece of me with her.

"I stumbled down to my aunt's house in the village, naked as the day I was born. Aunty Ada was absolutely speechless when she saw me."

"What did Isolde tell you about herself?" Gwen knew the answer, but this was her role in the story that her father had told her since she was a little girl.

"Only that her name was Isolde, and that she lived nearby, but too far away for me to imagine. She tended to speak in riddles. I didn't mind. It just made her more mysterious." He gazed out the window for a moment. "I wandered the hills for weeks after that, looking for her. Eventually I gave up—if she were still around, she obviously didn't want to be found. I left Cambridge with a bruised heart. Months later, I called Aunty Ada from a flea-bitten hostel in Vienna. She was frantic, saying a baby had arrived on her doorstep overnight. The baby had a piece of paper tucked into its blankets, a sketch that looked like mine, she said. I was confused, but agreed to travel to Cambridge right away to help. She showed me the sketch when I arrived. It was a portrait of Isolde that I'd drawn and given to her during our week together. I knew then that the baby was mine. Isolde had left me a perfect little creature, the creation of our magical time together. I don't know why she left you there, but I'm so glad she did. I can't imagine my life without you." He leaned over and kissed Gwen's cheek.

Gwen kissed his cheek in return, and he closed the laptop lid.

17

"I hate to see you on such a fruitless errand. If you do go to England, promise me you'll enjoy yourself and not spend too much time chasing phantoms."

Gwen sighed.

"I promise. It'd still be nice to see where I was born, though."

Her father heaved himself off the couch with a grunt.

"Well, it's a beautiful country. I don't think you'll be disappointed." He moved into the kitchen. "Where's that pizza she ordered?" he muttered.

"I brought it into the studio for you! Honestly, Dad, open your eyes." She rolled her own at him as he made his way to his room. She opened the laptop, stared at the browser screen for a few moments, and then resolutely closed the window. The sketch, however, she carefully folded and tucked into a side pouch of her backpack.

Chapter 2

Three months later, Gwen and Ellie stared up at a castle. It squatted heavily on a small rise, surrounded by a deep ditch filled with water in which two swans floated languidly. A gravel drive wound sinuously up to a bridge crossing the moat. A copse of trees lined the edge of a brilliant green lawn and disappeared from sight behind the castle.

Ellie's face glowed with a happiness that approached awe.

"This is amazing."

Gwen couldn't help herself. She started laughing.

"This is literally your dream come true, isn't it?" She grabbed Ellie by the crook of her arm and pulled her down the drive, their wheeled suitcases dragging and making crunching noises against the gravel.

Inside the massive wooden doors was a whirlwind of

luggage and bodies. Gwen and Ellie were quickly herded into a reception area by a friendly but harried woman, where they registered and received their room assignment.

Gwen looked incredulously at the paper she clutched in her hand.

"They gave us a map of the castle. This place is so big we need a *map*."

"Isn't it gorgeous? Here, let's take these stairs. Spiral stairs are the best." Ellie ran toward a doorway in the vast stone wall nearby, her suitcase bouncing behind her. Dim light from a tiny slit window illuminated a narrow spiral staircase winding upward.

Gwen consulted her map four floors later, her breath coming in short pants.

"I shouldn't have packed so much." She called forward to Ellie, "I blame the weight of my bag on you."

Ellie was already halfway down a hallway, her own map dangling from her hand.

"You'll thank me later when you can dress for any occasion." Ellie started reading the placards that hung from the numerous doors lining the hallway.

"The Silver Room, the Velvet Room—ooo, I bet that one's nice—the Amber Room, the Green Room! Here's ours." Ellie pushed open a heavy door on the left side of the hall. Gwen hurried forward, anxious despite herself to see their new home for the next month. She reminded herself not to get too excited. Already her breath came more quickly than was sensible. She had to let Ellie express enough enthusiasm for both of them—Gwen couldn't afford to lose control. Luckily, Ellie was excellent at expressing herself.

"Oh Gwen, it's perfect!"

Gwen rounded the corner. Her eyes were instantly distracted by an excessive amount of green. The bedspreads were a rich forest green, green brocade curtains draped over deep recessed windows, and even a painting suspended on the stone wall beside the dresser was a tasteful nature scene with a prominent green willow dominating the frame.

Ellie dropped her bag and leapt onto the nearest bed. Her ecstatic expression became slightly marred by a hint of disappointment. She turned to Gwen, and spoke in a tone of someone presenting unwelcome news.

"It's a modern bed." Ellie patted the offending piece of furniture. "I thought it might be straw. More authentic, you know."

Gwen started to laugh.

"Seriously? You're staying in a medieval castle, in England, and that's not enough?"

Ellie joined her in laughing, and for a while they couldn't stop.

***

"What do you think?" Ellie's eyes were wide with excitement, her shining face waiting for Gwen's reaction. "For the fancy dress ball later this month."

In her hands she held out a long dress, slightly wrinkled from its cross-Atlantic journey in a suitcase. Gwen thought that 'gown' might be a more appropriate term for the garment. It had a crushed green velvet overdress, with a lace bodice and huge trailing sleeves. The dropped neckline sported lace that sparkled with

21

fake diamonds. It was a perfect medieval dress.

Gwen's chin dropped.

"You have got to be joking."

"You don't like it? I made it for you. It should fit." Ellie swished the skirt back and forth.

"It's incredible, Ellie. You've outdone yourself as usual. But can you really imagine me waltzing around in it?" Gwen shuddered as visions of the spectacle she'd make of herself blossomed before her eyes.

"Yes! You'll be perfect in it. Honestly, Gwen, you've got to let your hair down sometime." Ellie held the dress up to Gwen, and pulled at a lock of Gwen's hair. "You should totally dye a piece of your hair green to match." She grinned wickedly. "Show a bit of your rebellious side. If you have one."

Gwen rolled her eyes.

"For the last time, I am not dying my hair." She turned with an air of finality to her own suitcase and continued her interrupted unpacking.

Ellie tossed the dress on Gwen's bed and flopped onto her own with a dramatic sigh.

"Isn't it all so perfect? I can't believe we're in England. In a castle. I'm going to explode from excitement."

Gwen picked up her dress.

"Well, don't explode over your handiwork." She carefully hung the dress in an enormous wardrobe beside the door. "How am I supposed to wear it with Ellie guts all down the front?"

Ellie smiled smugly.

"I knew you'd come around. And I didn't even have to guilt-trip, much."

Gwen smacked Ellie's ankles, the closest part of Ellie she could reach.

"Come on, let's go explore before dinner. Dinner," she added significantly, "in a *great hall*."

Ellie leapt up.

"I love this place!"

Gwen laughed and pushed her out the door.

***

Gwen and Ellie wandered through the wrought-iron gates of the castle, scuffing their shoes in the gravel drive and turning onto a narrow lane bordered by short stone walls. They reached a fork in the road.

"Left or right?" Ellie asked.

Gwen looked to the left. The road passed between large poplars and disappeared round a bend. Beyond, she knew, lay the village of Amberlaine, which they had passed through on their way to the castle a few hours before. To the right the road led straight up a shallow hill, lined by houses. A strange sensation started tingling in her chest. She took it for curiosity.

"Right. We can explore the village later."

They strolled beside the road, laughing and chatting. Squat cottages tucked into hollows in the hill emanated quaint comfort. Some even had chickens pecking near the front stoop, like an idyllic setting for a glossy magazine called *Rural Chic* or *Modern Cottage*. Gwen had a sudden fantasy of turning into one of the driveways, maybe the one on the left with the purple door, and having her mother open it. She'd say, 'Oh, Gwen, I've been waiting for you for so long,' and open her arms wide for Gwen to fall into them. Gwen could imagine her cheek brushing against wavy hair scented with flowery shampoo.

The purple door Gwen had been gazing at opened. A dark haired woman stepped out, face shaded with a hand against the afternoon sun. Gwen's heart leapt then throbbed with longing. Her breath came quicker and quicker. Ellie gasped beside her.

"What's happening to your hands?" Ellie grabbed Gwen's wrists and turned them face up. Small flickers of blue flames danced across her palms and up her fingers. Gwen stared in horror then took a deep breath to calm herself. The flames dimmed and died. Ellie let go of Gwen's right wrist and touched Gwen's left palm gingerly.

"Are—are you all right?" She flipped Gwen's hand and looked at the back. Gwen extracted herself from Ellie's grip, avoiding her gaze.

"Yeah, I'm fine." She made a show of wiping her palms on her jeans. "That was weird. Maybe there's a storm coming. Lots of static charge in the air." Ellie looked at her, and Gwen was aware of how flimsy the excuse sounded. "You know, like that St Elmo's fire old sailors saw on the rigging during a storm?"

"Maybe." Ellie sounded unconvinced. "You're sure you're okay? Because that was really weird."

"I'm good, I promise." Suddenly remembering the woman with the purple door, Gwen snapped her head around to look. The woman was feeding the chickens, but now her face was visible. The woman looked nothing like the sketch of her mother. Gwen shook her head inwardly. She'd let her emotions get the better of

24

her. She couldn't afford to lose control like that again, not in front of Ellie. Only her father knew about her strangeness, and that was more than enough. A memory surfaced from the last time she had lost control fully, before she'd learned to rein in her peculiarities. She had been eight, and Janelle was the lady who cared for her after school, back when her father had an office job to pay the bills. Janelle was the one who painted her toenails in every color of the rainbow, who taught her how to make chocolate chip cookies and who poured the milk Gwen dipped them in, who hugged her close when she scraped her knee in the park. And then one day Janelle had left, and that evening Gwen's sobs shook the little apartment, draining water from every tap no matter how tight her father twisted the knobs. After that night, staring in horror at the endless running water, seeing her father's face swim before her teary eyes, wary and afraid—she had vowed to herself that she would never let the strangeness out again. She couldn't afford to let it happen. Ellie was her best friend, but would their friendship be able to withstand that test? Gwen didn't want to find out.

"Come on, let's keep going." Gwen linked her arm with Ellie's, and together they set out again. Gwen carefully kept her eyes away from the woman with the purple door.

They rounded a bend. On the right, a path opened into the woods marked with a sign stating, 'Glengarry Barrow, ½ mile.'

"What do you think? You game?" Gwen turned to Ellie whose eyes gleamed with excitement.

"A real barrow? Of course I'm game." Ellie bounded

toward the path. Gwen followed then stopped, rubbing her chest. The tingling was still there, stronger than before. She took another deep breath to calm herself just in case, although she didn't feel in danger of releasing fire or explosions or whatever else her body wanted to throw her way.

"Come on, Gwen! What are you waiting for?" Ellie's disembodied voice floated back to her.

"Coming!" Gwen called back. She squared her shoulders and started walking.

***

"Wow. Isn't it amazing?" Ellie's large eyes were even wider with wonder as she gazed at the barrow.

"It's a hill. A little green hill." Gwen was less than impressed. The hill, thirty feet across and twenty feet high, sat on a grassy plain with the hedgerow of a farmer's field on one side and a grove of poplars on the other. It was an unremarkable sight. "Is this really what we came to see?"

"Oh, Gwen!" Ellie wailed in dismay. "Use your imagination! Do you even know what a barrow is?"

"Um, no," Gwen admitted. "All this history stuff is more your thing. What's a barrow, then?" Gwen asked less with interest and more with the hope that Ellie would distract her from the tingling, which had spread from her chest into her arms and torso. She tried to ignore it.

"A barrow is an ancient burial mound, Bronze Age or something. I don't think archaeologists really know all that much about them. There are lots of legends about them and the *aes sidhe*, though."

"Excuse me? The 'ais sheth-uh' who?"

"The *aes sidhe*. Faeries to uneducated heathens like you." Gwen stuck her tongue out at Ellie. Ellie continued, serenely ignoring the gesture. "Also known as elves, the good folk, or the people of the barrows. Apparently they live in another world that you can get to through the barrows. There are lots of stories of poets and bards being lured by faeries into their world."

"Huh." Gwen looked at the grassy knoll with new interest. She wondered how much her father knew about faeries. She bet he'd love to hear about the similarities between these legends and his own story about meeting her mother. "So, is there a door into this thing?"

Ellie gasped and grabbed Gwen's hand.

"Let's find out!" She started dragging Gwen around the barrow. The tingling in Gwen's chest grew stronger as they rounded the other side. The setting sun bathed the whole western slope of the barrow in a brilliant orange glow, except for a deep gash in the middle. The excess of light only highlighted the profound blackness of the entryway. Both girls' jaws dropped as an empty silence blanketed the slope. Gwen's tingling reached full body proportions, and she started to shake.

"Let's go," she whispered. She tugged Ellie's jacket sleeve. Ellie backed away slowly from the doorway, her eyes fixed on it. Then she shrieked and grabbed Gwen's arm, and they fled in panic from the silent barrow.

Chapter 3

Gwen and Ellie careened onto the road, gasping for air. Ellie burst into semi-hysterical laughter.

"What the hell just happened? Are we really such wusses?" She clutched a tree for support, doubled over with laughing.

Gwen joined in, her body still shaking from adrenaline. What had just happened? Why had she felt that strange connection between her and the barrow? Unease settled over her like a damp blanket.

Ellie finally stood upright.

"Whew, that was crazy. I haven't got that freaked out since we went to that stupid haunted house at the fall fair. We are such suckers for spookiness."

"Did you feel the tingling when we got close to the barrow?" Gwen dusted off dead leaves that clung to her jeans, trying to stay casual. "It felt really weird."

"Tingling?" Ellie looked at Gwen with concern. "No, it was just creepy. You know, like a ghost was going to pop out and say BOO!" She stepped toward Gwen and put a hand on Gwen's forehead, smiling slightly. "Are you feeling okay?"

Gwen batted Ellie's hand away, forcing a smile. "I'm fine. I think we need a pick-me-up, though. Banish the ghouls. Let's see if there's anywhere to get a drink in the village."

They wandered back down the road, past the house with the purple door—the woman was nowhere in sight—beyond the imposing stone pillars of the castle gate, and down the hill to the village. Gwen tried to shake her disquiet while Ellie chatted happily, appearing to feel nothing beyond a momentary fright. Gwen wondered if the tingling had something to do with her strangeness. After her slip-up on the road, anything was possible. And now Ellie's stories of faerie mounds felt a little too real—what had *really* happened that week her father met her mother?

The village of Amberlaine appeared, compact and snug in the twilight. They strolled past cottages and shops. A hanging sign, motionless in the calm evening, read 'The Green Man.' A carved likeness of a strange, wild man with leaves curling around his face rested above the lettering. Dimly-lit windows were too foggy to see through, but a hum of lively chatter drifted out the half-open door.

"This looks like the place to be," Ellie said. She turned to Gwen. "Thirsty?"

"I don't know," Gwen said with trepidation. "I was thinking of a café."

29

"This is England, silly. It's all about pubs here."
Ellie grabbed Gwen's elbow and marched her to the
door. "It'll be fun."

Ellie strode confidently to the bar like a regular,
Gwen awkwardly trailing behind her. Ellie rested her
forearms on the well-worn counter and leaned in,
smiling. Gwen shuffled close to Ellie, half-turned from
the counter to surreptitiously scan the pub's clientele.
There were a number of students she recognized from
the castle's reception area, two of whom waved at Gwen
when they caught her eye. She gave a small wave back.
The rest were mostly young, likely students from nearby
Cambridge, with one group of middle-aged men clearly
reliving their student days.

The bartender approached the two girls with an easy
grin. He was about their own age with a shocking head
of messy red hair, a pointed chin and nose, and high,
sharp cheekbones. Bright green eyes twinkled under
eyebrows that looked on fire. He distinctly reminded
Gwen of a fox.

"Hello, loves. Wait, I always guess what my patrons
want. You," he said, pointing his finger at Ellie and
making a show out of screwing up his face in
concentration. "You—want a single-malt whiskey, on
the rocks. A double. And you," he pointed to Gwen,
"definitely a port. Or is it a sherry?"

Gwen snorted and Ellie gave a peal of laughter.

"Hardly! I want something sweet. The fruitier, the
better. Anything with a little umbrella," Ellie added,
giggling.

"You think this is a beach resort, do you?" the
bartender said, grinning. "I'm sure I'll find something to

suit. And yourself?" He directed this at Gwen. "Did I also mistake you for an old professor?"

Gwen blushed at the attention.

"Whatever you have on tap is fine."

He smiled mischievously.

"My choice? Don't worry, I won't pour you a Guinness." He winked and strode off to the taps at the other end of the bar. Ellie looked at him, and back at Gwen's profile as she looked out into the pub.

"That's so weird. You and the bartender totally have the same look. Maybe he's from the same part of England your mum is from." Ellie knew all about Gwen's unusual birth circumstances.

Gwen eyed him with renewed interest, and then turned to Ellie. "What do you mean, the same look? I don't look like I'm on fire, thanks very much."

"No, no, you know, your face, your features. You're both all pointy and sharp. You know how great you look in photos, all cheek-boney and dramatic."

"What do you know about sharp, little Miss Apple Cheeks? You and your trustworthy face, all round and innocent."

"Little do they know, eh?" Ellie giggled.

The bartender came back carrying their drinks.

"There we are, señorita," he said, placing Ellie's drink in front of her with a flourish. He'd somehow fashioned a perfect little umbrella out of newsprint and a toothpick, and it rested on top of a ruby red drink. Gwen smiled and Ellie gave a delighted giggle.

"Oh, it's perfect!" She beamed at the bartender, who grinned.

"How on earth did you make that so quickly?" Gwen

31

plucked the umbrella out of Ellie's drink and examined it, marveling.

"It's magic. I'm a magician, of course. Day job. Not that it pays enough to give up my night job, but there you are." He studied her face as she examined the umbrella. Gwen caught his eye and blushed, putting the umbrella back fussily to cover her embarrassment. The bartender placed another drink in front of her.

"And for you, our special ale tonight, brewed with bilberries."

"Thanks." To fill the awkwardness, she said, "What's a bilberry?" She busied herself taking a sip. It was actually quite pleasant.

"They grow in the forest, they're small and purple— I think they're related to blueberries?" He cocked his head to the side in question.

"Oh! Well, then maybe I should drink more, to help me remember my classes tomorrow. Blueberries are good for the memory, you know. Not that I have problems with my memory, but, you know, never too much of a good thing!" Gwen snapped her mouth shut, horrified at her babbling, and took another sip. The bartender laughed.

"So you're telling me we should drink ale for our health? I like the way you think." Another patron waved him over. He waved back and said to the girls, "My name's Aidan. What do they call you?"

"I'm Ellie, and this is Gwen," Ellie said cheerily. Gwen glanced at her.

"Call me if you need anything, another drink, another umbrella." He winked at Ellie. "I'll make sure to have a swig of the bilberry ale so your names are in my noggin for good." He tapped his head, grinned at Gwen, and moved to the other customer. Gwen felt a nudge from her right.

"What did I tell you?" Ellie breathed in her ear, giggling. "British boys!'

***

Ellie was nearing the end of her glass, and getting sillier. Gwen was relaxed, but more from being comfortable in the pub and less from her drink, which she'd only sipped at. Ellie slid off her stool and stumbled a little, laughing.

"Gah, I'm such a lightweight! I'm just going to the bathroom. Or, as they say here," she affected a terrible posh British accent, "the loo."

Gwen laughed and pushed her in the right direction.

"Go on, you sodden tart." She watched Ellie weave her way between tables.

"Well, at least one of the drinks went down well." Aidan eyed her half-full glass as he cleared away Ellie's glass and the slightly damp newspaper umbrella.

"Oh, I didn't—I mean, it's really good. I'm just not a big drinker." She looked sheepishly at Aidan. He laughed.

"Sure, but here 'not a big drinker' means only three drinks an evening. I think my granny drinks more than you on Sundays. But you're American, right?" He looked at her expectantly.

"Canadian, actually. Vancouver, on the West Coast." She fiddled with Ellie's empty beer mat.

"Oh, Canada! Have you ever seen a bear, then?"

33

Aidan's face lit up with excitement. "The closest we've got to wildlife here are badgers. Oh, or a wolf?"

"I've seen a few bears. My dad and I go hiking sometimes. No wolves, though. They're not quite as reckless as bears are." She relaxed into conversation, the strained embarrassment of earlier drifting away in the face of Aidan's interest in her world. "We were hiking high in the mountains at Whistler, once, and a huge black bear started stalking us and…"

A customer hailed Aidan. "Thirsty men over here while you're chatting with pretty girls, Aidan!"

"I'll be right back. Keep your bear story ready." Aidan pushed off from the counter. "All right, who's first?" he asked the waiting men.

Ellie slid into the stool beside Gwen.

"So, what'd I miss? Were you chatting with Aidan? I think he likes you."

"Ellie!" Gwen's face grew warm and she shoved her shoulder against Ellie's. "I only just met him. We've exchanged maybe three sentences."

"Oh, let me have some fun. You've got to loosen up a little, Gwen. You're so on edge sometimes, you worry me." Ellie looked seriously into Gwen's eyes, but ruined the effect by hiccupping. They collapsed into giggles.

Aidan passed by behind the counter, eyeing them curiously.

"Aidan. What do you do for fun around here?" Ellie suppressed another hiccup behind her hand as Gwen tried not to laugh. Aidan thought for a moment, then his expression cleared.

"Come by the pub Friday night. We're getting in a live band and having a bit of a dance."

"Dancing!" Ellie said. "Excellent. I adore dancing. Are you working that night or are you coming with your girlfriend?" Ellie looked expectantly at Aidan.

Gwen gasped and kicked Ellie.

"Ellie!" she hissed, half appalled and half admiring of Ellie's initiative. Aidan threw back his head and gave a shout of laughter.

"Your friend doesn't beat around the bush, does she?" he said to Gwen, chuckling. "Yeah, I'll be working. And no, my non-existent girlfriend won't be there."

"Good." Ellie nodded smugly. "We'll see you then." She checked her watch and grabbed Gwen's arm.

"Gwen!" she said. "Dinner! In the great hall! We're going to miss it if we don't go now!" She clutched Gwen's shoulders and leveled her gaze into Gwen's eyes. "We *can't* miss it."

"Okay, okay." She opened her wallet and looked at the strange bills inside. "One of these?" she asked Aidan. He grinned.

"That'll about do it. But I suggest you learn our money before someone less honest than me swindles you."

Gwen gathered her coat.

"Well, bye then." She gave a little wave to Aidan. "Nice to meet you."

"I still need to hear the end of your story," he said. "See you Friday."

Gwen smiled shyly as Ellie pulled her to the door.

"See you later, then."

Aidan gazed at her as she left, a half-smile relaxing his face.

35

"Say," said a customer sitting nearby who had been watching their exchange. "Do I get half-price beer if I pretend not to know what money looks like?"

***

Gwen flipped through her English literature textbook as classmates zipped open backpacks and pulled out pens. The chattering of students and scraping of chairs echoed off the vaulted ceilings of the grand guest bedroom-turned-classroom. Ellie gazed enraptured at a tapestry hanging on the wall to Gwen's right that depicted a hunting scene. Gwen wondered idly why the lions in medieval art always looked so bizarre, with strange curling manes and grotesque humanoid faces. The angry eyes of the lion seemed to bore straight into her own. Strangely unsettled by the tapestry, Gwen turned away with a twinge of unease.

The professor stood up and the class fell silent in response. He smiled, and said, "Good morning. I hope you've all had a chance to do your pre-reading. Today we'll be discussing the Faerie Queene by Edmund Spenser. Can anyone tell me how the first book begins?"

A few people raised their hands. Gwen tuned out and looked at her phone, out of sight of the professor in her lap. She'd done the readings and already knew that the knight and the lady were riding their horses through some forest. She'd found the language pretty thick, but had better luck understanding when she'd read the text out loud. She searched for 'faerie' on her phone, curious about the title. The first link was simply entitled 'Fairy.' She skimmed down the article, reading about characteristics ('appearing human with magic powers') and origins ('spirits of the dead, or demon-figures, or a race separate from either humans or angels'). She kept skimming, and paused at the words 'sidhe (fairy mounds).' She clicked on the hyperlinked 'sidhe,' frowning slightly.

The aes sidhe (lit. the people of the mounds) are a mythological race similar to fairies or elves. Legend has them dwelling underground in fairy mounds (sidhe), in a world parallel to our own.

On a hunch Gwen searched for the word 'barrow.' Her heartbeat increased slightly.

In Great Britain, earthen mounds or barrows were commonly built to bury the dead from the Neolithic to the Bronze Age.

Gwen shut off her phone, her palms clammy. What did this have to do with the overwhelming sensations she'd felt at the barrow? And why did she get the sense that the barrows had something to do with her long-lost mother? She started paying attention to the professor again.

"... and you'll notice the shift in setting. The Red Cross Knight and Una are traveling across an open plain initially. But when the storm comes, they are driven into the dark forest where the monster Error dwells. This is a very common theme throughout literature, not only in the Faerie Queene. The forest is symbolic of wilderness, wildness. It is untamable, chaotic, a manifestation of our primal sides, where everything is not as it seems. The forest is often seen as separate from reason and intellect, the antithesis of the orderly pastures and tamed fields of civilization. The forest is where the Red Cross Knight truly begins his quest to conquer the base vices personified by the monsters and magicians in the forest."

Ellie passed a note to Gwen.

I always knew I was a 'wild' one. Guess it's from all our Canadian forests.

Gwen suppressed a smile.

***

"Are you sure this looks okay?" Gwen tugged at her emerald green mini-dress. The stratospheric hemline exposed far too much leg for Gwen's liking, and the color was very striking. Although it wasn't as conspicuous as Ellie's outfit—Ellie had paired a short black skirt with a hot pink sequined shirt, and topped the ensemble off with dangly earrings. The earrings winked at Gwen in the setting sun, and brushed against Ellie's neck with trailing feathers as they walked.

"Stop fussing," Ellie said. "You look gorgeous, and green makes your eyes pop. Honestly, you look great, in a demure sort of way."

"I only look 'demure' because I'm standing next to you," Gwen said. Ellie rolled her eyes.

"One day I'll get you to let your hair down— metaphorically speaking," Ellie added as Gwen swished her hair at her. "Oh look. They put out streamers."

Friday night in Amberlaine was livelier than during the week. Shops were still open, and light spilled out from most store windows. Shoppers and restaurant-goers mingled and wandered down the main avenue. The Green Man pub was on the shadowy side of the sunset-lit street, but cheerily festooned with haphazard streamers. The door was open and drums punctuated the still air. Ellie grinned at Gwen.

"Ready? Promise me you'll dance lots?"

Gwen sighed. She wasn't fond of dancing, and had hoped to just enjoy the music. She always felt so awkward and wrong-footed dancing. She knew she looked like a fool next to Ellie, whose years of dancing lessons paid off with smooth, sure moves. She gave a wry smile.

"I'll do my best."

"That's my girl." Ellie beamed at her. "Come on, the music waits for no woman."

Inside, someone had strung up white twinkle lights around the windows and bar, lending a soft glow to the scene. Tables were shuffled to one side to create a dance floor in front of the band, which included a guitar, an electric bass, a drum kit, and a fiddle. The dance floor had five people bravely twirling and swaying, but the tables were filling fast. Three more people squeezed by Gwen and Ellie as they stood at the door.

"We'd better get a table, pronto," Gwen said as she eyed the last two available. Aidan weaved between crowded tables, delivering drinks. As he turned, he saw them and grinned at Gwen. She gave a small wave back, smiling.

"Who needs a table? We're here to dance." Ellie shrugged off her coat, shimmied Gwen out of hers, and threw them over an empty chair beside the door. "There. Now let's go."

Ellie made a beeline for the dance floor, Gwen reluctantly following. Ellie turned, walking backward, and took Gwen's hands in her own.

"Let's show these Brits how dancing's really done," Ellie said. Gwen groaned as Ellie whirled her around.

"There aren't enough people dancing yet," Gwen hissed as Ellie wriggled her hips vigorously to the beat. Gwen tried to imitate her, but knew she was failing miserably. "I like it better when there are more people. Then no one looks at me."

"Where's the fun in that?" Ellie said as she twirled, her arms in the air. Gwen sighed and contented herself with gently swaying her hips to the beat. She envied Ellie's complete disregard for the opinions of others, how she did what she wanted without worrying if she looked foolish or extraordinary. Gwen wished she didn't care, but being ordinary was paramount. She didn't want to think what might happen if anyone found out exactly how *un*ordinary she really was. No one knew except her father, and keeping a low profile kept it that way. She watched Ellie moving rhythmically, anticipating changes in the music and accompanying them with twirls and shakes, managing to look flowing and exacting and sensual all at once. Gwen concentrated on matching her own shuffling to the beat.

After a particularly exotic move involving a lot of hand movements across Ellie's body, Gwen said, "Now you're just making stuff up."

"Of course I am!" Ellie said merrily. "Just do what the music tells you!"

Their appearance on the dance floor seemed create a critical mass, and people flocked to the floor in droves. The song ended and everyone cheered. Gwen turned in relief to go to a table, but Ellie grabbed her hand.

"Oh no you don't," she said. "Lots more dancing to

do yet."

"But perhaps you'll have this dance with me?" A voice spoke from beside them as the music started up again.

Gwen and Ellie turned to look at the newcomer. Bright green eyes in a narrow pale face gazed steadily at Ellie from below smooth black hair. Gwen raised her eyebrows. He was very handsome, in a strange, exotic way that Gwen couldn't place. He made such a sharp contrast to Ellie's apple-cheeked curviness that Gwen would have laughed, except for the way he looked at her friend. There was intensity in his gaze that was more than admiration. A thrill of disquiet snaked down her back.

Ellie appeared oblivious to this, as she quite readily accepted his offered hand.

"If you can keep up." She arched an eyebrow at the stranger, who gave a confident smile and twirled her away, his arm around her waist. Ellie shrieked with delight.

Gwen took the opportunity to exit the dance floor and head for the bar, dropping onto a stool with a sigh. Aidan came up behind the counter looking flustered, a bar towel draped across one shoulder.

"Hi Gwen. Glad you could make it, you and your very enthusiastic dancing friend." He pulled a glass out from under the counter. "What'll it be tonight?"

"Do you have ginger ale, or some kind of pop? Soft drink?" she asked, feeling lame. She was already on edge and felt exposed without Ellie by her side. She didn't want to risk losing control of herself.

"How about a ginger beer?" he said, reaching into

41

the cooler behind him. "I promise there's no actual beer in it." He cracked the bottle open and poured a glass for her. "It's got double the ginger, though, since I poured it."

Gwen laughed as she caught his wink. She took the proffered glass and said, "Is it just you working tonight? It's awfully busy here for just one."

"Tell me about it." Aidan ran his hands through his hair, leaving it standing on end and even wilder than before. His head distinctly looked like a flaming bush. "The person I hired cancelled at the last minute, and the owner's out of town." He looked toward the dancing crowd and the band. "The live music night was my idea, and I really want it to go well. I love music." He gazed at the band, his eyes wistful.

"Do you play?" Gwen asked, interested. She had played the clarinet briefly in high school, but had sold her instrument immediately after graduation.

"Yeah, lots of things. Guitar and harp and piano and flute—I wanted to study further, but my mum didn't think music was a real career." He laughed without much humor. "So you can imagine how proud of me she is now."

A group of dancers peeled out of the throng and headed to the bar.

"Damn," Aidan muttered. "The vultures are circling." He glanced sidelong at Gwen. "I reckon I shouldn't say that in front of a customer."

Gwen giggled, then looked out at the crowded tables, littered with piles of empty glasses.

"Do you want me to help out tonight? I can clear tables while you deal with drinks."

Aidan's eyes lit up with hope, and he looked down at the counter to hide them.

"I couldn't ask you to do that," he said.

"Luckily you didn't have to ask, because I offered," Gwen said briskly. She reached out and grabbed the bar towel off Aidan's shoulder then took a tray from behind a line of bottles. Aidan's face flooded with relief and gratitude. She smiled at him and jerked her head down the bar.

"Your customers await," she said as she turned to go.

"Thank you so much," he said hoarsely. He cleared his throat. "I'll give you free drinks for life!"

Gwen called out over her shoulder, "Good thing I liked that ginger beer." She walked around the dance floor to the nearest tables and started piling glasses onto her tray, then straightened, looking for Ellie. She finally spotted her through a gap in the crowd, in a thoroughly un-demure position with the stranger who had asked her to dance. Ellie's arms were entwined around his neck, and their bodies were pressed against each other as they moved to the beat. Gwen couldn't see the stranger's face, buried into Ellie's neck. Gwen frowned, and turned resolutely away to continue clearing tables.

***

Gwen sat down at the bar with a sigh a couple of hours later, dropping the bar towel on the counter. She kicked off her heels, despicable spiky things that Ellie had made her buy to go with her dress. She closed her eyes and tilted her head back in relief as her toes wiggled in the open air. When she opened her eyes again Aidan had flopped down on the next stool over and leaned his arms on the counter. He hung his head in exhaustion.

"Wow, what a night," he said into his lap. Gwen looked at the few remaining dancers. The band had finished its last set ten minutes before, and only a few diehards remained swaying to canned music. Gwen noticed with a frown that Ellie was still firmly ensconced in the stranger's arms.

"Everyone seemed to have a good time," she said.

"Everyone except you. Oh, Gwen, how can I ever repay you?" He turned his head to look at her with a woebegone expression. She laughed.

"It's fine. Two are faster than one."

"Except when riding a unicycle."

Gwen let out a burst of surprised laughter, glancing at Aidan's grinning face. She nodded at the dance floor. "And anyway, you rescued me from a dancing marathon with Ellie. I never know what to do out there."

"I hear you loud and clear. Music I can do. Dancing," he paused dramatically, "well, let's just say there have been incidents." He nodded sagely.

Gwen leaned over to nudge him with her shoulder. "No details?"

"Ha. You think I'm going to tell you all my shameful secrets? You've got to find those on your own. I prefer to remain a man of mystery." He grinned at her and she rolled her eyes, smiling.

They both looked at the stragglers for a minute. Gwen cast around for something else to say.

"Ellie and I walked to Glengarry barrow the other day," she said. "Do you know anything about it?"

Aidan pulled himself upright with a groan.

"Oh, yeah, old Glengarry. It's said to be the burial mound of a Pictish king, three thousand years ago. It's mostly a picnic spot on the weekends, and a teenager hangout at night. Not that I would know about that."

"Yeah, I'm sure." Gwen raised an eyebrow at Aidan's mock-saintly face then looked down at her hands, whose fingers twisted together nervously. She tucked them under her legs. "It really creeped me out. I felt…" she paused.

Aidan looked at her curiously. "Felt what?" He almost looked a little wary.

"Oh, just weirded out." She couldn't bring herself to mention the strange sensations the barrow had brought out in her. "We just got all worked up about it. Silly, I know." She changed the subject. "What do you think of that guy with Ellie?" She nodded in their direction. "Do you know him?"

Aidan shook his head.

"No, never seen him before."

"I think he's creepy." Gwen pursed her lips in distaste.

Aidan laughed.

"Are you sure you're not just being protective of your friend?"

"No, really," she insisted. "He doesn't look at her like he likes her. He looks at her like he's a lion, and she's dinner." She swallowed. "Kind of predatory."

Aidan frowned, looking at the two. Ellie's eyes were closed and the stranger nuzzled at her neck, eyes half-lidded. He said, "Maybe I could walk you two back to the castle? It's pretty late, and I'll be closing the pub shortly."

Gwen bit her lip, more relieved than she cared to admit.

"Would you? I'd feel a lot better," she said.

"For my savior? It's the least I can do." He stood up, and reached toward Gwen's face. She held still as his hand brushed beside her cheek then presented her with a budding rose. She stared at it in astonishment, and he grinned and tucked it behind her ear.

"How—how'd you do that?" She reached up to touch the flower.

"A magician never reveals his secrets," he said, looking at her mischievously.

Chapter 4

Gwen drooped over a plate of eggs and sausage. Surrounding her in the great hall were similarly bleary-eyed students trying to wake up after a late Friday night. Ellie dropped her plate across from Gwen on the long trestle table and climbed onto the bench heavily.

"Saturday mornings should be outlawed," she said grumpily, stabbing a sausage with a vindictive thrust of her fork. Gwen grunted in reply. She hadn't drunk the previous evening, but hard work, a late night, and an early breakfast time had all conspired to make her long for her bed with a passion. She could imagine its soft warmth, enveloping her in a dark cocoon...

"Gwen! Are you even awake?" Gwen jerked upright as Ellie's voice pierced her daydream. "I asked if you had a good time last night. Aidan seemed attentive. He walked us home and everything."

"Mmm." Gwen made a non-committal noise. Ellie clucked her tongue.

"Fine, don't tell me anything." She sniffed. "I, on the other hand, had an amazing time. Corann is such a great dancer, and we just really clicked last night, you know? And his eyes are so intense, it's like they see right through me…"

With growing discomfort Gwen listened to Ellie prattle on. She'd seen plenty of Ellie crushing on boys over the years, but this was different. Ellie wasn't usually so effusive about the boys she liked. She was always quick to laugh when other girls 'got all soppy,' and she was usually self-aware enough to see when she was getting soppy herself. Gwen could hear no trace of satire in Ellie's descriptions this time. She prodded a little.

"This guy sounds too good to be true," she said, trying for a jovial tone. "Where can I get one of those?"

To her great surprise, Ellie's face darkened.

"Sorry, he's taken," she said stiffly. She cut her eggs with a determined air, keeping her eyes fixed on Gwen's.

Gwen was shocked to her core. Ellie had never acted like this in all the years Gwen had known her, from the very first day in elementary school when Ellie had thrown her arms around the shy Gwen and declared them best friends. The Ellie Gwen knew would have recognized Gwen's words as the joke they were, and responded with a jibe of her own. Gwen looked down at her plate, a little stunned.

"I'm sorry," she said, not sure what she was apologizing for. "I didn't mean to upset you."

"Okay," Ellie said, sounding mollified. She went

back to her breakfast.

"So, are you seeing Corann again?" Gwen ventured, not wanting the silence to grow awkward. Ellie looked up with a big dreamy smile on her face, the offense of a moment ago apparently forgotten.

"Yeah. We're meeting at the big oak by the crossroads just before the village, Tuesday night. He's going to show me around the woods."

Gwen's stomach sank.

"Why don't you go for coffee, or somewhere in Amberlaine?" she said. "It's nice to have other people around, especially since you don't really know him yet."

Ellie's face soured.

"You don't know what you're talking about," she said with a sneer. "We have a connection. You're just jealous because someone likes me and you're too timid to go after anyone yourself."

Gwen looked down at her plate, her eyes swimming. She automatically took a deep breath to calm herself as her emotions threatened to take over.

"I'm just worried for you. That's all."

Ellie sighed deeply and Gwen looked up to see her rubbing her eyes. She looked at Gwen, confusion and guilt playing across her face.

"I'm sorry, Gwen. I don't know why I said that." She passed a hand over her face. "I think I'm going to go back to bed. You okay on your own?"

Gwen nodded.

"Yeah. I'll see you later." She watched Ellie walk to the doorway, wondering. Was this normal behavior upon meeting someone special, or should she be worried? Not for the first time, Gwen fervently wished for her mother.

49

By that evening, Ellie was back to her old self.

"So when are we heading back to the Green Man? Your British boy is waiting for you," Ellie teased when she and Gwen met in the great hall for dinner.

Gwen rolled her eyes as she set her tray down on the table and climbed on the bench.

"Honestly, Ellie, you read too much into things. I helped him out, it was no big deal." Gwen gave a show of indignation at Ellie's teasing, although inside she was relieved that they were back to their old friendship. Gwen carefully left the subject of Corann alone, unwilling to broach the topic and revert to the strain of the morning.

Ellie had no such qualms.

"I'm so excited for my date on Tuesday," she said happily, cutting into her meat pie.

Gwen said nothing, pushing her beans around her plate without enthusiasm. She suddenly found herself thankful that their stay in England would last only a month.

***

Gwen watched Ellie get dressed on Tuesday night.

"Is that what you're wearing?" Gwen drew her lips into a thin line. Ellie's blouse left little to the imagination as it draped open, an eye-catching pendant dangling low around her neck.

"Don't be such a prude, Gwen." Ellie threaded large

50

hoop earrings through her ears and looked at herself in the mirror, beaming. She turned to Gwen.

"Don't wait up."

Gwen bit her tongue around the warnings she wanted to speak. Instead she said, "Have fun," and watched Ellie bounce out of the room with a sinking feeling.

***

Gwen awoke with a start. She had been dreaming of endless green hills and stone doorways. The click of the latch alerted her to another presence. She sat up and looked toward the door.

Ellie's voice whispered in the darkness.

"Sorry I woke you."

Gwen sighed in relief. Ellie was here, safe and sound. Gwen's worries had been unfounded.

"That's okay. Did you have a good time?" She glanced at the glowing hands of her watch—it was one o'clock in the morning.

"Oh, it was amazing." Ellie giggled and fell into bed. "I told you it would be fine."

Gwen just got up and gave her a silent hug, happy to see her in one piece. Despite the uneventful date, Gwen's unease still lingered.

***

The next Saturday, after a school excursion to a nearby castle, Gwen and Ellie found themselves wandering to the Green Man after dinner with a few

51

classmates.

"That trebuchet was wicked cool," one of their classmates said, his eyes glowing. "Man, I would've loved to see it in action."

Ellie pushed his shoulder playfully.

"War-hungry boys!" She turned to Gwen. "I did like the crenelated towers. They gave it a perfect fairy-tale look."

"It was a pretty great castle," Gwen agreed.

"But not nearly as nice as ours," Ellie said smugly, in a proprietary tone.

They entered the pub and jostled around a table in the corner. Gwen quickly looked to the bar, but instead of Aidan, a middle-aged man with a snub nose and a round belly pulled drafts out of the taps. Gwen's shoulders drooped only slightly, but enough for Ellie to notice.

"I'm sorry, Gwen. I guess tonight's his night off." She put an arm around Gwen's shoulders and gave her a squeeze.

"I got the first round," one of their classmates said, to appreciative noises from the others. "Hey Gwen, want to give me a hand?"

"Sure thing," she said, following him to the bar. When they returned, balancing a cluster of glasses each, she was annoyed to see Corann had materialized in a chair beside Ellie.

When the drinks were poured Gwen pulled two glasses toward herself and Ellie.

"I already got one, Gwen." Ellie pointed to the full glass in front of her that Corann had smoothly placed there moments before. Ellie barely glanced at Gwen as she laid a hand on Corann's arm, giving him a coy smile. Corann leaned toward Ellie's ear and murmured something Gwen couldn't hear.

Gwen bit her lip then turned her attention to the rest of the group. She could have a good time without Ellie.

By the third round the others were getting rowdy. Gwen continued sipping on her first drink, feeling a little lonely. Just then Corann and Ellie stood up, Ellie grabbing her coat.

"We're going for a walk. You don't mind, do you, Gwen?" she said carelessly. Her cheeks were flushed and her eyes weren't quite focused. Gwen frowned.

"Yeah, I guess. I'll walk back with this lot." She gestured at her classmates, but Corann had already put his arm around Ellie's shoulders and steered her toward the door.

***

Aidan stared into the open cupboard, his eyes raking over the shelves, empty except for an upside-down can of tuna. He sighed, closing the cupboard door harder than necessary. He bent down to examine the contents of another cupboard.

Behind him an ordered chaos reigned. A coat and three socks lay on an unmade bed in the one-room flat. A cluster of shoes and boots gathered in a heap by the door. A large window was centered in a red brick wall, unaccompanied by any other decorations. A tiny table with a rickety single chair held the remains of breakfast, but the dishes beside the sink were clean and neatly stacked in a drying rack.

53

Aidan took one last look into a tiny fridge under the counter before slamming it closed in disgust. He marched to the door, grabbing the coat from the bed on his way. The clattering of his descent down the stairs echoed through the flat as the door swung shut.

Once outside, Aidan took a deep breath of the cooling night air. He directed his steps in the direction of the main road. He hadn't been walking for one minute when a voice broke through the stillness.

"Aidan!"

Aidan turned and peered into the twilight. A trio of young men approached from the opposite side of the street. Aidan's mouth opened in an easy smile as he recognized the owner of the voice.

"David. Good to see you, mate."

David greeted this with a wide smile of his own and a clap on Aidan's shoulder. "Aidan. It feels like forever since I last saw you. Graduation last year, wasn't it? How've you been? What are you up to these days?"

"Oh, this and that," Aidan replied. "I'm working at the Green Man at the moment."

"We were just heading there, for old times' sake. Oh," David turned to his two companions, "I forgot to introduce you. This is Will, and this is Simon." They nodded at each other. "They're my mates from uni. Say, do you want to come with us? Make a night of it?"

Aidan looked regretful. "Thanks for the invite, but I've got to be heading off. Good to see you though, David."

"You too, mate. I'll have a drink for you."

Aidan watched as the others walked toward the pub, chatting casually and familiarly. Aidan's hands clenched into fists. He shoved them into his pockets, his jaw tight and his eyes sad. Then he sighed and directed his steps toward a nearby fish and chip shop.

***

By the fifth round her classmates were singing and Gwen had had enough. Murmuring excuses that no one heard, she grabbed her coat and slipped out the door. The cool evening air hit her face with welcome freshness. Breathing deeply, she walked along the street, away from the castle for a change. She came across a small park lit by a single streetlight and sat down on a bench. The glow of the half-moon played tag with the streetlight's beam in the rustling shadows of a sprawling maple. She let her mind go vacant, trying not to think of her worries about Ellie.

Footsteps padded nearby in the still night. Gwen tensed, suddenly aware of how dark it had become and how alone she was. She turned to watch the newcomer, and was relieved to recognize Aidan's tousled red mop and lanky frame. He stopped in surprise when he saw her.

"Gwen?" He cleared his throat. "What are you doing here?"

She stood. "Just thinking. The pub was getting too rowdy for me."

"Where's your partner in crime? The one with the disco fever?" He looked around, as if expecting Ellie to pop out from the bushes.

"She's out with that guy again. The one she was

dancing with the other night at the pub. His name's Corann." She tried to sound nonchalant, but Aidan gave her a sympathetic glance anyway.

"Where are you headed? Can I walk you somewhere?" Aidan asked.

"I think I'll head back to the castle. I'm sure I can manage on my own—but I'd love the company if you're not busy." She stuck her hands in her pockets and lifted her shoulders up, waiting for his answer.

"Of course. Lovely night for a stroll." He walked over to a garbage can nearby and tossed in the grease-soaked newspaper he'd been holding. "Shall we?" He spread his left arm in the direction of the castle.

They fell into place together, a comfortable silence settling around them. Gwen peeked at Aidan, and he smiled back. To cover, she asked, "Was it fish and chips tonight, then?"

"Yeah," he said cheerfully. "Just the ticket for Saturday night."

"Were you out with friends, since it's your night off?" she asked, curious to know more about him.

He shrugged and put his hands in his pockets.

"I usually keep to myself. It's easier that way." His face was sad for a moment. He covered it with a grin. "Besides, a bartender can't afford to have too many friends, or else he wouldn't sell any beer."

Gwen chuckled, but wondered about his answer. She said without thinking, "But you're so…" She trailed off awkwardly.

He broke into a wide smile.

"So what? Say it. I could give you some excellent suggestions," he said, his head turned to look at her.

"Friendly," she said with a hint of defiance. "I was going to say friendly."

They walked for a bit in silence. The castle gates appeared around a bend in the road.

Aidan said, "I hope you have a good time at your fancy dress ball next week." He kept his gaze forward.

Gwen turned to him in surprise.

"Did I tell you about that?"

"Oh, I have my ways." He whistled a lively tune then turned and winked at her as they drew up beside the castle drive. He made a flamboyant show of taking her hand and bending down to kiss it. Keeping hold of her hand, he looked up at her. "Your castle awaits, my lady."

His fingers were warm and dry, and Gwen could still feel the mark of his lips on the back of her hand. She tried to match Aidan's playfulness, but her heart beat faster than usual. She surreptitiously took a deep breath to calm herself and stay in control, just in case.

"Thank you, my lord." She gave a little half-curtsey. "You are too kind."

He slowly released her hand. They looked at each other for a moment, then Gwen glanced down. "Thanks so much for walking me back."

"Hold out your hand," Aidan said. He put his palm down on hers, and when he lifted it up there was a glowing ball of bluish light balanced on her hand. Gwen gasped.

"So you don't get lost in the dark on your way to the door," Aidan said. "Don't examine it too closely—you might discover my secret. And a magician should never reveal his secrets."

Gwen held up her hand, and light streamed out in

front of her.

"Wow, cool," she said, marveling. "I want to learn magic tricks."

Aidan stood back, crossing his arms.

"You'd better get moving. The light won't last forever." He looked cautious, or unsure of himself. It was an odd look on one who always seemed so confident. He stood watching her as she walked up the drive, the light falling on her path. She looked back when she reached the doors, but he had disappeared.

Chapter 5

Gwen lay on her stomach on the bed, idly flipping through her literature textbook with a notepad and pen beside her. Ellie rummaged through the wardrobe, the late afternoon sun catching motes of dust in the air and landing on the warm mahogany of the open wardrobe door. Gwen picked up the pen and started chewing on the end absentmindedly.

"So, in *Lanval*, is the forest symbolic of the wild, or of Sir Lanval's inner turmoil?" She flipped the page again. "This stupid essay is due next week, and I still don't know what Marie de France was going on about."

"It's the Thursday before our long weekend! Leave the twelfth century literature alone. We've got four days without classes, and we're going to make the most of them. I have a full schedule of sight-seeing planned for us. And don't you remember it's the ball tonight?" Ellie held a faux diamond necklace against her neck and peered into the carved mirror above their chest of drawers.

"I guess we should get ready." Gwen snapped her book shut and rolled onto her back. She thought about her dress without enthusiasm then felt guilty. She heaved herself off the bed. "There'd better be other people dressed up tonight," she warned.

Ellie clucked her tongue.

"Don't fuss. Tamara and Braden and Jessica all have costumes." She discarded the necklace and picked up another, this one with peacock feathers and beads. She stopped and whirled around to face Gwen.

"Gwen. Do you have that sketch of your mother with you?"

"What?" Gwen was taken aback. "Why?"

"Please, can I just see it?" Ellie said. "I want to check something."

Confused, Gwen opened her drawer and dug around her underwear and bras. At the bottom her fingers touched raspy paper and she gently tugged the sketch out. She carefully opened it and handed it to Ellie. Ellie took the picture gingerly, Gwen was pleased to note, and peered at it.

"Wow." She exhaled sharply. "That is so weird."

"What?" Gwen was more than curious. Had Ellie seen someone? Someone who could be her mother? Her guts clenched involuntarily.

Ellie shook her head in amazement, handing the sketch back to Gwen.

"Corann always wears this locket around his neck. Well, last time we went out, I asked him what was inside. He gave it to me to look at." Gwen stared at her, impatient. "I opened it, and there was a little portrait inside. It was a perfectly painted miniature of a woman's head. She looked so familiar at the time, but I couldn't place her. Then," she said triumphantly, "I remembered. It was a dead ringer for your mother." Ellie winced. "Sorry. Maybe a poor choice of words?"

Gwen stared at Ellie, at a loss for words. Finally she blurted out, "How—why did he have the picture?" Her mind was chaos. "Why didn't you tell me sooner?"

"I'm sorry. I guess I just forgot." Ellie looked contrite. When Gwen didn't respond, she continued. "I asked him who she was, and he said she was the ruler of his realm."

"What the hell does that mean?" Gwen felt cheated and a little panicky. The mystery of her mother, long since relegated to the unsolvable category in her mind, suddenly loomed large. She tried to control her breathing, closing her eyes to calm herself. She couldn't let go now, not with Ellie in the room.

She opened her eyes. Ellie looked at her with wariness and sympathy, and said, "I know, right? I mean, the only ruler here is Queen Elizabeth, who's at least three hundred years old." She paused, and said, "But look, I'll ask Corann for more details, okay? I promise." She took Gwen's hands in hers and shook them for emphasis. "I promise we'll find out what's going on."

"Thanks," Gwen whispered.

Ellie gave her a big hug, and said, "Come on, let's get ready. It'll be time before you know it, and we haven't even done our hair yet!"

As Gwen applied makeup in the carved mirror, she tried to make sense of what she'd heard. She couldn't reconcile the fact that her mother, the ethereal and perfect mother living in her imagination, could be embroiled somehow with creepy Corann. Gwen's mouth twisted in disgust. Something wasn't right with him. Her gut told her that the way Ellie acted around him was more than puppy love. The personality change, the vacant eyes—it wasn't right, and it wasn't Ellie. And why hadn't Ellie told her right away about the picture in the locket? Something was not right at all. Gwen had never let herself consider that her mother would be less than perfect, and that only the gravest circumstances could have made her leave her baby. But now that Corann might know her, and know her well—Gwen's mind floated in a sea of unpleasant new possibilities.

"Hey, we're in luck." Ellie turned her back so Gwen could lace up her dress. "Corann's coming tonight, so I can ask him about your mother then." Gwen's fingers paused at the laces. Her first reaction was to question Ellie again on the wisdom of encouraging Corann. That urge was quickly drowned out by an overwhelming desire to find out about her mother. She swallowed her reservations and continued lacing.

***

The great hall dazzled with lights. Sconces on the walls flickered, bringing tapestries to life, and a central chandelier illuminated the swaying dancers below. A band was set up on a dais above the dance floor. Although dressed in costume, the performers were belting out contemporary covers. Ellie looked disappointed.

"I thought they'd have period music," she said, sticking out her bottom lip.

"Yeah, but nobody knows how to dance Shakespeare-style," Gwen said, laughing. "Oh, except you."

Ellie sniffed then pointed at a small crowd against one wall.

"Let's see what's happening over there." She pulled Gwen forward by her arm.

Gwen might as well have been naked as they crossed the room. Her embarrassment was almost as large as her billowing dress, which trailed long green sleeves lined with fawn-brown velvet. She knew she was being silly. She and Ellie were not the only ones dressed up in historical costumes. Ellie glanced at her face and must have guessed her thoughts, because she leaned close and whispered, "You look beautiful—honest." She stepped back and said louder, "And who is your seamstress? She did an excellent job." They giggled together and Gwen relaxed a little, despite the disquiet in the pit of her stomach that had been her companion ever since Ellie mentioned the locket. Her mind kept fretting over questions like a dog worrying a bone.

There were gasps from the crowd in front of them, and then applause. Curious, Gwen and Ellie nudged forward to see. In the center of the circle stood Aidan, dressed in a short black cape with silver stars woven at intervals across the fabric. He wore a solemn, mysterious expression which didn't entirely hide the spark in his eyes. A blue flame flickered in the center of his palm, similar to the flame he had given Gwen on her walk up the castle drive. He raised his hand and the flame trickled down his arm like water, without setting his sleeve alight. He let it run behind his head, bending his neck and moving his shoulders to let the flame travel to his other arm, where it ran down to his outstretched palm. He held out his arms and Gwen clapped along with the others, marveling.

He put his hand out as if to stop their applause then threw the flame high into the air. Gwen was still trying to figure out the physics of that when Aidan threw his head back, opened his lips, and caught the flame directly in his mouth. He gave an exaggerated swallow then stuck out his tongue for inspection. More applause and Aidan bowed, smiling. Then he frowned, clutching his stomach. Gwen and Ellie looked at each other, alarmed. Aidan's body heaved once, twice. The third time he opened his mouth.

Flames spurted out high above the crowd. Girls screamed and there were shouts of astonishment. Then, as Aidan raised his arms in presentation and grinned at them all, the crowd cheered wildly. Gwen released Ellie's hand from a death grip and cheered with the rest. Aidan bowed his way out of the circle, and Gwen turned to Ellie.

"That was incredible. How on earth do you think he did it?"

Ellie's excited face started to answer, but then her eyes caught something behind Gwen. Gwen watched in alarm as Ellie's expression drained away, replaced by a vague blankness. Gwen turned, unsurprised to see Corann directly behind her with eyes only for Ellie.

"I'll catch you up later, hey?" Ellie said as she moved past Gwen toward Corann.

"Ellie." Gwen grabbed her arm. "Don't forget to ask him about—you know." The possibility of finding her mother burned in Gwen bright and hot.

"Sure sure." Ellie's eyes weren't looking at her, but at Corann. "See you later."

Gwen was hardly appeased by this half-hearted reply but let Ellie go. She watched as the two made a beeline for the dance floor. Suddenly she fervently wished she hadn't worn the stupid costume.

"Gwen?" said a tentative voice behind her. She turned around to see Aidan in his star-strewn cape. He looked taken aback and a little vulnerable as he looked at her. Maybe the dress wasn't so bad after all. "You look—amazing." He collected himself and cleared his throat. "So. Surprised to see me?"

She laughed.

"Yeah. They mentioned we'd have entertainment, but I had no idea it'd be you. And those tricks—that was incredible." The blue flame flowed down Aidan's black sleeve in her mind's eye, filling her with a strange longing. "I'd love to be able to do that. Where did you learn?"

Aidan shifted his feet.

"Oh, here and there," he said evasively. He looked around the hall. "I'd better go do some magical mingling. I'm on the clock for another hour or so. But will you stick around until I'm done? I'd love to have a drink with you."

"I'll be here," she said, gratified, and he grinned and left. She looked at Ellie again, sighed, and went to find some of her classmates.

***

Across the room, Gwen could see Ellie with her new flame. Or, more correctly, Gwen could see Ellie's hair and the laces of her costume back, with Corann's hands roving up and down. Gwen gave a sigh.

"Oh, lighten up," Aidan said with a grin as he joined her with two glasses. "So she's having a bit of fun."

"I guess. Thanks." Gwen took the offered drink, still looking toward the opposite corner. The cold condensation on the glass brought her back to attention. "What's the drink?"

"Relax, it's just juice. Although it wouldn't kill you to have one beer, you know. You're not a recovering alcoholic or something, are you?" He glanced at her sideways, eyebrow raised.

She gave a short burst of surprised laughter.

"No, nothing like that." She sipped her drink to cover the awkward pause. "So, are you all done with the gig?"

"Yeah. They only paid me for the first two hours. Now everyone's too pissed to fully appreciate my talents." He flashed Gwen a smile. "Except you, of course." He reached into the drapes of her costume's sleeves and pulled out a slice of lime, which he carefully balanced on the rim of her drink.

Gwen laughed and bumped his shoulder with hers playfully.

"Nice one. Do you have a whole pantry hidden in your cape or what?" She took a sip from her glass. "So,

66

are you waiting to be discovered? Why aren't you in the big time? You're awfully good."

Aidan laughed.

"You think I should be the next David Copperfield? Poor man, I couldn't do that to him. I'd hog his audiences, I'd steal all his groupies—no, I'd better leave Davy in peace."

Gwen giggled then glanced back at the pillar hiding Ellie and Corann. Ellie dangled a flask in her right hand, her left supporting herself on Corann's shoulder. She looked confused, and gazed straight through the pulsing crowd as if the hall were empty. Corann bent down to whisper in her ear. She nodded, eyes glazed, and took Corann's proffered hand. Corann led her past a suit of amour and out into the night. Gwen grabbed Aidan's forearm.

"Did you see Ellie? She didn't look well."

Aidan's forehead creased. "I agree. I wonder…" He left the sentence dangling.

"You don't think—he drugged her?" Horror swept through Gwen's gut. Terrible images flashed through her mind—Ellie unconscious, beaten, Corann on her... "I'm following them."

"I'm sure she's just a little tipsy." Aidan gazed toward the door. "But maybe checking on her is a good idea."

Gwen barely heard the end of Aidan's sentence as she trotted to the open door. Peering out into the blackness, she opened her eyes wide, willing herself to adjust to the dark. Through the dim she spotted Ellie's sky blue gown shimmering between trees, a dark shadow accompanying her.

67

"Well, come on, then," Aidan said beside her. She turned in surprise.

"You don't have to come."

"I'm not going to let you go out there on your own with some potential weirdo on the loose. That sort of thing looks bad in the tourist pamphlets." He grinned. "Come on."

They ran down the steps and across the lawn to the forest. Already the dew was thick, and Gwen could feel it soaking into her cheap cloth shoes. She had just lost sight of Ellie when a pale light flickered to life ahead of them. Gwen and Aidan stopped immediately.

"What's that?" Aidan said quietly. The light flickered like a fire, but glowed with a pale white-yellow gleam. At the sight Gwen recalled the sickly light of a chemical fire in her chemistry class, a sort of unearthly, unwelcoming light. She wondered if that was what marsh gas looked like, lit up.

"I guess Corann has lit our trail for us. How thoughtful of him." Aidan moved forward toward the pale flicker. "Come on, or we'll lose them."

They moved forward into the woods more carefully now. There was no path in this area of the forest, and they had to pick their way over fallen logs and rustle through dead leaf litter. Gwen cursed inwardly at her floor-length gown as it caught on yet another sharp branch. An uneasy sensation began tingling in her chest. She attributed it to worry for Ellie.

"The light's stopped," Aidan said suddenly, drawing up short.

Gwen wavered for a moment.

"Maybe we should stay quiet and have a quick look.

Maybe she's fine."

"Yeah, I doubt she'd thank you for interrupting if she's actually here of her own accord." Aidan glanced at Gwen and smiled wickedly, and she found herself blushing and glad for the darkness.

"C'mon. I'll be as quiet as I can in this infernal dress."

They crept forward again until a clump of hawthorn blocked their view of the light. Gwen got on her knees and shimmied forward until she had a view of Ellie and Corann. She tried to ignore the tingling now in her arms and torso. Aidan hesitated a moment then bent down and followed suit.

Ellie was in a shallow depression beside a steep slope, a hedgerow nearby flickering with movement in the unearthly light from Corann's lantern. The light caught the edges of a crude stone doorway. Aidan stiffened beside her.

"This is Glengarry barrow," he breathed. Ellie stood still, arms down and palms up, as if in supplication. Her eyes were closed and her chin lifted, expressionless.

"What does that mean? And what is Corann doing?" Gwen whispered back. Corann ignored Ellie, instead pacing back and forth in front of the doorway behind her, his face frowning in concentration. After a few paces, he stopped and stared at the sky, where a waxing moon rose above the horizon. Corann gave a satisfied smile, and turned again to the doorway. He placed the lantern on the ground and reached one hand to each of the doorway's top corners. Immediately the impenetrable darkness within the doorway glowed with the same light as the lantern, which flickered weakly as if in response.

Corann lifted his hands in triumph and turned to Ellie, who remained unmoving. The light grew brighter and brighter.

Gwen found herself squinting, shielding her face with her hand against the light.

"What's going on?" she said to Aidan, her heart pounding. She didn't understand how Corann had made the doorway glow, or why Ellie was motionless in the clearing. Gwen heaved herself up, eyes shut tight against the light, and brushed away Aidan's restraining hand on her arm. She stumbled around their protective bush toward the other two, leaving Aidan behind. "Ellie! Ellie!" she yelled as she tripped over her hem and sprawled headlong on the grass. She squinted toward the barrow. Ellie and Corann's silhouettes grew smaller as they walked into the light through the doorway. Gwen closed her eyes in pain at the brightness. Seconds later, the light disappeared and darkness reigned at the silent barrow.

Chapter 6

Gwen stared into the black emptiness of the stone doorway, disbelieving. How could Ellie just disappear into nothing? Her brain refused to comprehend.

Cracking twigs popped behind her, and strong hands hauled her upright.

"What the hell just happened?" Aidan's voice was hoarse. In the light of the rising moon, he appeared as pale and wide-eyed as Gwen felt. He looked around the clearing, still gripping Gwen's upper arm with clenched fingers. Gwen carefully pried them away and ran the last few steps toward the doorway.

"Ellie! Ellie! Where are you?" Gwen cried out. There was nowhere Ellie could hide. The stone lintel opened to nothing but a blank wall of dirt. Gwen felt around desperately, scrabbling at the dirt and running her fingernails along the edge of the stone doorway. Her body was almost shaking with head-to-toe tingling.

"There's no way in. Trust me. I grew up here and I've been all over this barrow. It's completely sealed." Oddly, Aidan's voice reassured her despite its message. It was a solid reminder of normalcy after Ellie's disappearing act.

"She can't have just vanished." Gwen stood back and surveyed the doorway, nails digging into her cheeks in agitation. "Unless she did…" Gwen thought of her own experiences of the bizarre. She knew there was more in the world than could be readily explained. Could Corann do strange things too? Her brain was both woolen and electrified all at once. "What did Corann do just before they disappeared?"

Aidan replied, his voice confused and wary. "He paced a bit then touched the doorway."

"That's right, at both corners." Gwen walked back and forth in front of the doorway.

"What are you doing?" Aidan stared at her, looking alarmed. He rubbed his arms distractedly as if he were cold. She continued pacing.

"What if they did actually—disappear into thin air?" Gwen said carefully. "I'm trying to recreate what Corann did. Ellie's missing under very unusual circumstances, and I like to keep an open mind." She turned to face the door. "Here goes nothing," she said, and reached up to put one hand on each corner of the stone lintel.

For a long second, nothing happened. Aidan's soft breathing was the only sound disrupting the quiet of the night. The image of Gwen's mother floated to the surface of her mind, unbidden, frozen forever in graphite lines. Did Gwen's strangeness come from her? How did

Corann fit into this enigma?

The dirt wall Gwen faced turned a fathomless black before beginning to glow with an increasing brilliance. Gwen stood paralyzed in front of the doorway, her arms outstretched. Aidan gasped.

Within seconds the light was dazzling. Gwen closed her eyes and stepped back, breaking the connection. The light continued to brighten. She backed away, bumping into Aidan who had his eyes closed against the light. She clutched at him.

"I have to go through," she said. "I don't know what the hell is happening, but that's where Ellie's gone. I'm her best friend, and if anything happened to her I'd never forgive myself." She didn't mention out loud that she was starting to feel responsible. Not only for not doing anything about the uneasiness she'd felt about Corann, but also from the growing sense that all this had something to do with her mother. How, she had no idea.

"I know." Aidan took a deep breath and let it out with a whoosh. "I'm coming too."

"What?" Gwen was taken aback. "Why?"

"I can't let you go in by yourself. And—I've always felt there was something strange about Glengarry. Now I want to find out what it is."

Gwen shook her head in disbelief but didn't argue the point. She had no idea how long the doorway would stay open for, and Ellie was getting farther away with every minute.

"Okay, let's do this." She shook her shoulders in an attempt to psych herself up. "Hold onto me. I don't want to get separated."

"Yeah, and we don't know what's waiting for us on

73

the other side." Aidan put his hand on Gwen's shoulder. "Sorry, not an appropriate comment right now." He squeezed her shoulder and she looked at him. His eyes were determined. "Ready?"

She nodded, and they walked into the light.

***

Gwen shuffled forward blindly, her arms outstretched. Aidan gripped her shoulder tightly, his hand a solid anchor in a sea of the unknown. They continued deeper into the barrow until the light dimmed to almost nothing. Gwen opened her watering eyes. At first the only sense that came clearly was hearing, as Aidan breathed heavily behind her and her own heart pounded in her ears. She blinked a few times and her eyes focused.

They were surrounded by a dense forest. The moon shed no light, hidden as it was behind layers of canopy. Gwen was strongly reminded of the forests at home, vastly more primeval and dense than the deciduous groves she'd seen in England so far. Massive conifers soared high above their vision, untouched for centuries. Heavy moss clung to tree trunks and dripped off low-hanging branches. The forest was dark and close, sounds dampened by an excessive undergrowth of fallen trees and shadowy bushes. A small pool glinted dully from an errant moonbeam between two fungus-covered stumps.

Gwen swallowed a shout to Ellie. She felt distinctly unwelcome here. It was silly, she knew, but she had the impression that the forest itself watched them. It was not a comfortable feeling.

"Where are we?" Gwen whispered.

Aidan's hand slipped off her shoulder as he turned to look behind them. Gwen also turned and frowned in disbelief. Before them was a doorway, crudely constructed of three rough-hewn stone slabs. It was a doorway to nowhere, with nothing behind it. Aidan ran his hands along the side of the frame.

"How the hell are we supposed to get back?" He stuck his hand through the entryway. When nothing happened, he walked through. His pale face looked at Gwen in shock and despair.

"Let me try my hands on the door," Gwen said, gesturing Aidan back through the doorway. When he obliged, she put a hand on each corner of the doorframe, expecting a light to start glowing. The entry stayed stubbornly dark.

Aidan stepped forward.

"Let me try."

Gwen moved, and he paced three times, then stepped into the same position. Nothing happened. He screwed up his face in concentration, looking as if he wanted to will the doorway into submission, but to no avail. The darkness of the forest pressed in on all sides.

The way back was sealed.

"I don't understand." Aidan gripped his hair in both hands and exhaled swiftly. "How did it work before? How did you and Corann do it?"

"I don't know," Gwen said miserably. She stiffened. "Ellie!" Gwen swung around, appalled at herself for momentarily forgetting the reason they were there. "Where did they go?" She scanned the forest, but it was silent, keeping its secrets.

75

Aidan paced around the doorway, distracted for the moment. He bent over a low bush briefly, spiky branches and spiny leaves black in the darkness. He straightened, pointing at a broken patch where the branches had been forced aside.

"They went this way, if I had to guess," he said.

Gwen started forward, and then turned to the doorway almost involuntarily. She and Aidan stared at it then glanced at each other with identical expressions of fear.

"I could mark it with some trick lights," Aidan said finally. "It might become a doorway again, so we shouldn't lose it. Although I reckon we'll need to find Corann first to figure out how it works."

Gwen nodded her agreement, and watched as he pulled something out of his pocket and reached up to the top of the horizontal stone. When he removed his hand, blue fire flickered brightly on the lintel.

"How long will it last?" she asked, desperate to find Ellie but unwilling to leave their only tie to reality, no matter how tenuous and untrustworthy.

"Oh, a good long while," Aidan said, avoiding her gaze. "Come on, let's find Ellie and that conjuror she calls a boyfriend. They can't have gone far. Just be sure we can see the flame from wherever we are."

They reluctantly turned and trudged into the undergrowth in the direction of the broken branches. They hadn't gone five steps before Gwen stopped, cursing under her breath.

"Stop a sec, I have to tie up this damn dress before I trip." She wrestled it up and hooked the sides securely into the waist sash Ellie had fortuitously deemed

76

essential to the costume. "Okay, I'm ready."

They continued through the forest, clambering over slippery logs and stepping into stagnant pools of water, soaking their shoes. After the third time she tripped over an errant vine snaking across her path, Gwen figured the forest didn't want her there. After her sixth fall, she knew it. The forest breathed malevolence, like an oozing dank life-form from some fetid bog. Massive tree trunks leaned toward them, encased in rough bark encrusted with diseased-looking fungus. Long strands of moss caught in her hair and brushed against her cheek in an unwelcome sensation, like the stroking of dead fingers. Her breath caught in her throat when Aidan stopped short in front of her, his hand out to stop her.

He whispered urgently, "There are eyes. In the bushes. Everywhere."

Horrified, Gwen looked around. Little glints of wetness appeared two at a time, multiplied many times over. She gripped Aidan's arm instinctively.

"Okay, let's just back up slowly, back to the doorway," Aidan said quietly. They took one step backward, and stopped abruptly when a howl pierced the thick air like a knife slicing open a curtain. Gwen stopped breathing. All the little eyes blinked and vanished.

"That was a wolf! I thought there weren't any wild animals in England," she hissed at Aidan.

"We're not in England anymore, can't you see?" Aidan's eyes were wide, and he darted his head back and forth as if looking for an escape route. The wolf howled again, directly behind them and closer now.

"What do we do now?" Gwen's voice came out in a

squeak. She clawed at the part of her mind responsible for rational thought, desperate to keep herself under control in the midst of her panic.

A beat passed.

"Run," Aidan said. He grabbed her hand and they broke into a frenzied scramble forward, over tree trunks and under branches. Gwen fell more times than she could count. As the howling grew louder, Gwen felt like a scurrying mouse with a cat on its tail. She tripped again and Aidan hauled her up, wrenching her shoulder in his haste. She cried out in pain, and then clapped a hand over her mouth. Aidan pulled her forward again urgently, putting his arm around her waist instead. There was a brief silence, broken only by their gasps of fear and effort and the unavoidable noise of their passage through the undergrowth. The howl returned, almost at their backs. Gwen splashed through a muddy pool, sure that it would be the last she would trek through.

A great snarling erupted behind her. The howling stopped and the snarling was interspersed with yelps and barks. Aidan stopped and turned. His jaw dropped. Gwen whirled around.

Not sixty feet behind them, two enormous animals fought in the gloom. White fangs gleamed and eyes and snouts glinted. Wet streaks appeared on the wolf's flanks as the other animal tore it apart with sharp claws. The wolf's attacks slowed, and it finally succumbed when the other animal sunk its teeth deep into the wolf's neck. The wolf fell to the ground with a final thud as the other animal extracted itself from the killing wound. It put a paw on the wolf's flank, and slowly raised its massive head to look directly at Gwen and Aidan. Surrounded by a thick mane of curling fur, an oddly misshapen lion's face glared at them. Then, emanating supreme disinterest, the lion bent its head and ripped open the wolf's stomach. It tore out a long string of glistening intestines and started chewing.

Gwen grabbed Aidan's hand.

"Come on," she breathed urgently into his ear. "While it's busy." She prodded Aidan out of his position of frozen disbelief and they stumbled away as quietly as they could. Gwen kept her ears tuned to the wet chomping noises of the lion's feast.

They pushed forward until the lion's sounds had long since faded. Gwen thought in despair of the doorway and the little blue flame, flickering against the darkness. There was no way they'd ever find it now. Were they stuck in this terrifying world-within-the-barrow forever? And how would they ever find Ellie, if she were even still alive?

Chapter 7

Aidan stopped ahead of her. They hadn't spoken since the lion, but he broke the silence.

"We should stop and rest." He pointed to a huge tree with a gaping hole in its trunk. "Let's check out that hollow for shelter." Gwen nodded tiredly and he pulled another flame out of his pocket.

They peered into the tree's chasm. It was empty, and looked roomy and dry. The tree was somehow still alive, growing around the crevasse in its middle. They crawled in and squeezed awkwardly together. They sat in silence, listening for noises outside. Finally Gwen spoke.

"Any wild ideas about where we are?" She stared out of the hole, searching for any sign of movement. The lack of noise did not reassure her. "I'm drawing a blank."

A minute of quiet ended when Aidan took a big

breath.

"I have a theory. It's mad, but this whole night's been mad." He paused. Gwen turned to look at him, but the darkness within the tree was profound. He continued. "There are legends about the barrows, Glengarry in particular. The stories go that the barrows are portals to another world."

"To the people of the barrows," Gwen whispered, her heart contracting. She felt rather than saw Aidan's head turn to look at her.

"You've heard the stories, then."

She gave a humorless chuckle.

"No, just looking up barrows on the internet." She didn't mention her father's story. She was sure it had no connection. There was no reason to tell Aidan. None at all. Her stomach squirmed guiltily. Could she have prevented all this madness somehow? Were the signs all there, and she didn't piece them together fast enough?

She hugged her knees more tightly to her chest.

"Do you really think we've stumbled into some kind of magical otherworld? That we were whisked away to a parallel land? That magic is real?" She stopped abruptly, remembering her own strangeness. Was it any less crazy than everything that had happened to them tonight?

Aidan was quiet for a long while. Gwen kept vigil. Eventually he said, "I can watch for now if you want to sleep. We can't move anywhere until morning." He paused, and then said quietly, "If there is a morning in this world."

Gwen closed her eyes and tried to ignore Aidan's last comment. Her nerves were still jangling, but the stress and exertion of the night had drained her.

"Are you sure? Anyway, I don't know if I'll be able to sleep sitting in this tree."

Aidan extracted his arm from between them.

"Lean against me, if you like," he said, arm raised. She tentatively put her head on his shoulder. He was warm and solid, and she found herself relaxing into him. He carefully laid his arm across her shoulders.

Gwen said sleepily, "This was all just a ruse to get your arm around me, wasn't it?"

Aidan laughed softly. He shifted slightly and they settled together. Gwen gave a deep sigh.

"I hope Ellie's okay," she murmured into Aidan's chest.

He squeezed her gently.

"I have a feeling she has one of the locals for a guide," he said.

Gwen shivered.

***

Gwen awoke clutching Aidan's chest as they lay in a tangled heap in the tree hollow. She sat up, carefully extracting herself from the sleeping Aidan. He looked exhausted, his lashes pale against the shadows under his eyes. Gwen let him be and looked around their temporary home in the dim light filtering through the tree's entrance.

The tree's walls were rough and crumbling, releasing a dry dust when she touched the sides. Above them stretched a whole city of spider webs, and she was intensely thankful that they had not encountered them the previous night. She got up gingerly and crawled outside, careful not to disturb Aidan. It was morning, and the forest was dim and cool with a thick fog enveloping the trees. Gwen could see clearly no farther than twenty paces before the trees turned to indistinct silhouettes and were swallowed by the mists. Gwen shivered and wrapped her arms around herself. The forest was no more welcoming by day than by night. There was no sign of strange animals or glinting eyes, it was true, but there was also no birdsong, and a dull thickness prevented sounds from traveling any real distance. The greens and browns of the vegetation were washed with a grey murkiness that the dim daylight did nothing to dispel. Hanging mosses dripped with moisture collected from the fog, the wetness splashing with damp squelches into muddy pools. It was an ugly, forbidding place, Gwen decided, and she wondered miserably where Ellie was in all of it.

A muffled thump made her whirl around, all her senses suddenly on high alert. Aidan knelt in the tree hollow's entrance, blinking and rubbing his eyes. She sighed in relief. He clambered out of the hollow, unfolding his lanky frame through the narrow entrance.

"Morning." He yawned then cleared his throat. "I'm awfully glad to see you. I thought for sure you'd been snatched away in the night."

"Oh, I'm sorry," Gwen said apologetically. She waved her hand toward the forest. "I was just seeing what we were up against."

Aidan scanned the forest, nose wrinkled.

"It doesn't look much better in daylight, does it?"

They surveyed the woods another minute, neither wanting to broach the topic foremost on their minds.

83

Gwen finally spoke.

"So what do we do now? Just start walking until we get somewhere?" She bit her lip.

"It's as good a plan as any, and a better plan than some." Aidan brushed at the dirt on his pants and straightened his shirt. "The forest can't go on forever. And we might come across a path eventually. Corann knew where he was going, so there must be some human habitation." He swallowed, looking into the trees. "Or other habitation."

Prickles of fear crawled up Gwen's spine. She tried to ignore them. Aidan turned on the spot, looking up at the sun. Gwen considered him, puzzled.

"Didn't your cape have silver stars all over it? For your magician's gig?"

Aidan looked discomposed.

"They must have fallen off. Cheap rubbish," he added unconvincingly.

Gwen frowned at him, but he kept his eyes in the trees. The stars hadn't looked stick-on last night. In fact, Gwen could have sworn they were part of the weave of the fabric.

Aidan said, "The sun's already been up for a while. We slept better in that moldy old tree than I thought."

Gwen's mind was still on the stars of Aidan's cape, but she let him change the subject.

"Let's get moving then. Hey, if this is a magic land, maybe we'll come across a breakfast tree, dangling with bacon and egg fruits." She tucked her skirts more securely into her sash in preparation for their trek.

"Don't talk about food." Aidan groaned and clutched his stomach. "I'm ravenous."

***

They scrambled through the logs and undergrowth as they had the night before. Immediately, a vine appeared out of nowhere to trip Gwen. She narrowly avoided tumbling headlong into a bush crowned with wicked looking thorns by clutching Aidan's arm as she fell. He twisted with the impact, and his head landed in the middle of a vast spider web strung between decaying branches.

"Gah!" Aidan made an inarticulate noise and fought furiously to remove the strands. Gwen tried to extract him and ended up with sticky palms for her effort.

Aidan turned to get away from the web, and jumped over a nearby log. Gwen followed him. Too late she heard his startled shout, and landed next to him in a stagnant pool of water inconveniently located exactly where their feet had landed.

"This forest has it in for us." Aidan ducked as a branch cracked overhead and dropped with a heavy thud a foot away.

"I swear it's alive." Gwen looked around at the silent trees and shivered.

After an hour of this trekking, Aidan tripped over another branch and went sprawling headfirst through a patch of bushes with dull green leaves.

"Gwen! I found a path!"

It was little more than a deer trail, but it was infinitely better than what they had been traveling though. Gwen hugged Aidan, and they grinned at each other for the first time since the ball. They continued on the path.

"Which way, do you reckon?" Aidan said, swatting away a branch that dangled low.

"Does it matter?" Gwen replied.

"Now, there's the self-defeatist attitude we don't want. Pick a way! Be confident!" Aidan grinned at Gwen, and she stuck her tongue out at him.

The going was much easier on the path. Branches occasionally cracked and fell near them, and once a young tree uprooted itself and crashed onto the path right behind Gwen, but they could move much more quickly along the flattened trail.

At mid-day, or as close to mid-day as they could tell in the murky half-light of the forest, they stopped at a slow-moving creek that didn't appear too foul. They eagerly scooped up water with their hands and slurped at the dank, muddy-tasting liquid.

Gwen found a fallen tree to sit on and kicked off her shoes with a groan. She lifted her foot onto her knee and examined it.

"Damn it," she muttered.

"What's up?" Aidan stretched back on a log, narrowly avoiding a slimy-looking fungus protruding from the bark.

"I got a blister from these shoes, which were absolutely not meant for hiking in." She prodded the offending footwear with her toe. "At least they weren't heels."

Aidan stood up, looking around. He strode over to a nearby cluster of bushes, rummaged near the roots for a minute, and emerged triumphant. He knelt down in front of Gwen.

"Let's see your foot, then," he said, holding out his hand. She reluctantly placed her foot in his outstretched palm, hoping it didn't smell, not that he would notice beneath all the mud and bog water. She stifled a nervous laugh. How could she be worried about what Aidan thought of her when they were trapped in an unending forest in another world?

Aidan produced the leaf he had plucked. He rubbed it against her blister gently, keeping his eyes fixed on her foot. It hurt at first, but the pain numbed almost immediately. When he stopped rubbing moments later, the redness had faded and the blister had shrunk to half its size. She peered at her foot, amazed.

"What was that plant? How'd you know that?"

Aidan tossed the leaf aside and stood up, ineffectually brushing his filthy pant legs. He spoke without looking at her.

"Oh, it's a common herbal remedy in the country. My—granny taught me." He took a step away. "If you're ready…"

Gwen slipped her shoes back on and pushed herself to her feet. "Yeah, let's get moving. The path has to go somewhere, right?"

***

The afternoon lasted forever. By the time shadows from the occasional sunbeam slanted through the gloom, Gwen's legs screamed at her for a rest and her stomach wouldn't cease its growling. Aidan's pace ahead of her had dropped from a brisk hike to a slow trudge, and his head drooped. Gwen's initial blister had improved thanks to Aidan's ministrations, but her other foot throbbed with another angry sore.

Gwen stopped in front of a bush that looked like the one Aidan had plucked for its medicinal leaves. She grabbed a leaf, balanced on one foot, and rubbed the leaf tenderly over the reddened sore. All she managed to do was aggravate the blister, and she sucked in her breath in pain. Aidan turned around.

"What are you doing?" he asked, puzzled.

"Trying your herbal cure for blisters." She winced as she put her foot down. "It doesn't work when I do it. Do I have the wrong leaf?"

He took the leaf from her. His expression fought between amusement and sadness. He bent down and took her foot again. Instantly, the pain subsided.

"Thanks," Gwen said, relieved but puzzled. "How did you do that? Why didn't it work for me?"

Aidan avoided her gaze.

"Come on, let's keep moving. This path to nowhere won't walk itself." He placed her foot carefully on the ground, taking his time letting go.

Gwen looked at Aidan's back at he walked away, utterly confused. Why didn't the leaf work for her? Aidan's cape fluttered with every step, showing a few rents in the smooth, star-free fabric. What was Aidan not telling her?

***

The already dim light had grown even paler when Aidan stopped and turned around. The look of hopelessness on his face made Gwen's stomach clench.

She looked past him at a tree with a large hollow in its trunk.

"No," she gasped. She ran forward. It was unmistakably the tree they had slept in the previous night. "How is this possible? We've been walking all day." She found herself breathing in great, gulping breaths.

"The path must have led us in a circle." Aidan's voice was flat with exhaustion and despair.

Gwen was almost beside herself with worry and pain. She took one last look at Aidan's hopeless face, and she couldn't help herself. Her eyes welled with unexpected tears. She covered her face in her hands as she tried to control her emotions.

A tentative hand rested on Gwen's shoulder.

"Don't cry," Aidan pleaded. "We'll figure it out."

She leaned forward and rested her head on his shoulder, letting the tears drain out. He put his arms gingerly around her.

Eventually she snuffled and said, "Sorry. It's been a long day." She lifted her head and looked at the wet spot on Aidan's shirt. "Oh, I got your shirt all wet."

"And it was such a clean shirt too," Aidan said in a mock-complaining tone. Gwen chuckled through her tears and straightened.

"And what are you two young things doing out in the woods alone?"

Gwen's heart stopped and she and Aidan whirled around.

Chapter 8

A man stood before them. Glossy brown hair fell in waves around his face, which was tilted to one side in question. He was dressed in a fawn-colored shirt which hung loose over brown pants tucked into well-worn leather boots, supple and well-fitting. A short cape completed his attire. Dozens of patchwork diamonds made up the fabric of the cape, in every shade of green imaginable. The cape swirled around his body like a living thing, incongruent in its complexity but camouflaging in its coloration. A green tattoo that might have been a leaf peeked out of his shirt collar.

Gwen's jaw dropped. Aidan moved in front of her slightly. Gwen wondered if he was trying to protect her then immediately felt guilty at the jolt of pleasure in her stomach. He didn't have to be here, taking risks for her. Ellie was her friend and her responsibility, not his.

The man raised one dark eyebrow in a high arch.

"You're both absolutely filthy. How did you end up so deep in the woods?" He looked them up and down.

"We—got lost," Aidan said stiffly. The man moved toward them and Gwen tensed. He reached out swiftly, like a snake striking, and pulled back the neck of Aidan's shirt to expose his left shoulder. The freckled skin was smooth and pale in the evening light. What was the man looking for?

Aidan flinched at the sudden motion and stepped back, pushing Gwen behind him.

The man laughed merrily, loud and clear in the deepening gloom. He said, 'Two baby birds fell out of their nest before they could fly."

"Who are you?" Gwen said, trying to sound strong and suppress the tremble in her voice.

"My name is Loniel, little bird. And this is your first time in the queen's realm, is it not? Otherwise you would not be so hopelessly dirty and lost." He looked between the two of them. "Open your inner eye and see the world as it should be."

"What the hell is that supposed to mean?" Aidan spat out. The man's grin widened.

"The birds are even younger than I thought. What very sheltered lives you must have lived in your nest, where no one taught you what wings are for." He pointed to a tree behind him. "Stare at the tree. Then look past the tree, through the tree."

Gwen looked at him skeptically. He laughed.

"It will help, little bird."

"What are we going to do? This guy is crazy," Gwen whispered to Aidan.

Aidan frowned at the tree.

"Just humor him until we know." They stared at the tree. The moss-covered bark was as solid as Gwen expected it to be.

"How do I look through a tree?" Gwen asked in confusion.

"I think he means to unfocus your eyes," Aidan said.

"Indeed, my nestlings. Now notice the edges of your vision. Can you see the pieces of lovely swimming almost out of sight?"

Gwen's fingers clenched and unclenched as she tried to control her breathing. They were being forced to do mindless tasks by some potentially dangerous stranger after an exhausting day of exertion and despair. Her throat constricted as she fought against the emotion welling up.

A flicker caught her attention. She could have sworn she'd seen a flutter of brilliant orange wings at the edge of her vision. She moved her eyes to look, and the orange vanished.

The man laughed.

"Focus, birdling. Once you see the edges change, let them take over your eyes bit by bit. *Will* them to take over."

Aidan stared intently at the tree, brow furrowed in concentration. Gwen looked back at the tree and unfocused her eyes. Gradually flickers of color presented themselves at the edges. She forced herself to keep looking forward into nothing. The colors began to bleed into the gloomy greys and greens of the forest. Finally the tree was the last dark vestige of gloom in a bright and cheery world until it too faded, replaced by a tall birch with white bark gently lit by rays of sunlight that pierced through a shifting canopy of brilliant green leaves. Birdsong filled the air, and a butterfly flitted past Gwen's nose. The sun's rays lit the little clearing with a soft, warm light, illuminating emerald green moss and cheery white mushrooms on the forest floor. A wide path cut a swath through the forest on either side of them, clearly maintained. Gwen looked around, amazed, and turned to Aidan whose jaw hung open in astonishment.

Loniel clapped his hands together slowly. He spread out his arms.

"Welcome to the queen's forest. She has it enchanted to discourage strangers and humans who stray here." Gwen dared not look at Aidan, who stiffened beside her. Was his theory true? Was this man one of the people of the barrows? And who was this 'queen' he mentioned? Gwen remembered Corann's locket with the picture of her mother. What was the connection? Had her mother travelled to this strange world too?

"Luckily for you," Loniel continued, oblivious to their discomfort, "I feel Breenan strangers should be welcomed to the realm. Humans, on the other hand, are only good for amusement." He cocked his head to the side. "Did you stumble over from King Faolan's lands?"

Aidan was silent. Gwen said, "It felt like we walked forever." It definitely wasn't a lie, but didn't answer his question. She was confused by his assumption that they weren't human, but it seemed clear that they would receive better treatment if she kept up the charade.

He seemed satisfied with her answer and glanced upward.

"But now it's time for merriment, since the sun has

93

set. Come and join me and my fellow merrymakers for dancing and a feast."

"Food?" Aidan's head lifted, and Gwen's stomach asserted itself noisily.

Loniel laughed.

"Of course. Just let me make you presentable." He held out his hands toward them. A warm breeze ruffled Gwen's skirts and flowed upward until it lifted her hair off the back of her neck. Her heart pounded as she turned to Aidan, who looked down at himself. His clothes were immaculate once again, and his face was clean and free of scratches. Where before he had looked half-wild and desperate, now he was once again the dashing magician of Thursday's ball. Gwen's forehead wrinkled in confusion as she glanced down at her dress. It was fresh and unstained, the rents torn by malevolent vines healed over and the fabric smoothed. She and Aidan stared at each other in astonishment. Loniel clapped his hands again.

"Much better. Now come with me to the feast." He turned to go.

"Wait." Gwen collected herself. She was shaky and on edge after Loniel's overt use of—magic?—but she couldn't forget why they were here. "I know it's a long shot, but have you seen two travelers pass by? The man has dark hair, pointed chin—the girl is blond with a blue dress on." She held her breath, waiting for his answer.

"Ah, yes. They passed by me late last night. The girl was human, correct?" Gwen nodded tentatively. The man said, "Aye. They'd be heading to the queen's castle."

"Please, can you tell us where to go?" Gwen's eyes

94

opened wide in her eagerness. "We need to find them."
Perhaps this horrible day hadn't been wasted after all.

"Much too late for traveling, little bird." He swept
his arm toward the path. "Come dance and feast tonight,
and tomorrow I will send you on your merry way." He
nodded his head down the path in the other direction.
"It's that way, so you know." He waved his hand at them
and smiled impishly. "Come, come. I won't take no for
an answer."

Gwen and Aidan glanced at each other.

"At least there's food," Aidan said in a light tone,
but there was tension in his voice. "And we can go to the
castle in the morning."

Gwen nodded tightly.

Loniel clapped Aidan on the back.

"Come roost at my fire, little birds."

***

Gwen and Aidan followed Loniel along the widened
path. The difference in the forest was monumental
between what they now saw and their journey earlier.
Gone were the pitfalls and serpentine booby traps. The
pools of water that were stagnant and dark before now
glimmered in the dusky air, clear and calm. The trees
grew straight and tall, not leaning broodingly toward the
path. The evening sun cast dappled shadows of bright
warmth and cool darkness, highlighting the brilliant
emerald of mosses on the woodland floor. The forest
was peaceful, so different from the malevolent force of
earlier. Gwen thought that perhaps she could even like
this forest, given time. Aidan smiled as she glanced at

him, his face calmer now. She slipped a hand into the crook of his arm and they walked that way for a few minutes.

Loniel stopped with a swirling of his cape.

"We've arrived," he said, turning to them in the dusky light.

Gwen looked around doubtfully. Aidan pointed to their left.

"Look," he said. "There's firelight." Gwen followed the line of his finger to a flickering glow of a fire below a ridge in the distance. Small figures were silhouetted between trees. Aidan said, "I guess we have to leave the path." He looked longingly at the wide trail. "I was enjoying walking in a straight line."

"Ah, but perhaps you will enjoy supper better?" Loniel raised his eyebrows, and let out a smug laugh. "Come, warmth and food await you. Let it not be said that guests went away unsatisfied from Loniel's fire." With that he left the path, effortlessly leaping from log to stump toward the fire's glow.

Aidan gripped Gwen's arm as she prepared to follow Loniel.

"Really? We're going to leave the path and follow this mad bloke into the forest?" He looked at Loniel's retreating back nervously. "Who knows what he wants? What he can do?"

Gwen rubbed her face with her free hand and sighed.

"I know. But what other choice do we have? I don't know if I can face another hungry night in a tree. We're already lost, and I don't know how else we're going to get out of here. We're just going to have to trust him."

Aidan's face was grim, but he eventually nodded

and let go of Gwen's arm.

Gwen sighed again and said, "Let's do this." She pulled her skirts up to her knees and climbed onto the nearest log.

The way was surprisingly easy after the trials of the day. They leapt from log to log, if not as gracefully as Loniel, then at least with as little effort. The bonfire grew larger, and the crackling of burning branches was interspersed with murmurs and laughter. They climbed the last small rise and looked down.

They were on the lip of a shallow bowl, clear of trees. A bonfire was in the center, roaring high and hot, and as many as fifty people gathered around it. Some fed the fire with logs and branches, laughing as the flames leapt up and consumed their offerings. Others passed around platters of food and earthen pitchers. Gwen's mouth watered. Some platters were piled high with slices and joints of meat, some dripped with grapes and other fruits, still others balanced pyramids of bread. Next to her, Aidan groaned in hunger.

Loniel laughed merrily, and gestured to a few of the platter bearers. They peeled away from the milling group and joined Gwen and the other two at the edge of the bowl.

"Sit, and eat to your heart's content. I will return when you are satisfied." He snapped his fingers at the platter-bearers, who placed their burdens on the ground in front of Gwen and Aidan and melted away.

Gwen sputtered, "Thank—thank you. This looks amazing." Aidan echoed her words. Loniel bowed, keeping his laughing eyes on them.

"For my little birds, of course." He turned and

moved to the fire, losing himself in the crowd. Gwen and Aidan looked at each other.

"Ready?" Gwen asked him.

"You have no idea." Aidan flopped on the ground. "Dig in, Gwen."

They fell on the food with gusto, tearing into the bread like animals. An earthen pitcher was filled with clear, cold water, fresh and satiating. As they ate and drank, they watched three figures drag drums from the surrounding woods. The drummers began to play, filling the clearing with pounding beats in intricate combinations. The crowd of people before them split into two. Half moved away and gathered around the edges of the clearing, while the others began to leap and twirl around the fire. Faster and faster they danced, weaving in and out, bending and twisting and jumping. It looked chaotic, but as Gwen watched she noticed a pattern to the madness.

More people joined the dance, and as the drums grew more insistent Gwen's heartbeat pounded faster. She glanced at Aidan. He watched the dancers, eyes half-closed. His fiery red hair gleamed in the flickering light, and his high cheekbones cast strange shadows on his face. Gwen's stomach stirred and she glanced away quickly, cheeks warm. She felt him look at her then and kept her eyes resolutely on the dancers.

The beat changed. The dancers paired off and swirled around in couples. Loniel materialized from a nearby cluster of onlookers, bearing a goblet and walking toward them. Gwen and Aidan glanced at each other, Aidan looking wary. Loniel approached with a wide smile.

"Have my little birds eaten enough worms to satisfy them?" Loniel waved away their thanks, interrupting them mid-splutter. "Now that you are fed, you must drink some of my signature libation." He offered the goblet to Gwen, who looked at Aidan. He shrugged slightly. She turned to Loniel.

"Please, I insist," he said, his strange tawny eyes intense. She looked into the goblet as he moved it toward her lips. The liquid glimmered darkly in the golden goblet. What harm could it do? The food had been fine. *Just a sip*, she thought, and opened her lips. Loniel carefully tipped the goblet so the liquid met her open mouth. She swallowed, the drink sliding down her throat in a cool cascade of pungent fruit and deep notes of honey.

"That's really good," she said, and Loniel smiled smugly.

"Of course it is, birdling," he said, bringing the goblet to Aidan's lips. Once Aidan had swallowed, closing his eyes briefly as if to make the flavor linger, Loniel stepped back.

"Now you can truly enjoy my little bonfire, without the peskiness of inhibitions. There isn't much in this land more potent than my famous libation. Enjoy, my sweets." He raised the goblet in a toast as he backed away, smiling wickedly.

The blood drained away from Gwen's face. What had Loniel given them?

"Did he give us some kind of drug?" she gasped, clutching the grass on either side of her. Aidan leaned back unconcerned, watching the dancers again.

"Don't worry about it. It doesn't sound deadly." He

99

bent his head closer to study her face. "Hey, what's up?"

"You don't understand," she choked out, squeezing her eyes shut. Her father's blood-drained face swam in front of her, white against the splatters of black on his cheeks. The silence, broken only by dripping ink from a lamp shade. "When I lose control, things happen. I can't stop them."

She opened her eyes to see Aidan looking at her with a wariness that surprised her. He asked carefully, "What kind of things?"

Her head was woozy and light. She blinked hard to clear her swimming mind. A strange wave of complacency quickly enveloped the shores of her panic, leaving only a lingering sense of unease around the edges. She stared at Aidan, trying hard to focus. His hair glowed in the flicker of the bonfire, the light dancing and making his whole head seem aflame. His eyes, normally a bright and merry green, were growing dark and shadowed in the dim. Only glints in the firelight let Gwen know that he still looked at her, waiting for an answer. She swallowed, trying to fight the calm. It seemed a ridiculous thing to do, now. She wondered why she bothered.

"Once, when I was seven," she said dreamily, "I cut a worm in half." She was half appalled that she was talking, and half entranced by Aidan's left eyebrow. "I showed a girl at school. She thought it was gross, so I put it together and brought it back to life. She screamed and ran for the teacher. Not that anyone believed her. Idiot," she added with disdain.

She focused on Aidan as he stared at her, his body completely still. He wore an odd expression of disbelief—and hope.

"What else?" He breathed out the words so softly that she had to lean closer to hear. She put a hand on his shoulder to steady herself. She could feel the heat of his body, and the tenseness in his shoulder. She whispered in his ear, horrified at her blabbing mouth, powerless to stop it. It was oddly satisfying, though. She hadn't expected that. To share her strangeness, her secret, with another person was almost exhilarating.

"I've exploded pillows and watermelons. I've made plates fly around the room. Once I made our houseplant sprout until it burst through the ceiling. I don't know what the matter with me is. When my emotions are strong, when I lose control, weird things happen."

Gwen leaned back to gauge the effect of her words on Aidan, hand still firmly on his shoulder. He seemed dazed, eyes searching hers. He swayed and blinked, the drink clearly taking hold.

"For real? You're not messing with me?"

The fire drew her in. Silhouettes leaped around it, dancing to the drum throbbing like a heartbeat. She had a wild need to jump and run and twirl, join hands with the others and soar over the flames like a phoenix.

"It's all true. Why do you think I never drink?" She ran her hand down the length of his arm, feeling gratified as he shuddered. "I'm tired of talking. Come dance with me."

"Do you know how?" He let himself be drawn up by her as she stood.

"Let's figure it out." Gwen suddenly pulled him close and grazed her lips against his, softly, like a feather floating on water. Astonished by her daring, heart

101

pumping faster than the drum, she twirled away.

She ran toward the dancers, her dress fluttering around her legs. She felt free and wild, the same way she felt walking in a windstorm, energized and alive. As she approached the ring of dancers they parted to draw her in. She was whisked into the arms of a man with a crown of leaves and white teeth glinting in the firelight. He was bare to the waist, and the golden skin of his left shoulder sported an intricate tattoo of vines and leaves. They twirled and leaped, and Gwen knew exactly what to do. A small part of her was astonished that she knew, but that part was very quiet in the roar of energy that filled her.

She was unsurprised when Aidan joined the dance a few minutes or hours later, she wasn't sure. Time had ceased to have meaning. As she turned, Loniel's grinning face swam in front of her, watching. His golden eyes were intense and all-knowing, and his grin was mischievous. She let the dance sweep her away.

Hours or minutes later, she found herself partnered with Aidan. His cheeks were flushed and his eyes were bright. They danced without speaking, Aidan's eyes fixed on hers. She found herself trying to extend her moves to have her hands lingering on his body. Her breath came faster than her exertions warranted, and a dizziness took over that had nothing to do with the whirling of the dance. The drums pulsed from the edge of the firelight.

A great cry erupted from the dancers on the far side of the fire. Momentarily distracted, Gwen looked over. Some were clapping and shouting, while others continued dancing around them. A couple broke away from the group, held hands, and ran straight toward the fire.

Gwen gasped. Were they going to burn themselves? At the last moment the pair leaped high and soared above the crackling roar of the bonfire. They landed gracefully on the other side as the others cheered, and joined the dance again. Another pair prepared to jump.

Gwen turned to Aidan with excitement and met his shining eyes. They danced closer to the cheering group as the drums beat faster.

In no time at all they found themselves at the jumping point. A laughing woman dipped her fingers in a small clay pot and swirled berry juice in twists on Gwen's cheek, and in broad stripes on Aidan's. Gwen briefly spotted Loniel close by, staring at them with a half-smile.

Aidan grasped her hand tightly.

"You ready?" he whispered in her ear. She shivered as his warm breath brushed her cheek. She squeezed his hand in reply and they turned to face the fire.

The flames roared high, the tallest reaching into the air far past Aidan's head. Gwen stared up at the stars, brighter than she'd ever seen, and then at Aidan. They ran as one to the fire, and leaped.

They soared straight across, higher than Gwen would have thought possible. She looked down midway into the blazing heart of the fire and had a moment's fear, but it vanished as quickly as it had arrived.

They landed hard on the other side to cheers from the crowd. Gwen couldn't keep her balance, and they stumbled haphazardly out of the ring of dancers. Aidan tripped as they laughed uncontrollably and they both went down, rolling together in a muddle. They stopped, still laughing, Aidan sprawled on top of Gwen.

Gwen gave a few more chuckles, but those soon died. She was suddenly, intensely aware of Aidan's body, the whole length of it pressed against hers. Her breathing was shallow. Half of his face was in shadow, the other half gazing at her intently. There was no laughter from him anymore, and he wore an expression of vulnerability and longing. Without thinking, Gwen leaned her head forward and kissed him hard on the mouth. Her eyes closed.

He responded slowly at first, then with a sudden eagerness, pressing her to the ground with his intensity. Gwen's world shrunk until nothing remained but the two of them, here, now.

The fire died with a hiss, and everything went dark.

Chapter 9

Gwen opened her eyes as Aidan raised his head. The fire was dead. Not just extinguished—even the coals were black, and no smoke rose up from the ash pile. It took a moment for Gwen's eyes to adjust, but when the area brightened slightly she was astonished that the clearing was empty. Every single dancer had vanished into thin air without a trace. Even Loniel had disappeared.

There was a tremendous crashing noise to her right. Aidan raised himself onto his hands and Gwen sat up. They watched in astonishment as a man burst into the clearing. He was filthy and disheveled, with a manic glint in his eye. His broad round face was scratched and the tips of his fingers were bloody and raw. He looked around wildly then stared intently to his left. Gwen looked in the same direction toward a bonfire burning merrily through the trees with figures leaping around it. The drums began to pound in the distance. Perplexed, she looked back at the man, but he was already scrambling toward the fire.

"Help! Over here!" the man shouted toward the dancing figures.

Aidan pushed himself up and tried to run in the man's direction, but he had difficulty keeping his feet. He yelled at the man, "Wait! Stop!" But the man was too intent on his target to hear Aidan's call. Aidan paused at the edge of the clearing and clutched a tree for support. Gwen watched as the man drew nearer to the fire. The fire winked out as if it had never been and appeared farther away, almost invisible between distant trees.

Gwen hugged her knees as Aidan came back and slumped on the ground.

"I don't understand," she whispered. Aidan looked at the cold fire.

"That's one legend that I have heard of," he said. "The fair folk will lure travelers through the woods by keeping their feasting fires just out of reach."

"Remember what Loniel said? About humans as amusement?" Gwen recalled the frantic eyes of the lost man. "I guess that's what he meant."

"I still don't understand why he thought we were one of them, one of the—Breenan? Is that what they call themselves?" Aidan frowned.

"I guess we're lucky enough to look like them?" Gwen said. "That man wasn't similar at all. And this proves your theory, I suppose. We are in an Otherworld."

"I don't want to say I told you so," Aidan said

morosely. "I really didn't want to be right."

***

They sat in the darkness for a while. The shock of the bonfire's demise had released Gwen from her strange mood, and the drink's effects drained away to leave her tired and sad. She was also feeling more and more embarrassed. She scrubbed at the berry juice now crusted on her cheeks. What had she been doing? The dancing was obviously under the influence of Loniel's intoxicating drink, but what of her advances to Aidan? Waves of hot embarrassment washed over her, but her stomach still clenched in anticipation. She suddenly wanted Ellie desperately. She needed her best friend to talk to. Confident Ellie always knew what to do, what to say. Gwen sighed aloud.

"Are you all right?" Aidan broke the silence they'd been sitting in, lost in their own thoughts.

"I was wondering how Ellie was," Gwen said.

"Hey, we'll find her tomorrow." Aidan reached a hand out for her shoulder and then pulled away, as if unsure. Gwen pretended not to notice. They watched the sky lighten beyond the trees in the east. Gwen lay back on the grass.

"We should get some rest." The night was much warmer in this new, friendlier forest, and she was quite comfortable lying under the paling stars. Aidan lay down, sighing deeply. She turned to look at his profile, his eyes staring up to the sky. She reached out and touched his arm.

"You okay?"

107

He turned his head and gave her a half smile.

"Yeah." He took her hand and gave it a quick squeeze, then released it. Gwen withdrew her hand and closed her eyes, feeling better.

***

Gwen awoke to the sound of birdsong. She was confused at first, and wondered why Ellie was whistling so early in the morning. She remembered where she was when her eyes opened to a green canopy of fluttering leaves far above her head. She sat up quickly with her head swimming, looking for Aidan.

He was across the clearing, humming softly as he leaned over a knee-high bush with glossy dark leaves. He straightened up when he saw her watching him. He held out his hand in an offering gesture. His palm was full of tiny dark berries, round and shiny. He loped over and flopped into a cross-legged position in front of her.

"Breakfast," he said, laying a large leaf on the ground between them and carefully depositing the berries onto the make-shift plate. "It's not much, but it'll have to do." He popped one in his mouth.

"How do you know they're safe to eat?" Gwen said dubiously, picking up a berry and examining it.

"I don't," Aidan said cheerfully, grabbing a few more. "But I read somewhere that we have a decent chance of survival if they're blue instead of red berries."

Gwen stared at him, eyebrows raised.

"What? I'm hungry," he said defensively.

Gwen examined the berry then shrugged her shoulders and popped it in her mouth. It was slightly tart, but juicy and flavorful.

"Well, I guess we'll go down together. Thanks for breakfast." She took a few more berries.

They ate in silence. Gwen was relieved that Aidan was acting like his normal self after the previous night, but she wasn't sure whether to talk about it or not. How much of what had happened had been because of that strange drink? She was still trying to sort out her own feelings. She certainly didn't have a clue what Aidan thought.

He broke the silence.

"I need to ask you something." He sounded nervous. Gwen picked up the empty leaf and started fidgeting with it, her stomach twisting. Aidan hesitated, and said, "What you said last night. About why you don't like to drink."

Gwen headed him off.

"I was intoxicated. You can't take anything I said last night seriously." She tried to laugh it off, but Aidan looked down at his hands without smiling. Gwen's forced chuckle died in her throat.

"You told me what you've done. I also saw your skin start to glow when we were—you know, before the bonfire went out. I know you told me the truth," he took a deep breath, "because I'm like you."

Gwen stared at him, uncomprehending. And what had he said about her glowing? Had she done something strange in the heat of the moment?

He went on. "You know I do magic tricks. What you don't know is that nothing I do is a trick. It's all real. I have magic, or whatever you want to call it." He gulped, still looking at his hands. "That's why I don't have any close friends. It's easy to fool strangers, but a friend would figure it out eventually." He slowly raised his eyes to Gwen's. "I've never told anyone before. I thought I was the only one." He looked desperately sad and hopeful all at once.

Gwen let out a breath she hadn't realized she'd been holding. She closed her eyes for a long moment, relishing the waves of relief washing over her. She opened her eyes and looked directly into Aidan's.

"It's lonely, isn't it?" She reached out and grabbed his hand between both of hers. After a moment, he placed his other hand on top.

They sat together for a minute, then Gwen released Aidan's hands, leaning to one side to prop herself up on her elbow. The hand-holding embarrassed her a little, but the feeling was drowned out by the relief and happiness of finding someone like her.

"When did you first find out?" Gwen looked at Aidan, intensely curious. Aidan looked down at his hands.

"I don't remember the first time. It's always been like this. Mum was freaked out by it, so she made me keep it under wraps. I learned to control it on my own, when she wasn't around." He twisted his pant cuffs, fidgeting. "I never knew my dad. Mum wouldn't talk about him. I figure he might have been like me." He looked at Gwen, eyes questioning. "Do you know where you got it from?"

"I never knew my mother," Gwen said slowly, wondering. "My dad definitely doesn't have any of this. He spent a week with my mother and found me on his doorstep nine months later."

Aidan raised his eyebrows, clearly shocked.

"I've tried to find her since," Gwen continued. "But it's like she never existed. I couldn't control the—magic—as a kid, but I've learned to keep a lid on my emotions. I try not to get too worked up about anything, and the magic doesn't show up. Too often."

"That's no way to live," Aidan said firmly. "I could show you how to control it, if you like."

Panic rose in Gwen at the thought of exposing herself to the strangeness, the magic. She said hastily, "Let's focus on getting Ellie back first."

***

Gwen and Aidan's walk on the path was as easy and uneventful as their scramble the day before had been horrendous and obstacle-filled. They walked side by side down the well-maintained path lit by rays of sunlight, breathing in the warm air and listening to cheerful birdsong. Gwen played with her vision, trying to replicate the eye trick that Loniel had taught them. She relaxed and unfocused her eyes, and the enchanted gloom of yesterday's forest took over her vision. She ducked in panic as a branch fell directly to her left. She heard Aidan laugh and switched back to the beautiful calm they walked through. The branch became a drifting green leaf.

"Dancing with yourself?" Aidan raised an eyebrow.

"Just checking out the enchantments. You can switch back to the old forest if you want."

"And why would I do that? If I never see that forest again, it'll be too soon." Aidan grimaced. "You have to

111

give this queen some credit, though—she certainly knows how to roll out the *un*welcome mat."

After an hour of walking they reached a large grove of poplars, carpeted by delicate bluebells. Gwen spotted a dark mass between distant trees. She pointed it out to Aidan, who stopped immediately.

"If that's the castle, then we'd better be ready." He held out a hand. "Can I clean you up? Your dress is dirty."

Gwen looked at him askance. Aidan's cheeks flushed.

"I can do it by magic," he said, avoiding her eyes. She lifted her arms in reply. Aidan waved his hand and a strong warm wind blew her skirts and buffeted her off balance.

"Whew!" She regained her feet. "That was enthusiastic." She looked down at her dress, clean once again.

"Hey, no complaining. I'm self-taught." Aidan turned his hand to his own outfit.

"No complaints. I'm impressed that you can use it at all, given my lack of skills." Aidan looked mollified. Gwen said, "So, do we just try to waltz in like we own the place, or do we sneak in?"

"Let's play it by ear. Although we did fool them once for being Breenan, so here's hoping we can pull it off again."

They continued forward, more cautiously now. The castle appeared piecemeal through the trees, an imposing stone fortress with grey walls that were clean and bright. Crenellated turrets sprouted haphazardly alongside spires and domes, with pennants and flags waving cheerfully from their peaks. Gwen frowned in confusion.

Aidan said, "It looks like the architect didn't know what he wanted."

"Or that there were too many different builders," Gwen said. She let her eyes unfocus to see the castle under enchantment. "Whoa, check it out the other way."

The castle was a decrepit hulking ruin. Vines climbing up the crumbling walls tore the stones apart. Huge boulders littered the ground in front. Moss crept over every surface, and trees grew close to the walls of the ruin.

"I hope our new vision shows the true condition. That looks like it should be condemned," Gwen said, switching back out of the enchantment.

"Looks like nobody is manning the doors, so that's good news." Aidan pointed forward. "Should we just go for it?"

"I don't really have any better idea," Gwen admitted. "Okay, head high, like we're supposed to be here." It struck her suddenly that her mother might be here. What if she had been taken to this Otherworld years ago, just like Ellie had been spirited away? Was it possible?

"Righto." Aidan offered his arm to Gwen. They strolled toward the open double doors, twice as tall as Aidan. As they drew near, music floated toward them on the breeze. They glanced at each other.

"Ready?" Aidan asked. Gwen nodded slowly and took a deep breath. They climbed up the steps and paused at the doorway. Gwen blinked a few times as her eyes adjusted to the dim light of the castle interior.

They were at the edge of an enormous ballroom. The only natural light came from the tall double doors Gwen and Aidan were standing in. The rest of the cavernous interior gleamed in the light of a thousand candles, dripping from wall sconces and swaying on elaborate chandeliers. Candlelight illuminated the people below. There were hundreds of them, almost all in swirling motion as they danced to a waltz played by a small orchestra on a dais in one corner. They were dressed in highly decorative medieval-style garb, long sleeves and colorful sashes brightening the ballroom floor. Gwen gave silent, fervent thanks to Ellie—her green velvet dress blended in perfectly. Many of the attendees wore masks bedecked with jewels and feathers and horns, winking and glittering as the dancers spun.

Candlelight glinted off intricate sword displays mounted on the walls, interspersed with huge woven tapestries. The nearest tapestry caught Gwen's eye, its glimmering golden threads depicting a hunting scene. Unlike the tapestry in her classroom in the human world, this one showed a hunt not of deer, but of men. Their open-mouthed terror made Gwen queasy, and when she spotted a child woven into the bottom corner she turned away in horror, her stomach clenching. How did she and Aidan think they would get away with this charade? And where was Ellie?

"Is this all these people do? Dance, I mean?" Aidan muttered in her ear. They edged sideways, trying to remain unnoticed. Gwen's determination to march in like she owned the place leaked away at the sight of the hundreds of dancers.

"I guess so. I wish we had masks. I'd feel a lot more comfortable with one." Gwen looked around, but no masks were forthcoming.

"Not everyone has one, so we aren't entirely out of place." Aidan's words were confident, but his voice was unsure. Gwen looked around at the crowd of dancers.

"Do you think Ellie is here? What do they want with her? Maybe we should check for dungeons or something, I don't know." Gwen's thoughts turned to what Corann wanted with Ellie. None of the scenarios she envisioned looked good. She scanned faces for Ellie's cheerful round features, but also kept the sketch of her mother in her mind.

"Wait a minute," Aidan said suddenly, scanning the crowd. "Wasn't she wearing a blue dress?"

"Yes! Blond hair, short, blue dress. Do you see her?" Gwen clutched his arm tightly, trying to follow his line of sight.

"Yeah, I think so. Dancing with the guy in the red shirt, with a bird mask. On the left side. There, she just twirled out."

Gwen breathed in sharply, hand to her mouth. There was Ellie, unmistakable, her hair still miraculously up in its styling from the ball of two nights ago. She was waltzing, and as she turned Gwen was horrified by the look of misery on her face. Gwen's grip on Aidan's arm tightened.

"Are they're forcing Ellie to dance? Look at her face!" Gwen's breathing was shallow in fear and indignation. Aidan shushed her.

"Try to look normal. There are Breenan looking our way."

Gwen tried to compose her features into a neutral expression, but her insides were writhing. She stole a glance around. One or two people in masks had their

115

faces turned to Gwen, but looked away without interest when Gwen calmed. She spoke quietly to Aidan out of the side of her mouth.

"I want to get closer so Ellie can see me."

Aidan looked around, readjusting Gwen's hand in the crook of his arm.

"Come on then. Try to look inconspicuous."

They set out around the perimeter of the ballroom. Gwen had never been so terrified in her life. The eyes of the Breenan peered through masks and over goblets, but no one seemed very interested in them and no one stopped them. Gwen had to remind herself to breathe.

"You know," Aidan said quietly as they side-stepped to miss a dancing couple, "I thought it might be worse. Being made to dance, well, I can think of worse fates."

"But did you see her face?" Gwen said. "There's something not right going on." Aidan gave her a look. She amended, "Beyond the obvious, that is."

When they reached the area where Ellie danced, Gwen pulled Aidan close to the wall next to a thick round pillar that disappeared into the gloom of the ceiling above their heads. Aidan looked around surreptitiously to make sure no one watched them, but Gwen had her eyes fixed on Ellie.

Ellie's look of vacant-eyed misery changed when she spotted Gwen. Her eyes opened wide with disbelief, and astonishment transformed her face. The shock made her stumble, and she grabbed her partner for balance.

The entire ballroom stopped still, and all heads swiveled to focus on Ellie.

Chapter 10

Gwen watched in confusion as the dancers parted to create an empty corridor. A woman appeared at the end, resplendent in a turquoise silk dress and a heavy necklace of glittering jewels. An elaborate mask of peacock feathers and diamonds was affixed to her face, outlining large, dark eyes. She strode slowly down the corridor, stopping in front of Ellie. The man in red gripped Ellie's forearm to face her toward the lady.

"My queen," said the man in red, bowing. "This human did not keep the rhythm."

"What's the matter, my dear? Is the dance too complex for you?" The queen's voice was smooth and low, yet Gwen had no trouble hearing it clearly.

"No, my lady," Ellie gasped out. She visibly shook.

"Is your partner not to your liking?" The queen glanced at the man in red. He gazed back, unconcerned.

"No, my lady, not at all."

"Perhaps your shoes are too loose. Yes, that must be it." She waved a hand toward Ellie's feet. There was a strange ripping noise, and Ellie gasped in pain. Tears sprang to her eyes and she sunk toward the ground, only held upright by the grip of the man in red. Gwen's stomach turned and it was all she could do to not cry out in sympathy. Was this terrible woman the queen Loniel has spoken of, the ruler that Corann has mentioned?

The queen smiled under her half mask. "There, that's better. Now we won't have any problems dancing, will we?"

"No, my lady," Ellie forced out, head hanging.

The queen turned to address the crowd. Dispassionate eyes gazed out from silent masks at the lady and the limp form of Ellie.

"The humans are fragile things," she said. The watching dancers laughed. The queen smiled before continuing. "But they are the key to fuelling the protection of our realm. I bring you these humans, and I take what we need from them. I do this for you, my people, for your safety and your comfort. For without my magic and my power, our realm would be overrun by our enemies. And so use this human, take from her what we need, and when she has no more to give, I will provide you with another. For I am your loving queen and I will protect my people with all my power."

The crowd bowed their heads in obeisance as the queen turned away and the man in red hauled Ellie up. As the dancers took their positions the orchestra began to play once again. The queen climbed a dais on the far side and sat in a carved gilded throne, looking down on the dancing multitudes. Gwen let out her breath, not realizing she'd been holding it. She turned to Aidan.

"We have to get her out."

Aidan nodded in agreement, his eyes wide.

Gwen's mind whirled in frantic chaos. How could they free Ellie from the vindictive queen and her terrible court? What did they want with Ellie? Had Ellie not escaped yet because she was punished by magic if she tried? Gwen tried desperately to come up with a plan, but how could she free Ellie from someone whose abilities Gwen didn't even understand? The rampant magic frightened her and made her feel powerless. What was the queen capable of doing? What Gwen had seen so far made her nervous for what else the queen was capable of.

Paralyzed with indecision, Gwen stood beside Aidan against the wall, watching Ellie dance. Suddenly the music stopped, and all the dancers moved gracefully into a wide circle. The queen stood up on her dais and walked to the center of the crowd.

"Loyal subjects and gentle guests, it is with sorrow that I must announce the departure of Prince Crevan's company." A young man with hair as flaming red as Aidan's stepped forward. The queen nodded to him and continued. "It has been our honor to host your people for the past half-moon. Your father is a close ally and dear friend of our realm. Although we may feel sadness at your leaving, we know you travel to a far greater destination—the sacred mountain, where your children will be reborn into the adults they are destined to be."

The crowd applauded, and a large portion disentangled themselves from the others and joined

119

Prince Crevan in the circle. About two-thirds of the group of fifty had red hair, leaving a scant few redheads left in the outer circle. The prince approached the queen to bow and kiss her hand.

As he did so, a Breenan man on Gwen's left leaned toward them and whispered, "You'd better get moving, boy. You'll miss your group, and the queen doesn't take kindly to visitors overstaying their welcome."

Aidan said quickly, "I'm not with them."

The man leaned over and yanked at the collar of Aidan's shirt to expose his left shoulder. Loniel had done the same thing before the bonfire. Gwen wondered what they were looking for, but didn't ask for fear of exposure. Aidan jerked back.

The man winked.

"Nice try, boy. But there's none of King Faolan's fold who are unmarked and living in the queen's court." He nodded at Gwen. "Is she one of ours? Is that why you don't want to go? Can't say I blame you," he said, leering at Gwen. Gwen tried not to wrinkle her nose.

"She's with me," Aidan said quickly.

"Then you'd best be off. Otherwise I'll be bound to tell our beautiful queen." His smile was nastier than Gwen had expected. "I wonder what she'll do with you. Could be quite a scene." Aidan swallowed and glanced at the queen. The expressionless mask revealed no secrets. The man said, "My favorites are the toenail extractions."

Gwen's eyes widened. She and Aidan looked at each other in horror.

Gwen said, "Look, the prince is leaving. We'd better get moving. Lovely to meet you." She dragged Aidan toward the double doors which Prince Crevan's group filed through. The man laughed behind them.

"Bloody hell," Aidan muttered. "Now what? Do you think he was having us on?"

"You saw Ellie's punishment," Gwen said. "I have a bad feeling he meant every word. I think we'll have to tread very carefully from now on." They trotted forward to the door. Gwen said, "Let's try to sneak off once we're outside."

Just then Gwen spotted Ellie. Their eyes locked, and Gwen's heart broke at the desperation and pain in Ellie's gaze. She held out her palm slightly in invitation. *Can you come?* she mouthed. Ellie shook her head, her eyes filling with tears. Gwen let her hand drop. *I'll come back. I promise,* she mouthed again. A hand pressed against the small of her back.

"Better hurry, young one." The Breenan who had warned them a minute ago pushed her and Aidan, cackling. She gripped Aidan's arm and they marched toward the door, Gwen giving Ellie one last pained look. They merged into the group behind three girls a little younger than Gwen, who were laughing and marching arm in arm together. Gwen avoided eye contact.

They stepped across the threshold, Gwen blinking in the daylight. The line of visitors stretched from the door into the forest to disappear between trees. The atmosphere of the visiting group was cheerful and festival-like. Small groups of visitors chatted happily together, all moving quickly down the path. Gwen noticed that most of the visitors were young, in their late teens. A few were middle-aged, smiling indulgently at the young people or walking gravely on their own. Gwen

121

turned to Aidan.

"What is this? Are we on some kind of school trip? Would that even be a thing here?" She kept her voice down, careful to avoid being overheard by the chattering girls ahead.

"No idea. But I don't know how we're going to escape undetected." He pointed discreetly to the side of the path. Blending into the trees like a shadow, a Breenan stood watching the line. In her hand she held a bow loosely cocked with an arrow. Thirty paces down the path Gwen spotted a man dressed in green, half-hidden by a thick bush. There was another, thirty paces beyond him. Gwen gulped.

"So that Breenan was right about guests overstaying their welcome."

"Yeah. So much for a friendly alliance between kingdoms." Aidan snorted.

"I'm worried that this *is* considered friendly here. I'm not looking forward to unfriendly." Gwen shuddered. "They can't have guards forever. Maybe we can escape soon."

"I hope so." Aidan sounded unconvinced.

***

Afternoon sun filtered through silver-leaved trees surrounding a meadow and danced on a small burbling stream winding through grass and hummocks of moss, illuminating the sleeping forms of a crowd of Breenan. They were draped over grassy mounds and tangled in loose piles of limbs as they slumbered in the lazy stillness.

122

Loniel remained watchful. He leaned into the hollow between two large roots at the base of a spreading oak. His eyes gazed at his sleeping revelers as he stroked the curls of a woman whose head rested on his chest.

Loniel turned his head sharply, his body tensed like a wild animal sensing its prey. The sleeping Breenan did not stir, but Loniel waited, eyes fixed on the forest to his right. He remained in place.

A few moments later, a Breenan man noiselessly entered the meadow. His elaborate dress appeared out of place beside the rustic garments of the revelers. He looked around until he spotted Loniel in the shadows and swiftly skirted the sleeping Breenan to reach the oak tree.

"Finegal." Loniel greeted the newcomer. "Welcome." The man bowed in reply and sat within the shade of the oak. Loniel continued to stroke the woman's hair.

Finegal looked around at the sleeping forms dotting the meadow.

"It was a wild night last night," he stated, looking to Loniel for confirmation.

"As always," Loniel said calmly. "We had some fun teasing a human. I eventually put him out of his misery. The amusement I gain from humans leaves a bitter aftertaste when I can't send them back to their homeland. Of course we wouldn't have this problem if the queen behaved herself." He leaned his head back against the tree trunk and looked at Finegal through half-closed eyes. "Did you do as I asked?"

Finegal nodded. "Indeed. The two lost children are on their way to the sacred mountain as we speak. I doubt

123

they will escape Prince Crevan's group. The queen has far too tight a grip on the forest for that. She doesn't trust Faolan at all, despite being allies." Finegal laughed briefly. "I think I gave your young couple quite a scare. I mentioned something about the queen torturing by toenail extraction, I believe. They were more than eager to leave the castle after that."

Loniel smiled widely, and then sobered.

"It's hardly out of character for her."

"Well, she wouldn't do that to a Breenan, but they didn't seem to know that." Finegal looked curiously at Loniel. "May I ask, what is your interest in these two? Why the determination to get them to the sacred mountain?"

Loniel did not immediately reply. He bent down and kissed the woman's forehead. She blinked herself awake.

"Wake the others, my love," he said quietly. "It is time to prepare for another night."

She smiled sleepily and moved away to the nearest group, her brown curls swaying gently. Loniel watched her go, and said, "They are more important than they know. They must fix what I cannot. But first, they must know themselves better." Loniel smiled at Finegal's confusion. "Just make sure they don't return to the castle until they've been marked."

***

Gwen and Aidan walked in silence, Gwen checking for guards in the trees. She noted with a heavy heart their continued presence and thought miserably of Ellie.

Aidan finally broke the silence between them.

124

"I'm sorry, Gwen." He sounded very forlorn.

Gwen turned to him in surprise.

"What on Earth for?"

"We wouldn't be traveling to who-knows-where away from the castle if it weren't for me." Aidan kept his eyes forward, his jaw tight.

Gwen was taken aback.

"It's not your fault they think you're one of them. And anyway, you really think I would just sneak off, rescue Ellie, and waltz back home without you? I'm not leaving you here on your own. We're only getting through this if we stick together." She touched his arm briefly. Aidan caught her eye and smiled wryly.

"Oh, I don't know. It's not so bad here. At home I'm a dreaded ginger. Here it seems I've got my own tribe."

Gwen laughed. They continued walking companionably, following the chattering girls.

A hand on her shoulder broke her reverie. She tensed, ready for an intruder, but when she turned to look at Aidan a different face greeted her with a beaming smile. The arms of the intruder draped across their shoulders in a friendly fashion.

"Hello. I don't know you yet, which makes you more interesting than most of these idiots already." The boy was thin and wiry, with the now-usual shocking red hair and high cheekbones. He went on. "Names? Where did you spring from?"

Gwen and Aidan glanced at each other, Gwen nominating Aidan to speak with a widening of her eyes. Aidan took the hint and said, "I'm Aidan and this is Gwen. We joined the group late." The half-truth rolled off his tongue easily. Gwen looked at the boy closely to gauge his reaction.

The boy seemed unconcerned.

"I'm Bran. I'm bored of the lot I came with, so I'm going to be annoying and stay with you a while." He laughed easily. Gwen looked at Aidan in desperation, and he returned her glance with a tiny resigned shrug. Bran let go of their shoulders and darted off to the side of the path.

Aidan whispered, "When life gives you lemons…"

Bran returned with a daisy-like yellow flower which he tucked behind Gwen's ear with a flourish. She smiled uncertainly.

"So, Bran," Aidan said, "Do you know how far the sacred mountain is?"

"Oh, we'll be there in the wink of an eye, but we'll go much further than we've ever gone before," Bran said cryptically, walking backward to face them.

Gwen gave a tiny sigh. Loniel had been evasive and riddling too. It was supremely unhelpful. She tried a different question.

"Our parents didn't tell us much about where we're going or what we're doing. We—we live very isolated lives, far from everyone else here." It was not a lie, but definitely misleading. Aidan gave a slight nod of approval.

"We're going to get our marks, of course. You know, the tattoos you get when you become an adult? They show your tribe affiliations and your parentage." Gwen's heart started beating too fast. Was this the detail that would give them away? He noticed the blank looks on their faces. "Come on, you must have seen them on elders before."

"Oh yes, of course," Gwen said automatically, but then recalled the strange green tattoo peeking out of the collar of Loniel's shirt. "I was just never told much about them."

"Are your parents hermits or something?" Without waiting for an answer Bran went on, "I can't wait to finally get my elder mark. My older brothers won't stop teasing me."

"That's not very nice," Gwen said consolingly. Trying to be offhand she said, "What do your brothers' marks look like?"

"The usual leaves and vines," Bran said dismissively. "I can read them, though. As can most people." He looked curiously at them. "If you didn't even know what the marks are, does that mean you can't read them either? I've never met someone illiterate." He dropped back and walked forward again, this time on the other side of Gwen. Gwen cast around for something to say.

Aidan beat her to it, obviously wanting to distract Bran from their inability to read marks.

"This thing at the mountain, where we get our marks. What exactly happens?"

"Dunno," Bran replied. "It's all hush hush until you actually go. I think there's some kind of ceremony, then we climb the mountain. There's a stone circle on top where we get our marks."

"Does it hurt, getting a mark?" Gwen imagined a team of tattoo artists perched on stones, waiting for them. It was a bizarre thought, but it seemed that in this world anything was possible.

"Worse than you can imagine, apparently. But it's

totally worth it. People finally take you seriously. I'm so done being a child." He whistled for a moment then jumped in front of them again, walking backward. Gwen had never met someone with so much energy. Bran asked, "So are you two related? Because you don't look it."

Gwen shook her head.

"Are you two an item?"

Gwen's cheeks reddened slightly and Aidan's eyes looked away in confusion.

Bran laughed heartily.

"Ah ha! A confused uncouple-couple! How precious. Has he kissed you yet?" This was to Gwen, who looked down to avoid Bran's eyes. He put a finger under her chin and lifted her head up. "A quick test of his feelings," he whispered to her, and quick as a bird he pressed his lips to hers.

Gwen raised her eyebrows in shock.

"What the hell are you doing?" Aidan pushed at Bran's chest with the flat of his palm, causing Bran to stumble back.

Bran merely laughed loudly, a broad grin on his face and mischievous eyes twinkling.

"He passed the test," he said to Gwen. "Later, hermits!" He turned and trotted up the line, where he disappeared around a bend in the path.

Chapter 11

They stopped in the middle of the path when Bran kissed Gwen. Aidan's face was stormy as his eyes followed Bran's retreating back. Gwen tried to keep her face emotionless, a difficult task. Her cheeks were burning with embarrassment and agitation, but those emotions were warring with a small warm core of pleasure at Aidan's reaction. She wondered whether he was being protective of her because they were stuck together in this strange land, or whether there was a part of him that was jealous, as Bran seemed to be implying. She busied herself with adjusting her ridiculous sleeves, trying to keep calm.

A trio of boys parted to walk past them. Aidan shook himself out of his preoccupation and Gwen started walking again.

"Are you all right?" Aidan said as they followed the

boys.

"Oh yeah, no harm done," she said brightly. She chewed the inside of her cheek briefly, trying to disentangle herself from the awkwardness of Bran's actions. It seemed the perpetrator was the only one immune to their effects, and Gwen could well believe Bran had very much enjoyed putting them on the spot. She said, "So what about this ceremony? What on Earth do they do to get these super painful tattoos?"

"What I'm wondering is what they're going to do to us when we get in that stone circle and don't sprout a brand new tattoo." Aidan glanced to the side. "Hey, do you want to try escaping? I don't see the guards anymore."

Gwen's heart beat a little faster.

"Sure. Pretend to tie your shoe or something." They moved to the side of the path and Aidan bent down. Gwen looked around, trying to affect an air of nonchalance. The last few dregs of walkers passed them by, glancing curiously or disinterestedly or not at all. Finally the last walker arrived. She was a tall, haughty-looking woman, aging but gracefully so. She wore a long overdress of soft brown leather, and an expression of suspicion.

"Move along, you two." She made a waving motion with her hand. "If we're caught in the queen's forest after dark, it won't go well for us."

"What will happen?" Gwen couldn't help asking as Aidan unfolded his length from the shoe he'd been tying and untying.

"I have no doubt you'd be run through with an arrow, or perhaps animals in the forest would be sent

130

after you. The treaties are very clear." She sniffed, pursing her lips. "Now, move!"

They moved without further delay, walking quickly to catch up to the others and to put some distance between themselves and the lady.

"Dammit," Gwen said when they were out of earshot of the lady. "How are we supposed to get back to the castle?"

"I guess we wait until we're out of the forest, then we ditch this lot," Aidan said, settling into a walking rhythm a short distance away from the last group. The forest was still and calm, and Gwen resigned herself to walking for the last part of the afternoon.

Gwen supposed her face had grown somewhat serene because Aidan said, "I'm glad to see you're enjoying yourself." He grinned. "It's not like we're taking a forced march through an enchanted forest in a magical land where a wrong step could end in our doom."

Gwen stuck her tongue out at him.

"You were the one telling me to make lemonade."

Still smiling, Aidan looked forward up the path. Gwen watched his expression change into tense wariness. He said, "Bran's coming back."

Gwen looked quickly forward. Bran loped back to them, occasionally stopping to exchange words with others on the path. He paused to conjure a large spider out of nowhere on the shoulder of a pretty red-headed Breenan girl, whose screams echoed loudly in the still air.

Gwen shook her head.

"I wonder if this ceremony gives them more than

just a tattoo to show their adulthood. Bran is such a child." She grabbed Aidan's arm. "Let's find out more about the queen and castle from him."

"Tread carefully," Aidan warned as Bran took a great leap and landed in front of them. His hair was wild and his eyes bright with excitement and activity.

"We're almost there, hermits!" He fell into step with Gwen and Aidan, inserting himself in the small gap between them. They made room for him, Aidan with less than good grace.

"Hi Bran," Gwen said, trying to sound welcoming. "Is everyone else as excited as you are?"

"Of course they are! I might be a little more enthusiastic than most," he conceded with a wink at Gwen. He turned to Aidan. "You're not still sore at me, are you? I promise I won't steal Gwen away from you. Not unless she wants me to." He glanced impishly at Gwen. She rolled her eyes at him with a smile, trying to keep him in a good mood.

Aidan said awkwardly, "It's fine. Hey, we, uh, came late to the castle. Did you have a good time there?"

"Oh, it was fine. Tons of dancing mostly. The queen can't get enough, apparently. Me, I prefer hunting." Gwen thought of the tapestry in the castle depicting a hunt for humans, and decided not to ask him what he hunted. Bran continued, "She's constantly on the lookout for new ideas. You know the humans are the creative ones, always making new things and thinking new thoughts. Most of us are content to do what we've always done. It works, and we've had plenty of innovation in the past from humans long ago. I don't really see why she wants more. But anyway, she somehow sneaks into the human world and steals away humans. She uses them to make up new dance choreography, paint pictures for her, play new tunes in her orchestra, tell her new stories. You must have seen that monstrosity of a castle. She's had at least three human builders working on it, and so had her mother and her mother before her. The whole line is batty like that."

"So why are humans the creative ones?" Aidan frowned in interest.

"Who knows? It's always been like that. We've got magic—they've got creativity." Bran shrugged. "That's how we're made. Honestly, I think we got the better end of the bargain. I don't know why the queen is so enthusiastic about new things."

Gwen cut in while Bran took a breath.

"So the humans that are taken, can they go back? Are they forced to be here?"

"Oh, I expect they die eventually. The queen works them hard, and humans don't have the greatest endurance." Bran spoke matter-of-factly, and Gwen tried to hide the distress on her face. Aidan took over for distraction.

"So they're trapped in the castle?"

"Some kind of containment enchantment, by the looks of it, so they can't leave the castle proper." Bran lifted his hand and gave a flashy flick of his wrist. A bright green apple appeared in his palm.

"Apple?" He offered it to Gwen.

"No, thanks." She couldn't stomach eating. Her stomach roiled at the thought of Ellie's fate. Aidan also refused the apple. Bran bit into it with a crunch.

133

"So, in your land," Aidan said, "you don't bring in humans for anything?"

"Oh, we used to," Bran said, swallowing a piece of apple. "Back a few hundred years ago, humans were always stumbling through the portals, passing through by chance along the old pathways connecting the worlds. But that was before the closing of the portals." He must have seen the blank looks on their faces, because he cried out, "Oh, come on! Did you grow up in a tree stump? Five hundred years ago, when Queen Kiera was slighted by her human lover. In retaliation she closed all the portals between worlds in a huge show of magic. She didn't want anyone else to be tormented like she had been."

"Whoa," Gwen said softly. Then she frowned. "But how does the queen nowadays get her humans for dancing and all that?"

"No one knows," Bran said, shrugging. "Kiera made it so the only one who could get through was her half-human child. So the kid could visit his human relatives, I guess? Otherwise, the ways are sealed for everyone except a very few people who have figured out how to open the portals. The queen, King Landon of Silverwood, the family of Sheehan by the sea, but it's a closely guarded secret. Humans don't just stumble into our world anymore like they used to. They're taken."

They walked in silence for a brief minute. Gwen digested the new information. Bran was obviously not accustomed to quiet, because he broke the silence quickly.

"Apparently the humans used to be quite fun. Lots were poets and bards, so they always had good stories.

134

Obviously many of our people took them as lovers, but the humans would react really strongly to our drinks, and it would leave them all dazed and crazy." Gwen stole a glance at Aidan, who returned it with a raised eyebrow. "Sometimes we'd take them to a different portal, and tell them that a hundred years had passed in their world. The humans were great for pranking." Bran sighed wistfully. "I live in the wrong age." He looked up suddenly. "It's almost sundown. We should be there really soon."

Trying to get more information out of Bran, Gwen said, "Our parents didn't tell us much about the ceremony. Why this mountain? How did the queen get control of it?"

Bran looked surprised.

"It's not on her land. The sacred mountain is neutral ground. No one owns it. Everyone can go for the rites. We just passed through her lands on the way."

As if on cue they turned a corner and saw the setting sun beyond thinning trees. The rays highlighted a dark mass of mountain rising up ahead of them. Most of the mountain was in shadow, but its silhouette was outlined in a fiery crown from the blazing sunset. The mountain seemed to Gwen to be more firmly placed, more intensely present, rooted more deeply than any other mountain she had yet encountered. It seemed larger than it was, with a dense presence that spoke of long history, eons of watching over this valley and forest, millennia of sunrises and sunsets, the flickering of lives winking into and out of existence as the mountain sat unchanged. A shiver tingled in her chest, just as it had at the barrow in the human world.

Gwen turned to Bran. He said happily, eyes ahead,

"Welcome to the sacred mountain."

***

"And we spin half a turn to your left, and then you step forward—there." With a twist of blue skirts, the Breenan man twirled Ellie according to her instructions. They paused for a moment, Ellie's brow wrinkled in concentration.

"Okay, now let's turn once more, and then you can dip me." Her partner nodded silently as he followed her words. Eyes watched impassively from the edges of the darkened chamber.

Ellie pulled away from her partner after their last move and turned to face the five Breenan watching them.

"Well? Are you satisfied with your new dance? Is it different enough for you?" She wiped her palms against shaking legs hidden by her skirts.

"A bit lack-luster, but certainly a novel combination." A rather severe-looking Breenan woman with hair tightly wound around her head looked appraisingly at Ellie. "You gave us your best choreography last night. It was quite exciting. But tonight..." The woman raised an eyebrow. "I don't know if the queen will be as pleased."

Ellie closed her eyes momentarily.

"I can't go on like this. Dancing all day, choreographing for you most of the night. What little food I get in the morning, you've drugged to disorient me. How can you expect me to create anything of value?"

The woman gave a short laugh.

"We have not poisoned your meals. You simply cannot tolerate our food and drink, human, which is why we let the effects wear off before you teach us novel dances. And yes, we expect you to provide us with new choreography. That is your purpose here. You know what will happen if you do not comply."

Ellie swallowed hard and looked away. Bitterly she said, "Fine. More dances, then." She grabbed her partner and hissed at him, saying, "Follow me." She proceeded to lead him in a fast salsa, close and hard. The watching Breenan leaned in, curious.

"That will do." A resonant voice echoed through the chamber. Ellie immediately stopped and whipped her head around to look at the newcomer.

The queen paced across the room toward Ellie and her partner, her long dress whispering on the wooden floor. Her face was unmasked and wore an expression of calculating curiosity. She stopped an arm's length away from Ellie, looking her over.

Ellie's jaw dropped when she looked into the queen's face. The queen looked back curiously.

"You look like you've seen a spirit. Or is it my overwhelming beauty?" Titters emerged from the other Breenan as the queen smiled indulgently. She grasped Ellie's chin in her hand and tilted her head up, examining her.

"Has she been fed recently?" she asked the others.

"No, my lady," one of the women replied. "She is quite alert."

"Then why the open mouth?" The queen twisted Ellie's head back and forth, then released her. "It's not an attractive look, my dear. Please don't make me fix it for you."

Ellie snapped her mouth shut so hard her teeth clacked together audibly. Her partner laughed.

"Well?" The queen waited for Ellie's answer.

"I—I thought I recognized you from somewhere. I've never seen you without a mask on. I must have been mistaken." Ellie's eyes darted from the queen's face.

"Indeed." The queen looked disinterested. "Well, do not let me detain you any longer. I'm sure you are eager to contribute your best work to beautify my ballroom." She stroked Ellie's cheek. Ellie tensed. "You will perform your best here tonight?"

"Yes, my lady," Ellie murmured, her eyes downcast.

"Good girl." The queen withdrew her hand and walked back to the doorway. She turned before leaving.

"I'll make sure to receive a full report from the others later." She smiled with all the confidence of absolute power, and left.

Ellie let her breath out. She turned to her partner and put her shaking hands into position. She said grimly, "Okay. Let's do this."

***

Panic threatened to take over Gwen's control. They had walked all afternoon with no chance of escape, and now they faced some kind of Breenan ceremony during which they would almost certainly be exposed as human. Gwen glanced at Aidan and noticed his cheeks were paler than usual and his face creased in a frown. She thought wistfully of the days before they entered the

138

barrow. She missed Aidan's bright-eyed grin. As if he read her mind Aidan looked at Gwen and gave her a wry smile.

"You ready for this?"

"No," she said honestly. They had slowed to let Bran move ahead. She whispered, "What do we do now?"

"We try to get back to the trees or we ride out the ceremony and wing it." Aidan nodded at a dense cluster of trees at the edge of the forest. But before they had walked two steps toward it Bran turned and called back to them.

"Come on, hermits! The sun's setting!"

Gwen bit her lip but there was nothing to be done. Bran waited for them, expectant face turned their way. They trudged toward him, Gwen forcing her expression out of its worried state.

"Just stick close to me, and we'll try to stay on the edge of things," Aidan said.

Bran clapped Aidan's shoulder when they joined him.

"Come on, let's get to the camp. One of the elders will give a speech, then the rites will begin." He rubbed his hands together. "I'm more than ready for this."

They followed the others across an open meadow that lay adjacent to the now brooding forest, grey grasses swaying in the shadow of the mountain. Their destination appeared to be a cluster of graceful willows, drooping on the banks of a small stream. As they drew nearer, light appeared from a fire burning on the river bank between swaying trees. Branches fell from the heights of each tree and spread out to form natural enclosures under shifting veils of leaves.

139

The fire popped and hissed in the darkening twilight, dancing flames bright in the gathering gloom. Most of the travelers were already gathered around the fire. Bran grabbed Gwen and Aidan's arms and dragged them to the others. There was a hushed expectancy to the group and all eyes were fixed on Prince Crevan, a lone figure on the far side of the fire. His eyes were shadowed and his face impassive. He waited to speak until the last of the walkers had jostled into position across from him.

"You have travelled far," the prince said, his quiet voice carrying clearly, punctuated by the crackling fire, "much farther than from your homes to the sacred mountain. You have travelled from childhood to be here, and it has been a long road. Tonight you will continue your life journeys, not as inconsequential children, but as full elders, with all the right and responsibilities therein.

"Tonight you will be transformed. And may the stones find you worthy." The prince stepped back out of the firelight. A moment's hush was followed by quiet murmuring. Gwen turned to Bran in a panic.

"What did he mean, 'May the stones find you worthy?' Is there some test we have to pass?"

Bran shrugged.

"Don't worry so much, Gwen. Occasionally the stones don't leave their usual mark, and leave the tribeless mark instead. It means there's something wrong with them, or they were never going to properly grow up. We don't talk much about the tribeless ones. If they escape, they make their way to the Forbidden Lands."

"And if they don't escape?" Gwen asked, dreading the answer.

"They're a danger to us all, and must be stopped,"

Bran said in what sounded like a memorized line. In his usual voice he said, "I don't know if they're just captured, or killed, or what."

Gwen looked at Aidan in despair. So this was their fate. They would be marked as somehow 'wrong,' and be forced to flee for their lives. Gwen felt like walls were closing in on her from every side. Aidan looked sick, and he swallowed hard.

Bran said, "Stop worrying, you'll be fine. Come on, Aidan, let's get changed." He put an arm around Aidan's shoulders and steered him away. "You go that way, Gwen," he called out over his shoulder, pointing behind her. "We'll see you soon."

Gwen opened her mouth to protest her separation from the only familiar person in this strange and dangerous world, but a solid hand clapped down on her shoulder. She turned and saw that the hand belonged to the grim-faced lady from the path. The lady jerked her head toward the girls filing through an opening in the branches of a willow nearby. Gwen turned one last time to look at Aidan. They exchanged a wide-eyed look of panic before Aidan was steered into a different tree. Gwen gritted her teeth and walked to the girls' tree, the lady's hand slipping off her shoulder as she went.

Inside the tree it was dim. The only illumination was firelight filtering through the long branches of the willow. The tree was crowded with girls. Gwen recognized the trio she had walked behind earlier that afternoon. An older woman passed out sacks and simple tunics, both cut out of the same coarse-woven brown cloth. Gwen accepted a bundle, and held out the tunic at arm's length. It was a shapeless bag of a dress, knee

141

length, with only a single sleeve. Gwen was puzzled, but tried not to show her confusion. She watched others sidelong to see what they did.

The other girls chattered as they unlaced each other's dresses and slid out of stockings.

"Everything off, girls! You must be reborn with nothing of your own, just as you first arrived in this world." The woman passing out tunics called out instructions over the babble. "Put your own clothing into the bags. Don't worry, you'll get it back after the ceremony."

The other girls undressed easily and without any apparent regard for modesty. Gwen was glad of the dimness as it hid her own embarrassment. She tried to shimmy out of her dress as quickly as she could, carefully avoiding eye contact as she slipped the tunic over her head. She struggled with it as her elbow caught in a fold, and wriggled furiously until she was free. Only then did she look down and see her bra lying on top of her dress, distinctly unlike the undergarments of the other girls. She shoved it into her sack as a nearby girl watched with open curiosity.

The tunic fit better than Gwen had expected. The left shoulder was bare by design. Gwen presumed the tattoo would be drawn there, like the tattoo of the dancer at Loniel's bonfire. She wondered how on Earth she would cover up the area when she and Aidan were exposed as frauds. She pulled at the hem of the tunic and crossed her arms, feeling exposed and uncomfortable without her bra. She tossed her sack against the tree trunk with the others and watched as more elders appeared through the branches, carrying shallow bowls of a dark, viscous

142

liquid. Gwen didn't have to wonder what it was for long, as the lady from the path started to speak.

"Before me stands a group of girls. Tonight, you will become women." She waved imperiously at the elders next to her and they began to walk around, dipping two fingers in the liquid and drawing spirals and swirls on each girl's cheeks and forehead. The lady continued, "This blood signifies your monthly blood, the first sign of your approaching womanhood. The blood represents the blood of childbirth, another journey you may take in your adult life. The blood also stands for the blood of death, of ones you love and of your own. As an adult you must face mortality. You will never escape it, so you must learn to embrace it."

A woman approached Gwen with the bowl. The metallic scent of warm blood drifted to Gwen's nose and her stomach turned. It was obviously fresh. The woman dipped her fingers and swirled the blood gently over Gwen's cheeks. Gwen looked into the woman's eyes, tawny as an owl's, and was strangely mesmerized by the ritual touch and the intensity of the woman's gaze. The woman lifted her fingers, nodded once, and moved on. Gwen blinked, feeling oddly bereft.

The last of the girls was blooded, and the lady said, "Into a circle holding hands, please." Gwen's hands were grabbed by her neighbors on either side, and she was comforted by the contact, strangers though they were. She looked around at the dim figures in the circle, rough tunics and painted faces looking like relics from another age. Part of Gwen protested at this ridiculous caveman ritual, half-expecting human sacrifice or worse. The other part was awed by this obviously ancient living tradition, sensing larger things happening than she could comprehend and feeling a kinship with these strange girls. She thought briefly of Ellie, who she knew would give anything to witness this.

"Eyes closed, and let your energies meld and flow around the circle. Feel the energy of your sisters. For you are now sisters, part of the great dance of life. Even if you never see each other again, you will always be together on your life's journey, for we all travel the same road." The lady paced around the tree trunk in the center of the circle. Gwen closed her eyes obediently, but her breathing quickened. Energies? What was she supposed to do? Gwen hoped keeping her eyes closed would be enough.

Then a great rush of energy poured through the hands she grasped. It took over her body so suddenly she gasped, and her chest and chin lifted involuntarily as the sensation filled her. Without thinking, she relaxed her mind and body and joined the river of energy flowing through her around the circle. She gave herself over to the sensation, not knowing or caring if she stood there for seconds or hours.

Finally the great tide of energy ebbed and she pulled back into herself. She opened her eyes, seeing the other girls blinking and looking at each other with shy smiles of recognition. Gwen caught the eyes of a girl across the circle. She smiled at Gwen with such warmth and inclusiveness that Gwen instinctively returned the smile. The peace and serenity from the ritual lasted until the lady said, "It is time."

Gwen remembered what was going to happen, and clutched her shoulder without thinking. Now she would be exposed as human, and all the feelings of kinship and goodwill that the other girls felt for her would evaporate into disdain or hatred once they knew, and she would be hunted down and punished for daring to enter their world. She felt sick and longed for Aidan's comfortable presence.

The girls filed out of the tree and Gwen waited her turn. As she waited, she overheard the lady speaking to another woman in low tones.

"It just felt strange, don't you agree?" The lady's voice was puzzled.

"Perhaps we have a tribeless one this year." The other woman seemed less concerned.

"No, it was different, but I don't know what it means." A pause, then, "Tell the guards to be on alert, just in case. We don't want a tribeless one getting away."

"Yes, my lady." The woman moved off, leaving the lady frowning by the tree trunk.

Gwen followed her neighbor out of the tree, barely breathing through her terror. They could sense her, and now she and Aidan had no chance of escaping with guards in place. The calm from the circle evaporated in the heat of her agitation.

The boys had exited their own tree and Gwen was relieved to spot Aidan's tall frame beside Bran, who looked positively beatific in anticipation. They were dressed in simple pants, roughly cut off at the knee and held up with coarse rope. Gwen's cheeks flushed hot when she looked at Aidan's bare chest and she turned away to compose herself, astonished that she could think of her attraction to Aidan in their present situation. She

145

mentally shook herself.

Prince Crevan clapped his hands together twice. All eyes locked on him. He said calmly, "Now, to the mountain, the stone circle, and your adulthood." He waved his arm toward the hulking mountain, and yellow lights sprang into being. They lit a clear path to follow from the willows to the meadow and up the mountain. There was a moment's pause, and then a few of the more adventurous boys and girls started forward.

Gwen quickly sidled toward Aidan as the two groups merged together. He spotted her and relief spread across his face.

"I'm glad to see you," she said.

"Let's not split up again if we can help it, okay? I can't take the stress." Aidan smiled weakly at her. His face had been painted with blood also, broad straight strokes glistening across his cheeks.

"Hi Gwen." Bran grinned at her. "Ready for the grand finale?"

"I guess I'd better be," she said wryly.

They followed the path with the group, picking their way tentatively along the dirt track with their bare feet. The mountain loomed up in front of them, ominous and dark. The pale yellow lights zigzagged up the face and disappeared over the top.

Gwen trudged along in silence. The ceremony in the tree, the eerie lights, the darkness, and her worries left her uncommunicative. From the silence beside her, she guessed Aidan felt the same. Even Bran seemed subdued by the circumstances. He hadn't said a word since they began their climb.

The way grew steeper very quickly. Gwen started

146

panting as she hiked upward, sweat beading on her forehead. Occasionally she used her hands to clamber over boulders in the way. The unearthly glow from the Breenan lights brightened the path, but not enough to prevent Gwen from stubbing her toes and stepping on sharp stones inconveniently lodged in the dirt. She paused a moment to catch her breath, standing on one leg to massage a particularly sore point on her sole.

Aidan stopped beside her, apparently unwilling to be separated again. She was glad of it. He said in a casual tone, "So, I was thinking, maybe when we get home you'd join me in a ramble. We've got loads of excellent walks around Amberlaine."

Gwen stared at him in bemusement until he grinned. She swatted his arm.

"I'm never leaving the city again after this. You can keep your rambling, thank you very much."

They joined the path again and continued to climb. Gwen was annoyed and very hot in the warm evening air by the time the first of their group crested the ridge. The line sped up slightly, everyone eager to complete the climb and arrive at their destination. Suddenly the unknown horrors of the ceremony were a little too close, and Gwen realized her teeth were clenched together tightly. She focused on Bran's feet in front of her and tried not to think about the ceremony ahead. She still had no idea what was going to happen.

In her distraction her foot slipped off a rock she had been climbing. She fell, bashing her knee and stumbling backward. She panicked—the way down was too steep for mishaps—but then arms surrounded her waist, stabilizing her. She gulped in air.

147

"It's okay," Aidan said softly in her ear. "I've got you."

They stood together for a moment, Gwen calming her breathing and enjoying the sensation of being held and feeling safe. It was a welcome distraction from her fear of their destination. She shivered slightly, hairs on her arms rising as the heat of his bare chest warmed the skin of her exposed back.

"Come on, hermits," Bran's voice called softly back to them. He stood on the ridge above them, backlit by a greenish-yellow glow. He beckoned to them. "We're here."

"Oh, for Pete's sake," Aidan said. "What'll it take to get Bran to bugger off? He's worse than an ant at a picnic."

"Well, one way or other it will all be over soon," Gwen said with a shiver. She patted Aidan's arm around her waist and he slowly let go. She carefully climbed the last few steps to reach Bran and looked down from the ridge toward the glow.

The top of the mountain was bare, with only an occasional tuft of grass and windswept rocky outcrop. In the very center stood a circle of stones. Gwen counted twenty-one rectangular megaliths, chest-height, sticking up out of the ground as if growing there organically. She couldn't help thinking of them as teeth in an open mouth. The same lights that had lit their path were scattered around the periphery of the circle, but inside shadows of the stones fell across each other in darker and darker layers.

The others walked with measured paces into the circle as if compelled. Bran's eyes as he passed Gwen were intensely focused straight ahead with none of his usual cheerful mischief. She looked at Aidan, half-afraid she'd see the same expression on him, but he just raised his eyebrows and shrugged.

Gwen saw their opportunity. "Aidan," she hissed under her breath. "Let's make our escape now. They all look pretty preoccupied."

Aidan looked to the circle, where the last of the stragglers were arranging themselves, all facing the rising moon. He nodded.

"Good call. Let's go."

They both took a step away from the circle. At least, Gwen meant to step away. Instead, she found her foot facing the stones. She tried again with the other foot, and again was one pace closer to the circle. She looked at Aidan in alarm.

"What the hell? Why aren't my feet working?"

Aidan's face was perplexed. He gave another experimental step, then a jump. Both brought him closer to the stones.

"Bloody hell," he said, frowning at his feet. "There's some kind of enchantment on us, maybe. We have to go to the circle with the others."

"Seriously?" Of all the trials and indignities they had suffered over the past few days, Gwen thought this might take the cake. They were stuck in this stupid world, following stupid rituals because of a stupid identity mistake, and now she couldn't move where she wanted to because of a stupid spell. She thought she might scream in frustration.

A strong wind blew her hair around her face and whipped their clothing into a frenzy.

"Whoa, where did that come from?" Aidan clutched at his rope belt, then looked at Gwen. "Was that you?" The frustration must have been apparent on her face because he quickly added, "Don't worry, Gwen. Let's just go into the circle and get this charade over with."

Gwen looked into Aidan's eyes as he gave her an encouraging smile. She exhaled and tried to let go of her anger, as much as she could. Aidan reached out a hand. She took it, and together they walked into the stone circle.

Chapter 12

Gwen and Aidan took their places at the back of the group. The rest stood motionless, heads raised, all eyes gazing unblinking at the full moon. Gwen and Aidan glanced at each other, then Gwen shook her hair out of her face, took a deep breath, and looked at the moon.

After a little while, she started to understand the fascination. It was very beautiful, perfectly round, and brighter than she'd ever remembered seeing it before. The stars nearby were faint in comparison, although the Milky Way was emblazoned across the zenith above their heads. The familiar stars comforted her—despite all the strangeness of her surroundings, some things were constant and forever. The moon's craters were clearly etched on its surface. She remembered vaguely that the craters were named as bodies of water, like the Sea of Tranquility and other poetic labels. Her frustration suddenly seemed a fuzzy memory. She imagined herself floating on a tiny sailboat in a sea of tranquility on the moon. She filled in the crater with an imagined ocean, calm and dark, glimmering with the moon's radiant glow.

She came back to herself as the standing stones began to glow with a pure white light, as if the moon had broken into pieces around them. As the light of the stones grew brighter, a strange tingling developed on her left shoulder. She reached up and touched the area, wondering, and looked at Aidan to see him doing the same thing. She craned her neck, but the light of the stones exposed only smooth unblemished skin.

Suddenly a surge of energy pulsed through her. She threw her head and hands back involuntarily and her mouth opened in a silent scream. The sensation was similar to the one she'd shared with the girls in the willow tree, but many times stronger. Energy poured through her, and she was paralyzed by it. She stared at the stars overhead, unable to breathe, unable to think. She only existed, merely a fragile vessel surrounding a piece of the universe pulsing inside her. Eons passed— the stars flickered and blazed and exploded before her eyes in life cycles too massive to comprehend. Gwen mindlessly witnessed the glory of the universe unfolding and accepted her unfathomably small role in the infinite.

She had almost lost herself, was almost not Gwen anymore, was only atoms of the universe, when there was a change in the energy filling her. It brought her back to her body with a sudden awareness. Then the energy turned from pressure to white hot agony, gradually focusing onto her shoulder.

Gwen screamed aloud. She couldn't help it. The pain was all-consuming, both a deep throbbing and a sharp stab all at once. She was forced to her knees, the weight of the pain pressing down on her like a giant hand. Her own screams mingled in a dissonant chorus of other screams and cries, but she quickly dismissed all external noises as secondary to the overwhelming torment.

Then, as suddenly as it had come, the pain left. Gwen found herself bent over on her knees, gasping for air as if she'd been running for her life. She stayed perfectly still, afraid to move for fear it might trigger the pain again. After a minute, when nothing happened, she cracked open her tightly shut eyelids.

The standing stones were dark and lifeless, brooding once more. The moonlight cast shadows of the stones again, and the stars twinkled innocently. The others began to stir, obviously as stricken as Gwen. They slowly raised their heads and shakily got to their feet.

Gwen straightened carefully. She looked over at Aidan who was on his hands and knees, head hanging. She crawled over to him and put a hand on his right shoulder.

"Aidan?" she whispered hoarsely. "Are you okay?"

He turned to look at her, still panting. His eyes were half-closed and a little dazed, but he nodded.

"You?"

"Yeah." She looked around. "Can you walk? We should get out of here."

Aidan's eyes opened wider and flashed to her left shoulder. She craned her neck to follow his gaze. A dark pattern stained the skin of her shoulder by the dim light of the full moon. It was extensive, larger than the length

153

of her hand, wrapping from her collarbone over her shoulder to her back.

"What the hell?" Her mouth gaped open in astonishment. She looked at Aidan's shoulder, where a similar darkness spread. "Do you think they look like the others we've seen?"

"I don't know—it's too dark. How do we have them at all, anyway?" Aidan looked around. "Just wait here until the others leave, then we can at least be in the back."

Gwen sat back on her feet and watched as the others trickled out of the circle, arms around each other's shoulders, some moving as if still in pain or afraid of its return.

When the last of the Breenan stumbled out of the circle, Gwen got unsteadily to her feet. She felt drained and weak, as if she were recovering from a long illness. Her shoulder was tender to the touch, but surprisingly little of the acute pain remained.

Aidan lurched to his feet, swaying a little as he straightened. He put a hand on his forehead and rubbed tiredly.

"I feel like I got hit by a bus," he said, rolling his shoulders in a stretch.

"I hear you," Gwen replied. They hobbled after the last of the group, a young man with his arm around a staggering girl. As they passed between two of the black stones, something jumped out at them from the shadows.

"Hi, hermits," Bran said. He grinned at them, but Gwen detected a tiredness that hadn't been in his face before. Maybe even Bran had been affected by the ceremony. She smiled weakly back, but inwardly groaned. How long would they have to stay with these people just because they couldn't shake Bran?

"So, it finally happened," Bran said, spreading out his left arm and twisting it to look at his mark. He held out his right palm. Instantly a bluish flame appeared in his hand. Gwen threw a sharp look at Aidan. It was identical to the flames Aidan made back in their world. Aidan stared at Bran's hand, his eyes dazed.

Gwen started to piece things together, in waves of comprehension that washed over her. Aidan's magic, her 'strangeness,' their acceptance into Breenan society based on appearance, their unknown parentage, the marks on their shoulders that looked suspiciously like Bran's...

"Excellent," Bran said, nodding in satisfaction as he examined his mark. "Let's see yours, then." Bran twisted around and held onto Aidan's shoulders with both hands, leaving the flame to hover in mid-air nearby. Aidan looked too shocked by what had happened to put up much resistance. Bran hummed a little to himself.

"Ah! You're one of King Landon's tribe, from the neighboring realm to mine." He looked into Aidan's dazed face. "But you didn't even know that, did you, hermit?" Aidan's confusion must have answered him, because Bran shook his head in disbelief and continued reading the mark on Aidan's shoulder. Gwen looked too, but there was only an incomprehensible pattern of vines and leaves. Bran's normally carefree face frowned suddenly, and Gwen's stomach clenched.

Bran said, "Wait a minute. It says here that Lord Declan is your father. But Declan is my mother's cousin, and I've been to his house many times. He has loads of children, but I've never seen you." He glanced at Aidan, who craned his neck to view the mark. Bran scrutinized the mark again. "And it doesn't say anywhere who your mother is. I'm sure I'm reading it right." He released Aidan's shoulders and stepped back. Confusion played across Bran's face, until understanding blossomed. It was swiftly followed by incredulity. "No. Are you—are you both half-human?"

Gwen and Aidan stared at him, dumbstruck. Gwen couldn't think of a single thing to say. Terrible visions filled her thoughts of what would become of them once the rest of the Breenan found out who they were. All she could do was stare in dread as Bran looked from her to Aidan and back again.

Suddenly Bran's face transformed as he let out a great burst of laughter. Gwen took an involuntary step back and Aidan put out a hand as if for protection. Bran bent over in convulsive laughter.

"That is the best—joke—ever," he said between bouts. "How did you get here? And you've been fooling everyone all this time!" His outbursts calmed gradually into chuckles.

Gwen tried to shush him.

"Please, not so loud." Others were looking curiously back at them as they climbed down the mountain. Bran continued in what Gwen would have generously described as a theatrical whisper.

"Wow." He gave them both an admiring glance. "I've pulled some stunts in my time, but nothing as amazing as this." He shook his head in wonder, still grinning. "No wonder you didn't know anything. Hermits indeed. So you're actually from the human

156

world?" His curiosity was almost palpable.

Gwen let out a long slow breath. Aidan bent his neck back, rubbing his hands over his face. Gwen said, "Are you going to tell anyone?"

"What, and ruin the joke? Not likely." Gwen's knees actually weakened in relief. Bran said, "So why are you here, anyway? And how did you get here? Most of the portals have been closed for hundreds of years. Only a few people can go through them, and it's a closely guarded secret how they do. So how did you manage, when only a few of the most powerful people in the land can do it?"

Gwen briefly put a hand over her eyes, letting the adrenaline pass out of her body.

"I don't know," she said. "I just touched the stone doorway in a barrow and the portal opened."

Bran moved toward her.

"Do you mind?" He gestured at her shoulder. She shook her head and he leaned in to inspect her new mark. After a minute he said, "Looks like you're from Queen Isolde's realm."

Gwen stood perfectly still. Had she heard him right?

"What did you say?" Perhaps Isolde was a common name here, or maybe he had said Isabelle.

"Queen Isolde's tribe, yeah. That was her castle, where we met. Wait a minute." He looked closely at her shoulder, and then into her face. Deep curiosity filled his eyes.

"Did you know you're the queen's daughter?"

Chapter 13

Gwen stared at Bran, uncomprehending. What had he said? The pieces were all there, but she couldn't assemble them into a coherent picture. Her mother's name was Isolde, her father had told her that years ago, and the sketch reminded her every time she looked at it. She'd surmised that her mother was either here in the Otherworld or had some connection to it, given the portrait in Corann's locket. She had thought that perhaps her mother had been lured here just as Ellie had been, and had maybe died here. She'd met the queen of this realm, presiding over the never-ending dance and punishing Ellie for the ridiculous crime of missing a step, forcing her to dance until her shoes were in tatters. Now Bran was saying that the queen's name was Isolde, and that she was Gwen's mother?

"No," Gwen whispered. "No no no no no." She

shook her head in small frantic jerks, trying to stop her mind from connecting the dots. Her mother was supposed to be a kind and lovely woman, not a cruel inhuman Breenan. She thought suddenly of her father, her kind-hearted generous father, and her mind recoiled at the thought of him ever being attracted to the queen. Queen Isolde.

Aidan put a hand on her unmarked shoulder. "Hey," he said, his white face peering into hers in concern. "Are you all right?"

"How could that—monster—be my mother?" she gasped, searching Aidan's face as if trying to find answers there. His concerned eyes offered only questions of his own. She whirled on Bran.

"Are you positive? You're sure you read my mark right?"

Bran put his hands up defensively.

"Yes, I'm sure." He eyed Gwen curiously, clearly taken aback by her reaction. "You know, Queen Isolde's not that bad. She's decent, although a little obsessed with novelty. And dancing, really too much dancing."

Gwen closed her eyes briefly, shaking her head.

"She's got my friend. My human best friend," she added, and Bran raised an eyebrow. "She's forcing her to dance all the time, with no rest, and punishing her with magic." She gulped, tears springing to her eyes. "I don't think she can last much longer."

Bran looked a little perplexed.

"You really care about this human." He eyed her with interest. "How strange."

"I am human," Gwen flared at him. She bit her lip, her brief anger retreating as quickly as it had come.

159

"Part-human, I guess." She looked at Aidan, shaking her head. "This is ridiculous." She turned to Bran, throwing caution to the wind. Bran knew where they were from, now, so why hide anything else? "That's why we're here. We saw Ellie, my friend, get taken through a portal in a barrow by a Breenan named Corann, and we followed them through."

"Oh, Corann's slimy, isn't he," Bran said, wrinkling his nose. Then he frowned. "What did you come through?"

"A barrow," Gwen said slowly. "A burial mound. That's why we call your kind the 'people of the mounds.' Our—kind." She briefly squeezed her eyes shut with the discomfort of admitting the relation.

Bran still looked confused, so Aidan added, "Because the barrows are supposed to be entrances to this world, the Otherworld. That's how we got through."

"Huh. So the portals are through some old person's grave?" Bran digested this for a moment. "Weird."

They all stared at each other for a minute. Bran broke the silence with a little laugh.

"I've wanted to meet a human since forever, but now I don't know what to say."

"I'll start, then," Gwen said, eager to learn whatever she could. "Tell me more about the queen." She couldn't bring herself to say the word 'mother.'

"I don't know much, really," Bran said, shrugging. "Our kingdoms are allies, but not really friends. I know she never married—she only takes temporary lovers. Rumor has it she once had a human lover…" He caught Gwen's eye and chuckled with embarrassment. "I guess that rumor's true. Anyway, she doesn't have any

160

children, none here at least. Her mother died years ago, so she's been ruling her realm ever since. That's all I really know."

Gwen gave a small sigh, unsatisfied with Bran's answer.

"What about my father? What do you know of him?" Aidan stared at Bran, eagerness and wariness warring on his face.

"Oh, Declan? He's a great laugh, he is. Going to his house is always a good time. Declan's an excellent hunter, and his forests are well stocked. He let me ride his best stallion once," Bran said dreamily. "A beautiful horse."

Aidan looked at him expectantly for a minute, then breathed heavily out of his nose in exasperation. "Anything else?"

"I don't know. I was a child when I last visited, and I mostly played with his many children. A lot of them aren't his wife's but she keeps a blind eye toward the others. They all seem to get along swimmingly, as far as I can tell."

Aidan's mouth worked, but when he spoke his voice was steady.

"So, just one bastard out of many." He looked to the stars and gave a deep sigh. Gwen was moved out of her own fog of horror to put a hand gingerly on Aidan's upper arm. He looked at her and gave her a tight smile.

"Revelations all around, hey?"

"Can we walk and talk?" Bran looked down the mountain at the retreating line of the newly-marked. "It's just that I'll be missed, and then you'll be discovered, and all the fun will be over. My brother will probably

161

send someone for me."

"Who's your brother?" Gwen frowned in confusion. She hadn't seen Bran interact with any of the elders, least of all in a brotherly way.

Bran said, "Crevan, of course. He's taking his marking duties very seriously. It's his first year leading." Bran laughed. "You should have seen the blood drain out of his face when I reminded him it was my marking year. 'You'd better not mess this up, Bran,'" he mimicked in a falsely deep voice. His eyes lit up with glee. "He's going to be livid when he finds out he had two half-humans in his group and he didn't know."

"Bran!" Gwen said, horrified. "You said you wouldn't tell anyone."

"Oh, yeah." Bran's shoulders drooped a little, and then he brightened. "Maybe later? When you're gone?" He paused. "Or are you planning on staying here?"

"No!" Gwen and Aidan said in unison. Bran raised his eyebrows. Gwen clarified. "I just mean, our home is in the human world. And from what I've seen, I don't think we'd be too welcome here."

Bran shrugged. "I don't know. Lots think that humans are inferior, sure, but back when the portals were all open, there were more half-humans around. In some realms they were welcomed, because they were often poets and bards. They were preferable to full-humans because they could handle our food and drink, and didn't get so dazed here."

"Well then," Aidan said, "Maybe we should stay, Gwen. You any good at singing?"

"Ha, right." Gwen shook her head at Aidan, half-smiling.

"So you're here to rescue this human of yours?" Bran said, scooping up one of the yellow flames beside the path and tossing it from one hand to the other. "How are you going to do that?"

"Well, we need to get away from this group for starters, then we have to get back to the castle." Gwen was suddenly very tired. There were so many obstacles between her and Ellie, and she still didn't know how to get Ellie away from the castle, nor how to get back to their world afterward.

"What's your plan? Are you going to storm the castle? Or make up disguises and sneak in? Or confront your mother and rely on the element of surprise?" Bran showed his excitement by tossing the flame back and forth rapidly. Gwen wondered how he had hands available to juggle as she slid down a rock face on her bottom, but his agility seemed unhampered.

"I don't know," Gwen replied. "Cross that bridge when we come to it, I guess." She pushed down the dread that rose with the thought, and focused on keeping her feet. She said, "We can't do anything until we escape your people."

"Yeah, we've been trying all day," Aidan added.

"Oh, that won't be a problem," Bran said dismissively. "I can distract them." He rolled the ball of flame down the hill, where it bounced against rocks and eventually collided with another flame, resulting in a small explosion of light. A few shrieks told them it had been noticed. Bran gave a small grin of satisfaction and turned to Gwen and Aidan.

"I want to come help rescue your human."

Gwen was puzzled.

163

"Why would you want that?"

"It'd be such a great prank. Probably the best ever."

"But you don't even know Ellie. Why would you risk it?" Gwen looked at Aidan, puzzled, and he returned a perplexed shrug.

"I don't care about your human. No offense. But to steal her away from under Queen Isolde's nose, helping her own half-human daughter, now that's the stuff of legend. Crevan would kill me," Bran said, a beatific smile on his face.

Gwen gave a little laugh of disbelief. She said, "Hey, if you can get us away from here and then find us later, you're certainly welcome to help." She caught Aidan's exasperated glance. She said defensively, "Hey, he knows a lot more about this place than we do. He might have some good ideas for rescue. Goodness knows I have none."

"Excellent." Bran rubbed his hands together. "That's settled then. Now let's get you out of here."

***

The fire blazed high and hot when they neared the camp. Shadows on the willows flickered tall and strange, accompanied by the sound of noisy chatter and the smell of roasting meat. Gwen's stomach gave a long, deep growl.

Aidan groaned.

"I could eat a horse. I think the last time we ate properly was at Loniel's bonfire."

"You shouldn't come to the fire," Bran said at once. "People are going to want to read your marks if you do."

164

"Dammit," Gwen muttered. She frowned with a sudden thought. "Can you read them at a distance? How careful do we have to be?"

"Oh, no, you have to get close and really want to read it," Bran assured her. "But people are going to want to do that here. Everyone has a new mark, so they'll want to compare."

Aidan's stomach grumbled loudly. She looked at him and gave a sympathetic laugh at his woebegone expression.

Bran said, "Okay, here's the plan. We come up behind the trees, you both sneak in and grab your bags, and we'll meet at that rock." He pointed at a lumpy boulder on the far side of a nearby willow. "Then we'll try to avoid Ula over there." He nodded to their left where a young elder paced, arrow notched loosely in a bow by her side.

Gwen nodded tightly and the three of them strolled toward the willows. Gwen tried her best to look casual. Bran jerked his head to the closest willow. She nodded back once and ducked under its skirt.

The room created by the tree's branches was empty, save for the pile of brown sacks. Gwen's heart sank when she looked at them. Which one was hers? She picked up the nearest bag and peered inside. Even in the dim light the fabric of a red dress was evident. The next one was a pale yellow. Her heart leapt at the third one, but the green fabric was wool, not velvet. She rummaged more quickly, aware of the Breenan party underway on the other side of the curtain of leaves.

She opened one of the sacks and was more than relieved to see green velvet and a distinctly human-world bra nestled inside. She grabbed the sack and jogged to the edge of the room. As she ducked out, two people burst into the tree. She just caught a glimpse of the figures entwined together in an embrace as the branches swung across her vision. The girl giggled, and Gwen let out her breath in relief.

Aidan waited at the rock, dancing from one foot to the other in impatience.

"There you are," he said as she arrived. "I promised myself we wouldn't separate again, and then we just did."

"Where's Bran?" Gwen peered toward the willows, the bonfire visible between trees. She jumped as a drum began to pound. Figures started to dance and leap around the fire.

"More dancing? Seriously?" Aidan shook his head. "Is that all these people do?"

Bran trotted up to the rock, a sack swinging from his shoulder.

"Here, take this." He passed the sack to Aidan. Bran reached up to his own head, grabbed a few hairs, and pulled. "Ow," he said, rubbing briefly. He took the hairs and twisted them between his fingers, staring intently at them. Gwen stared too, curious. She noticed with astonishment that the red hairs were turning thick and metallic under Bran's fingers. Once completely transformed, he deftly twisted them into a ring and passed his fingers around it one last time. He held it up for them to see.

It was a brilliant copper ring, smooth and unblemished. Gwen's mouth gaped in astonishment. Bran grabbed her hand and slipped the ring onto her right thumb.

"There. Wear that and I'll be able to find you."

"That was amazing." Gwen said. Bran looked pleased with himself, then looked around.

"Okay, Ula is right over there. I'll cast a deflection enchantment on you so you can get away from the firelight. It's not perfect, but if I distract Ula at the same time, you should be able to reach the trees. Follow the forest edge to the right and you'll come across a small stone hut. You can stay there overnight. We'll be leaving in the morning heading west, so we won't pass it. You should be safe there."

"How do you know about the hut?" Aidan said, a hint of suspicion in his voice.

"My brothers have explored this area on hunting trips. I'm good at extracting information." He grinned. "Okay, ready?"

"Thanks, Bran," Gwen said suddenly, realizing they were parting. "Thanks for everything."

He winked at her.

"Don't worry, you haven't seen the last of me." He reached out and put a hand on her forehead and on Aidan's. He closed his eyes for a few seconds. Gwen stole a glance at Aidan, who watched Bran intently. She was shocked when Aidan started to fade. His body wavered like a reflection on a pond, and then his color faded to mere shadows. Gwen gasped and looked at her own hands, which had dimmed to a similar ghostly grey. Bran took his hands away and beamed at them.

"There. That should do for a few minutes. I knew that spell would come in handy one day. Now go, quick! Before it wears off." He wiggled his eyebrows at them, then turned and strolled purposefully toward Ula. Gwen grabbed her sack and Aidan's arm and together they stole across the darkened meadow.

As they tiptoed through the grass, Gwen overheard Bran speaking to Ula. He engaged in a little light chitchat, and then moved quickly into, "So you know I'm of age now, and you're the prettiest woman here. Can I ask you to dance?" Gwen suppressed a snort of laughter and glanced in their direction. Ula's back was to them, and Bran reached out and played with her hair. Gwen looked at Aidan, who raised his shadowy eyebrows incredulously.

"Smooth." He shook his head.

**

They met with no further obstacles crossing the meadow, and arrived at the forest's edge just as they started to regain solidity and color.

"Do you think we're in the clear?" Gwen whispered.

"Let's keep a low profile, just in case," Aidan replied.

They crept along the forest's edge. The full moon lit their path like a spotlight. After a few minutes of walking Aidan touched Gwen's arm.

"Just ahead," he said quietly.

A small stone hut stood at the forest's edge, painted by moonlight. It was tiny, no more than one small room, but it was shelter. They made straight for it.

There was no door, just a gaping black hole for an entryway. No windows illuminated the interior. They paused before the threshold and Gwen looked at Aidan.

"I'll make a light, shall I?" Aidan flicked his fingers and his usual blue flames sprang to life. He leaned down and rolled it like a bowling ball through the doorway. The flames slowed to a stop in the center of the room, lighting up bare stone walls and a packed earthen floor.

Gwen nodded in approval.

"Nice trick. You've been taking notes, I see."

"You like that? I think the biggest thing that's been limiting me is my imagination." He walked forward cautiously and Gwen followed, looking up for spider webs. The room was bare and moderately web-free, and Gwen sank down on the ground.

"Wow, what a night." She stretched her legs out and wiggled her toes as Aidan flopped down next to her.

"It's been ridiculous," Aidan agreed. "But I'm starting to expect the unexpected, these days." He peered into the sack that Bran had thrust upon him. "Hey, Bran snuck us some food and drink. He's now been upgraded from minor annoyance to best friend." He opened the bag and offered it to Gwen. "Dig in."

She reached in and pulled out pieces of the roasted meat she had smelled earlier, along with an earthen jug sealed with a cork. Her mouth started watering, and she tucked in with gusto. She hoped the meat was pork, but it was wild and gamey compared to pork at home. Were there still wild boar in these woods?

The moon had moved around to filter through the doorway by the time they finished eating. Aidan lay back on the dirt floor with a groan.

"This feast and famine diet takes getting used to." He rubbed his stomach. "I was hungry enough to eat a horse earlier, and now it feels like I ate one. A large one, that's still kicking."

Gwen chuckled and leaned back against the stone wall, cool against the skin of her bare shoulder. She stared out of the doorway at the moonlit landscape, full of silver and shadows. Her mind threatened to get back to the topic of Isolde. To delay, she tried to focus on Aidan.

"Are you okay?" she asked him. He lay on his back staring at the ceiling, hands on his stomach. His bare chest rose up and down rhythmically, but paused when she said, "About your father, I mean."

He let out his breath in a whoosh.

"I don't know. It explains everything—my magic, why he didn't stick around, why Mum never talked about him. I never had a great opinion of him, so I guess I'm not shocked that he's got so many kids with and without his wife. I just don't know what it means to be a—half-breed, or whatever we're called."

Gwen gave a humorless laugh.

"Do you think the Breenan are a different species?"

"Mmm," Aidan said. "When we get back I'll look up their taxonomy. I'm sure someone's done a study."

Gwen poked at him with her foot. They fell silent again. Gwen's fingers found the ring Bran had made, and started idly playing with it.

"How do you think this ring works?" she asked casually. Aidan looked over at her hands and frowned.

"It's a piece of him, or was, so he probably has some sort of connection to it. But do you think it's a great idea to keep it? If he can follow us, it means he can lead people to us."

Gwen held up the ring and looked through it to the

moonlit meadow out the doorway.

"I don't see that we have another option. Last time we tried to rescue Ellie, we ended up here. We desperately need the help of someone who knows the Otherworld. Sometimes you just have to trust people."

"I guess," he said doubtfully. He turned his gaze to the ceiling again. "I usually manage fine on my own. And Bran's such a loose cannon."

"I know," Gwen said, putting the ring back on her thumb. "But if he can help us rescue Ellie from—from my…"

She couldn't finish the sentence. Her hands balled into fists, and she took deep breaths to calm herself. Aidan looked at her then scrambled over to sit beside her against the wall.

"How are you?" He searched her face in the dim light of the blue flame. She kept her eyes trained to a clump of grass in the distance.

"I dreamt of my mother for so long. She was supposed to be lovely and amazing, and only left me because she was forced to. Now I find she's cold and heartless and torturing my best friend."

She gave a little gasp of disbelief as the import of her own words hit.

"How could she leave her own baby? How could she leave me?"

Gwen drew her knees up to her chest and hugged them, rocking a little with the strength of her squeezing. An arm moved across her shoulders as Aidan drew her into his chest. She remained tense for a moment then released her body in a long breath.

"I thought I'd gotten over that years ago."

He carefully smoothed her hair back from her forehead. She closed her eyes.

"I told myself that the only way she would have left me and not come back was death or kidnapping. I was really starting to think she had been captured and brought here as a slave like Ellie had been. It made so much sense. This doesn't make any sense." She paused a moment. "And what the hell did my dad see in her? How could he…" She trailed off, shaking her head in incomprehension.

"She must have been a looker. You said they were together only a week. That's not very long to get to know someone."

She gave a little laugh. "I haven't known you for very long. I feel like I would know if you were into torture and murder."

He gave her a little squeeze. "We've been through a lot. If they were only—having a good time, it was probably easy for her to keep the charm turned on. Or she might have enchanted him, like Corann did to Ellie."

"I like that idea much better. I don't care if it's true or not, I think I'll believe it anyway." She adjusted herself against Aidan's chest. She closed her eyes, comfortable, the cool breeze from outside drifting over her bare legs, contrasting against the warmth of Aidan at her back.

"So why did she do it? Come find your dad, I mean." Aidan sounded puzzled.

"Hey, don't make fun of my dad. He's a good-looking guy." She reached around to prod Aidan in the stomach. He laughed.

"No offense meant. I can believe Isolde came to our

172

world for—entertainment. What I don't get is why she stayed pregnant and had you."

"Well, they're kind of medieval here. Maybe birth control isn't a thing."

"You can't tell me that with all this magic, they can't deal with an unwanted pregnancy. It could be against their beliefs or something, I guess. But Bran said Isolde has had other men since, but no other children. I think she wanted to have you."

Gwen digested this for a moment.

"That doesn't make any sense. Why would she keep me, but then leave me on my dad's doorstep? She can't have wanted me that much."

Aidan sighed. "I don't understand. I just think there's something else going on, that's all."

They sat there for a while. Gwen felt sleepy. She was a little cold, but Aidan's solid warmth behind her compensated.

"Why do you think you could make the barrow portal open?" Aidan's quiet voice roused her from sleepiness. She pondered his question.

"Well, Queen Kiera's curse allowed her child to come through. Maybe that's a loophole for all half-and-halfs."

"Interesting," Aidan said. She could feel the vibrations of his voice through his chest, lulling her to sleep. "I wonder why Isolde and Declan can do it too."

She was too tired to think, too tired to answer. She let the whole exhausting day slide away as she fell into sleep.

Chapter 14

Gwen awoke chilled. She and Aidan must have rolled apart in the night, because she was sprawled on the ground with her cheek pressed into the dirt. She pushed herself upright, arching her back in a stretch, and leaned against the wall rubbing sleep out of her eyes.

The morning sun streamed through their doorway with a vibrant orange glow. It lit the hair of the still-sleeping Aidan so that he looked more on fire than usual. His head was tucked into his folded arm and his legs sprawled out, stomach pressing into the dirt. She felt protective, suddenly. His bare back rising and falling with each breath, his face relaxed into that of a boy—birdsong trilled loudly outside and Gwen fiercely willed it to stop, to not disturb his sleep.

Aidan's mark was clearly visible stretching across his shoulder and down to his shoulder blade. She studied it, but couldn't see how Bran was able to read the swirling pattern of dark green vines and leaves. She wondered briefly if perhaps he had made their parentage up, but quickly dismissed the notion. The half-blood observation, the name Isolde—Gwen knew Bran was right.

Thinking of Isolde brought Gwen's mind around to Ellie, forever dancing. Her stomach clenched with the memory of Ellie's anguished face and tattered shoes. Gwen felt so inadequate, so unmatched in the face of all the Breenan and their magic, so unprepared to mount a rescue attempt. She needed to learn how to fight fire with fire.

Gwen waited, basking in the warmth of the morning sunbeams, until Aidan blinked himself awake. He brought his hand up to shade his eyes, and looked at the watching Gwen with a sleepy smile.

"Morning," she said, smiling back.

"Morning," he replied, pulling himself into a sitting position and yawning widely.

They pulled out leftover food from Bran's sack for breakfast.

"Aidan," Gwen said after they had eaten and he was picking through the sack, looking for crumbs.

"Mmm?" He popped an errant grape into his mouth.

"Can you teach me how to use my magic?"

He paused in his search, looking at her.

"Well, sure. But I got the impression you weren't that interested."

"I'm just nervous. Every time I've used it, it's been kind of traumatic. It's usually explosive or startling. But—" She breathed out with determination. "I need to

175

figure this out. Everyone else here uses magic, and I feel very out-gunned."

"These people have been using magic since birth, I expect, so I doubt we'll ever be able to compete. But I think it's a great idea for you to control your magic. You shouldn't be afraid of it." He grinned at her. "It can be really fun." He crossed his legs and sat up straight. "Okay, close your eyes."

"What? We're doing this right now?" Panicky sensations fluttered in Gwen's chest, even though she had asked for this.

"Why not? Eyes closed."

She shut them obediently.

"Okay, now feel around in your chest with your mind."

"What the hell is that supposed to mean?" she demanded, her eyes popping open.

Aidan clucked his tongue. "Just try it. Imagine it."

Sighing, she closed her eyes again. She pictured a tiny hand crawling around her lungs and heart. She paused when she felt—imagined?—a warm humming under her imaginary fingers. Her posture or expression must have changed, because Aidan said eagerly, "Do you feel it? Your core?"

"Maybe? It's all warm and tingly." She paused. "That sounded really dumb."

"No, I know what you mean. Okay, now reach into it, and pull some of it through your arm into your hand."

Gwen flexed her imaginary fingers and tentatively pushed them toward the core. They stopped short as if a wall stood in the way. She prodded, then jabbed. She could have sworn she felt a dull thud on impact.

176

"I can't get in. There's something stopping me."

"Hmm." Aidan sounded puzzled. "Try pushing harder."

Gwen imagined her inner hand jabbing hard at the wall with its index finger. The wall didn't budge. Frustration built up, mixed with a little fear. What if she pushed too hard, and she couldn't control it? As her emotions rose the wall yielded, just slightly.

"Hey, I felt it move!" Gwen said, elated.

Aidan said, "Okay, now give it another push."

Her frustration melting away, she pushed again only to find the wall as firm as before, the warm tingling ensconced on the other side. She opened her eyes.

"It's back to being a solid wall," she said glumly. "I did feel it move, though, I swear."

"That's really strange," Aidan said, frowning in confusion. "I don't understand what's blocking you." He cocked his head to one side, looking at her with narrowed eyes. "You said earlier that your magic came out when your emotions were heightened. Do you think after years of suppressing them, you've gotten too good at it and can't let go of your control?"

Gwen raised her shoulders, questioning.

"Maybe? What do I do about it?" How could she stop doing something that she didn't know she was doing?

"You need to relax a little. It's okay to feel, to get angry sometimes, to lose control. If you can let go anywhere, it's in this land of magic. It's practically expected here."

Gwen stared at him.

"I don't know how. I don't know where to begin.

And even if I did, I'm afraid of what I might do."

Aidan looked at her for a minute.

"You were using magic at Loniel's bonfire. You were glowing. It wasn't scary at all. It was beautiful."

They stared at each other for a long moment until Gwen looked down, her heart pounding.

"I guess I should have grabbed a flask of Loniel's drink, if it makes me relaxed enough to make magic." She got up and dusted off her legs.

Aidan got up as well.

"The point remains that you can do it, when you let down your guard. Just don't let your emotions be your enemy." Aidan's voice was cool. She turned to look at him, but he had bent down to pick up his sack and was already heading out the door. "I'll go get changed outside. Come out when you're ready."

Feeling like she had failed a test she didn't know she was taking, Gwen quickly slipped out of her tunic and into her undergarments and dress. The neckline of the dress was low and wide, leaving most of her new mark exposed. She traced it with her fingertips, exploring this new adornment. It was so large that when she placed her hand over her shoulder, she could only just cover the mark with her fingers and palm. She rubbed it lightly, and then with more vigor. The mark stayed put. As far as Gwen knew the tattoo was permanent. She wondered whether she would have the nerve to show her father.

When she came outside, blinking in the bright morning sun, Aidan was waiting for her.

"Ready for an invigorating morning stroll?" He grinned at her. The awkwardness of a minute ago was forgotten, or else Aidan purposefully ignored it. He

178

exuded his characteristic easy joviality, and Gwen was puzzled but grateful. She wondered if she weren't the only one with a tight guard on her emotions.

She smiled back tentatively.

"Yeah, we'd better get moving. It'll take all morning to get to the castle."

"I figured we could practice magic on the way," Aidan said, fastening his cape with a theatrical swirl. "That way maybe you'll be distracted enough to not focus so much on control."

"Sure," Gwen said, wanting to be agreeable. She didn't have high hopes, though. The wall felt very solid.

***

They traced their way back along the forest's edge, keeping a careful eye out for signs of the others. All was quiet except for birdsong. Gwen pointed at the cluster of willows in the distance when they neared. The fire was cold and dead. No figures stirred near the trees, not even a pacing guard.

"They must have left really early," Gwen said.

"Do these people ever sleep, or do they just dance?" Aidan said incredulously.

They quickly found the path, a clear opening in the dense forest. Gwen adjusted her dress and prepared herself for the long walk. As they walked, and as the sun rose higher in the sky and created dappled shadows along their way, Gwen practiced magic.

Or at least, she attempted it.

"Try to imagine your core as before, but this time with your eyes open," Aidan instructed. "We need to keep walking, and having your mind on two things might help with distraction."

Gwen tried to imagine the hand again. It came more easily this time, and she had little difficulty finding her tingling core. Accessing it, however, proved as fruitless as it had earlier.

"It's—just—not—working," she said, jabbing her core with every word. She tried slapping it, grabbing it, and punching it. Her only reward was a faint sense of nausea. Frustration rose in her, fuelled by desperation. She took a deep breath to calm herself.

"No!" Aidan leaped in front and faced her, grabbing both her arms. "Don't control it! Feel your frustration, let it take over!"

She stared at him, wide-eyed with astonishment. He shook her arms slightly.

"Try it again." She reached in and met the usual resistance. "Still can't do it? Is it frustrating? Look how easy it is for me." He let go with one hand and held up the other in front of her face. Blue flames licked the center of his palm. He extinguished the flames and put his hand back on her arm. "Doesn't it bother you that you can't do that? Don't you want to? Aren't you so frustrated you could scream?"

Gwen stared into Aidan's eyes, confusion and uncertainty swiftly replaced by anger and frustration. Why was he saying these things to her? It was cruel of him to be flaunting his magic in her face, taunting her with her inabilities. Her breath became shallower, and she reached inside to poke her core once again, if only to prove Aidan wrong. She met the usual wall. That resistance, along with Aidan's intense face in hers, combined to make her feel trapped. She sprang away.

"Stop it!" she shouted, hands in fists at her sides, facing Aidan head-on. Her heart pounded and her breath came in shallow gasps. A little burst of heat flared in her chest.

Aidan looked down at her hands.

"There we are," he said softly.

Gwen looked down. Her fists were covered in orange flames, flickering brightly, crawling over her curled fingers. Her mouth dropped open in astonishment, all anger ebbing away. As it did, the flames flickered and died. She stared for a moment at her fire-free hands, then looked up at Aidan.

He gave her a wry smile.

"I'm sorry, Gwen. I didn't know how else to break you out of your box." He looked contrite.

Gwen looked down, flexing her fingers as if looking for the flames.

"Did you see that?" she asked quietly. She looked up again. "I made fire."

He gave her a real smile then.

"Yeah, you sure did. It wasn't so bad, was it?"

She tucked her hands under her arms.

"I guess not." She prodded her core, disappointed yet unsurprised that the resistance was back again. "So I need to Hulk-out every time I want to use magic?"

"Oh, I'm sure it just takes practice." Aidan turned around and they started walking again. "We'll get you there eventually. There are other emotions besides anger we can try."

Gwen looked sharply at Aidan, but he kept his eyes forward and his face bland. Gwen let the comment slide, her face a little hot as she recalled the night of the bonfire.

They walked in silence for a while. The sun warmed up the forest pleasantly and the path was over easy terrain. The light had a warm green glow from filtering through the canopy of leaves above.

"So how do you reckon we'll get back home after we rescue Ellie?" Aidan spoke into the silence, waking Gwen from her mindless reverie.

"I have no idea. Try to find that doorway again and keep trying to get through, I suppose." She sighed. "Let's just get her away from—the queen first."

"Yeah, about that—" Aidan glanced sidelong at Gwen. "Any thoughts?"

"Well, if Bran doesn't turn up before we get there, I suggest we clean up, join the crowd, and dance Ellie out the door."

"Ha, all right." Aidan looked at Gwen, and frowned. "You're serious." She nodded. "Wow. There are so many holes in that plan..." Aidan left the sentence dangling. "Let's see. I can manage cleaning our clothes again."

"I could kill for a wash," Gwen said. "If you spot a lake, let me know."

"Wouldn't that be nice. Okay, do you know how to dance? Whatever they're dancing, I mean?"

"Umm, no," Gwen admitted. "Ellie's the award-winning dancer, not me." She grimaced at Aidan. "First big hole. Can you dance?"

"I'm not the greatest dancer. Luckily for us, I developed an enchantment for bad dancers. It was after a particularly humiliating incident in year nine which we don't need to get into now." Gwen giggled. Aidan looked at her from under his eyebrows with mock sternness. "Nothing from the peanut gallery, thank you. Anyway, the spell works by mimicking and mirroring the moves the other dancers do, and sort of suggesting your body does complementary moves. You still have to follow, but at least you know what to do."

He stopped and faced her.

"Let's try it." He reached out and put his fingertips on her forehead, closing his eyes with a concentrated air. A moment later his eyes popped open. "Right, hopefully that worked. I've never put that spell on someone else."

Gwen raised an eyebrow.

"I don't feel anything. What do I do now?"

"Whatever you feel like doing." He stepped back, paused, and twirled on the spot. As soon as he began his turn, Gwen felt an urgent need to turn herself. She twisted in a circle and stopped to face Aidan. She stared at him in disbelief.

"Seriously?" She held herself tense, unsure what her body would do next. Aidan grinned and started clapping and flapping his arms like a bird.

"You are *not* making me do the chicken dance," Gwen burst out, starting to laugh as her own arms started flapping. With a huge effort she crossed them across her chest and tucked her hands under her arms.

Aidan kept flapping as he backed up. The spell lessened with every step he took.

"It dies off it you move away from people, don't worry." He walked back, waving his hand with a twist. "There, spell canceled." They continued down the path. "And you saw for yourself you can resist it, if you need to."

"Where have you been all my life?" Gwen said. "I could have used this spell every time Ellie drags me out dancing. Which is all the time. You think practice would make perfect, but no."

"Well, we can clean up and dance, but what if Ellie can't come with us? What if she's enchanted to never leave the castle?"

"Then I beg Isolde for mercy. See if she has any drop of maternal instinct." She bit her lip. "I'd rather not do that, but if I have to, for Ellie's sake I will." She snorted. "Not that it's likely to work, but it's our last resort."

***

The sun peaked in the sky and beamed down through every parting in the leaves. The forest was warm and humid, moisture from the undergrowth evaporating into the air. Everything was lazy and hot as Gwen sweated in her dress, long since hiked up into her sash. She daydreamed of a shower, blissfully cool water pouring out of the showerhead in an unending stream, the dirt and grime of the past few days sliding down the drain. She was so immersed in the vision that she bumped into Aidan. He had stopped in front of her, his head tilted to one side as if listening.

"Do you hear that?" He looked to their left. "I hear water."

Gwen was suddenly, intensely aware of her dry tongue. She licked her lips, feeling cracks. A faint trickling and splashing gave scintillating hints of a river nearby.

"I thought it was just my imagination. Oh, let's go find it."

"It doesn't sound too far," Aidan said, indecision warring with longing in his voice. "Okay, let's go. I just don't want to go too far from the path."

Gwen barely let him finish his sentence before climbing over a nearby log in the direction of the sound. There was a small crest ahead of them, and beyond that the tops of willow trees peeked out from a thicket of leafy bushes. She picked up her pace.

The water sounds grew louder and more resonant as she climbed the ridge. Twigs snapped loudly under Aidan's feet behind her as they climbed, but her focus was entirely on the water. She rounded the top of the crest and her mouth widened in a blissful smile.

A river flowed below the ridge, its waters clear and deep. Broad banks of moss curled over the water's edge in puffy pillows. The river bank widened directly below Gwen. Farther upstream the river grew shallow as it rippled and splashed over boulders in a series of mild rapids. The sun filtered through the willows and beamed down into the clearing. The river curved gracefully as if presenting itself to Gwen, and meandered out of sight around a corner downstream. She sighed in relief and contentment.

Aidan hauled himself up beside her, panting, and stopped short.

"That's a sight for sore eyes," he said, wiping his forehead with a sleeve. "You ready for a swim?"

"Am I ever," Gwen replied. She paused. "No bathing suit, unfortunately."

185

Aidan gave an exaggerated sigh and gestured extravagantly toward the river. "Ladies first. I'll just sit on the other side of this hill and ward off flies."

"Eww." Gwen laughed and swatted his arm. "Just go down the river a few steps and wash there. You don't have to go too far."

Aidan looked downstream and nodded.

"Scream if you need anything."

Gwen smiled as Aidan trudged away, then turned to the sparkling river. It beckoned, inviting her with gentle burbles and flashes of sunlight. She waited until Aidan was out of sight and glanced nervously up and down the banks, but there wasn't a living creature in sight. She walked down the gentle embankment and stopped by a large boulder at the water's edge, feeling immensely self-conscious.

She took one more glance around then quickly untied her sash and slid her dress to the ground. Undergarments off, she stepped gingerly to the edge of the river and stopped. A strange tingling ran up her spine and the hairs on the back of her neck stood up. She crossed her arms over her chest and looked around. Was someone watching her?

Nothing stirred along the river except a solitary robin peering inquisitively at her. Feeling foolish, but horribly exposed, Gwen lowered herself into the clear water. It was freezing and she gasped in shock. Then, taking a big breath and squeezing her eyes shut in anticipation, she let herself fall backward into the deeper pool in the center of the river.

Her body exploded with sensation in the cold water swirling with bubbles. She instinctively kicked to the surface and gasped as her face emerged into the summery air. She paddled for a minute, panting, trying to pretend she couldn't feel the frigid water surrounding her body and rushing past with each kick.

Gradually the sensations faded, and Gwen began to enjoy her swim. The sunlight dazzled her eyes and warmed her head, and the gentle flow of the river kept her paddling to stay in one place. She felt she could stay for a long time, here in this sunny piece of paradise. But then she thought of Aidan and time passing, and regretfully dunked her head again to wash it as best she could. Once she had rinsed away the last few days of grime and sweat and fear, she hoisted herself onto the bank. The moss was spongy and soft under her knees. She nestled her fingers into its fuzzy bulk, enjoying the sensation.

Suddenly conscious of her nakedness, she looked up to find her clothes. The boulder that she had laid them on was empty. Thinking they had fallen to the other side she stood up and dripped over to the boulder. A quick circumference yielded nothing. Puzzlement gave way to alarm.

A voice behind her said, "Are you looking for these?"

Chapter 15

Gwen whirled around to look for the owner of the voice. She crouched behind the boulder with all her senses on high alert, frantically searching for the speaker.

There was a tall bush directly ahead, its large leaves creating patterns of light and shadow on themselves, which melded and mixed with shadows cast by the gently swaying willow nearby. Gwen looked once, then closer. A figure stood casually in the shadows of the bush, his body so camouflaged by the dappled shade that he almost seemed a part of it, as if he were growing there amongst the leaves. He stepped forward and Gwen saw why she had been confused. As the light hit the man, it revealed a torso completely covered by swirling green tattoos of vines and leaves, similar to her own mark. But where hers wrapped across her shoulder, the man's mark spread down his arms and across his stomach to end just above his trousers, and a tendril or two even snaked and climbed up his neck. Gwen tore her gaze away from the markings and looked at the man's face.

"Loniel?" she gasped.

"Hello, little birdling," he said. "I said we would meet again, and so here we are." He smiled impishly. "In the flesh, as it were."

Gwen was acutely aware of her naked body, crouching awkwardly behind the boulder. Trying to muster what little dignity she had left, she said, "Have you seen my clothes? I thought I'd left them here." She tried to ignore the fact that Loniel had probably been watching her for some time.

"You mean these ones?" He pointed to his right. On the bank were her dress, undergarments, and shoes, all neatly laid out and impeccably clean. He continued, "They were filthy, so I took the liberty of cleaning them."

"Thank you?" she said, half-questioning. She looked from Loniel to the clothes and back again. "Umm…"

Loniel tilted his head to one side and looked at her with knowing eyes.

"You want me to look away, don't you?" He sighed, smiling, as she nodded. He turned and started to whistle. Gwen ran over to her clothes and hastily threw them on, cheeks red. She was tying her sash when Loniel said, "I forgot how modest humans are. You shouldn't be ashamed. Bodies are beautiful things."

The words took a moment to sink in. Gwen's hands paused at the bow of her sash.

"What did you say?" she gasped.

Loniel turned his head to look at her, letting his body follow in a fluid wave. He raised an eyebrow.

"You may be able to fool the rest of them, but you can't hide from me." He looked appraisingly at Gwen's fearful face. "Fear not, little halfling. I mean you no harm."

"How do you know? I mean, who are you?" She looked at his chest then back into his eyes. "Or what are you?"

"Ah, a more pertinent question." He reached his arms out languidly and turned in a circle for Gwen to see the full extent of his tattoos, which spread across the upper half of his back and curled around his sides. He returned to face Gwen. "You and I are not so different. Your father is human, and your mother is queen in these parts, if I read your mark correctly." His eyes strayed briefly to her shoulder, exposed in the low-cut dress, then back to her face. "My mother was also from this realm, long ago. My father was of a different race entirely, from another world parallel to this one. Connected, not unlike the close linkage between this world and the human one."

Gwen frowned, digesting this information.

"So, are there lots of worlds, all linked together?"

Loniel shrugged.

"Perhaps. I haven't explored enough to say. What is relevant is that you, little halfling, have strayed over to this world and have caught my attention."

A chill ran down Gwen's back at these words.

"What do you mean?"

"When we met, you were searching for a human girl, were you not? In a blue dress, as I recall." He gazed at

Gwen through half-closed golden eyes. "I presume you followed Corann and his prize from the human world, given your wild demeanor that afternoon. You wish to rescue your human girl from Isolde's court, do you not?"

Gwen shook her head slightly in amazement. Somehow he had guessed everything.

"I suppose there's no point in hiding, since you seem to know everything already."

He laughed softly.

"Indeed. I make it my business to know. And when you've lived as long as I have, it's not difficult to piece things together." He gave a half-smile at Gwen whose confusion must have been apparent on her face. "Yes, exceptional long life runs in the family, on my father's side. I have seen many centuries pass, and the people here bloom and wither like leaves on a tree."

Gwen looked at him curiously.

"Why did you stay here in this world? Why wouldn't you go to your father's people? It must get lonely here by yourself if everyone always dies on you."

"Ah," Loniel said softly. "You cut right to the heart with one blow, little bird." He looked at her, considering. "I was born and raised here, so this place feels like home. But my longevity is inconsequential. My father's people will have nothing to do with me, and I am viewed with shame—an abomination. You see, they came to this world to use these people for their own amusement, but the Breenan were always inferior, always beneath. My father fell in love with my mother, which was incomprehensible to most. When she died, he killed himself so as to not live without her. Birth and death are rare in that other world, and I was a perfect

191

vessel to pour in their blame and grief of losing one of their own. Their memories are long and their grudges unbending. There is no place for me there, nor at this point would I wish for one."

Gwen took her hand away from her mouth, where it had ended up during Loniel's tale.

"Oh, Loniel, I'm so sorry. That's horrible."

He looked at her with amusement.

"Dear little halfling, do not pity me. I have had many centuries to accept my lot. The past holds no more pain for me. My birth caused the others to vow never again to enter this world, lest another be born of the same shame.

"I stayed in this world and lived my life. I even visited your world from time to time, since the Breenan had discovered the locations of the portals. I was pleased when some humans ventured here, falling through the cracks between worlds. They are so amusing when they are confused. They always enjoy themselves, especially at my bonfire." Here Loniel raised an eyebrow suggestively, and Gwen blushed. "I was less pleased when the Breenan began to feel superior to humans, to treat them as slaves and to hunt them for sport. It was history repeating itself, but with the enslaved race now snaring their own prey in turn. The lessons of the past were too far removed. I was frustrated, but unsure what to do.

"Then a queen of the Breenan came to my bonfire one night, heavy with child, sobbing as if her heart were broken. She was a descendant of my mother's brother, truth be told, although she did not know it. Her name was Kiera, and she had found her human lover with another woman, a human woman. She was distraught,

192

and wanted to close all the portals to prevent any other Breenan from following her path and falling in love with a human.

"'For I know you have the power, Loniel,' she said to me, 'and it is for the best. No one should suffer the fate I have suffered.'

"I pondered her request. It seemed extreme, but perhaps it was a solution to the greed and callousness of the Breenan, and it might protect the humans from further enslavement. And then she said something that removed any doubts.

"'Just make sure my son may travel between worlds. He is of both kinds, and I would not want to take away his human side. He deserves to be of both worlds.'

"Such a request from this last bastion of kindness of the Breenan, I could not refuse. And so it came to pass that Queen Kiera closed the portals between worlds, with a little help from yours truly." Loniel gave a bow. "And that is how you, my little halfling, were able to enter this world. I agree with Kiera, that all halflings should be able to be of both worlds, if they so desire."

Gwen's head whirled. Her first thought was to wonder how old Loniel really was. A second, more relevant question came to her mind.

"How did Corann get through with Ellie? And how did Isolde come to find my dad?"

Loniel's lips pursed.

"Isolde and a few others have discovered and exploited the loophole. I believe Isolde has a locket with the necessary magic, which she lends to Corann to collect humans for her own purposes. The defense, and indeed the very fabric of her realm are dependent on

193

magic produced from the dancing and music in her court. A pretty notion, dreamt up by her grandmother, but a risky one. It relies on a steady input of new human talent to feed the magic." He stepped toward Gwen. "Your feathers are still wet, little bird," he said. He moved behind her. She stood stock still, tense. There was something about Loniel that was wild and uncertain, despite his calm words. He touched a hand to her temple. "May I?"

She nodded slightly, not quite sure what she was allowing. He stroked her hair gently. As he did so, her hair lightened as it dried under his touch. He continued talking, close to her ear.

"In fact, that locket is the reason I am here. I wish to prevent Isolde from luring any more humans into her realm. I would take the locket myself, but unfortunately she has a cunning magical barrier surrounding her castle. You would think that with my far greater magic she would not be able to keep me out, but there you are." There was a smile in his voice as he separated strands of her now dry hair. His wrist appeared on the edge of her vision as he worked, its green markings distinct against his golden skin.

"Is that what the marks represent?" Gwen asked, interested. "The amount of magic people have?"

"Partially. Also parentage, as you know by now." He put his hands on her shoulders and leaned into her ear. "Will you steal the locket, and destroy it? Will you prevent future enslavement of your people?"

Gwen's breath was shallow. Ellie's desperate face appeared in her mind's eye. Could she stop this madness from happening again?

"How can I get it from her? She's so powerful. And cruel…"

Loniel moved to stand in front of her and continued to manipulate her hair, teasing strands and tucking things in.

"I'm sending her a message," he said vaguely. "There, you are complete."

Gwen reached up to touch her head.

"Ah ah," he admonished. "No touching." He looked into her eyes. "Remember, you have deep power that your mother cannot access, if you choose. You will find it, when you are ready to find it."

Gwen's brow knit in confusion at his cryptic words. Loniel smiled wide and stroked her cheek.

"Safe travels, little bird," he said, and walked away into the bushes, fading into the leaves without a trace.

Aidan called out. "Gwen? Can I come over?"

"I'm ready!" she called back.

The noise of cracking twigs preceded Aidan's appearance as he climbed over a log partially fallen in the river. His wet hair lay against his head, and his face was scrubbed clean. He stopped when he saw her.

"Wow," he said softly, then cleared his throat. "You look amazing. How did you do your hair like that?"

"I had help," she said.

**

"Honestly, I leave you for twenty minutes, and this is what happens," Aidan said, shaking his head. They were on the path again, heading for the castle. Gwen had just filled him in on Loniel's visit. Aidan was sufficiently awed by Loniel's longevity and otherworldliness, but was less than impressed that he had been watching her swim.

"That's creepy," he said flatly.

"Yeah, definitely." Her mouth twisted in distaste, and her cheeks flushed with embarrassment. "They're not so up on modesty here."

Aidan raised his eyebrows, but refrained from commenting further.

"So now we've got to get this locket off the queen, as well as rescue Ellie." Aidan scuffed his foot against a protruding tree root. "And get home. Luckily they're all easy tasks. We should be back by supper."

"Ha, ha," Gwen replied. "Loniel said he was sending Isolde a message. Maybe that will help? Let's focus on one task at a time. Ellie is first."

"Agreed. Let's carry out the plan as is," Aidan said.

They walked for another hour, Gwen with her skirt carefully tucked up into her sash as usual to preserve Loniel's cleaning. The cool freshness of morning had faded into the warm sultriness of a summer's afternoon when Gwen paused.

"Do you hear that?"

Aidan stood still, listening intently. "Is that music?"

Drifting across the stillness of the woods was the sound of a trumpet, high and clear, its notes faint but discernible. Gwen and Aidan looked at each other.

"Loniel?" Aidan guessed.

"A trumpet doesn't really seem his style," Gwen said, considering. "He seems more of a primal drums kind of guy."

Aidan huffed through his nose, but otherwise

ignored the comment. He said, "Well, it sounds like it's on our path, so I guess we'll find out."

"Tread carefully," Gwen warned, and they continued, walking more slowly and deliberately.

The music gradually grew richer and more complex as more instruments unveiled their tones. Trombones followed the trumpet, then a smattering of clarinets and flutes followed by a faint but growing swell of strings.

"Violins and flutes and cellos," Aidan said slowly. "This is a whole orchestra."

"Do you think…" Gwen trailed off. "We must be awfully close to the castle."

"Yeah, sounds like the queen took a little field trip this afternoon."

Gwen bit her lip.

"Are you ready?" she asked Aidan, turning to him. His cape was twisted at the clasp, and she reached over to fix it. Her hands trembled slightly as she undid the clasp, thinking of their task ahead.

As she finished, Aidan grabbed her hands in his and held them still.

"We can do this."

They gazed at each other for a few long moments. Gwen felt like they were saying so much without any words. After a long moment had passed she tucked her head down to their clasped hands between their chests, wondering what had just happened. She squeezed his hands and let go, looking back into Aidan's eyes as she did so and smiling shyly.

Aidan reached a hand to her temple and brushed back an errant piece of hair. She suddenly wished he wouldn't stop.

197

"There are so many flowers in your hair. It looks beautiful." He took his hand away and it left a hollow near Gwen, like the absence of heat in winter. "Let's go show it off."

Spontaneously she tucked her arm into his.

"Let's do this," she said, and together they walked down the path toward the music.

***

Gwen realized when they had walked past the next bend that the music came from a spot off the path.

"Guess we have to break trail again," Gwen said, removing her hand from Aidan's arm to hike her skirts up higher.

"Wait, there's a path here." Aidan pointed to a well-worn trail through the undergrowth, its inception hidden by a carefully positioned shrub. "Looks like the queen's not a fan of bushwhacking."

"That's one thing we have in common," Gwen muttered.

The path quickly widened into a large sunny clearing. Stately birches ringed a meadow of wildflowers, blooming white and yellow and violet amongst waving grasses. The sun streamed down, bathing everything in a bright glow. The meadow was alive with Breenan dancing in the hazy light. Their forms swayed and flowed like a mirage as Gwen blinked in the sudden brightness. A small, open-sided pavilion stood on the far left of the meadow and the dark-haired queen perched on a carved wooden seat within. Gwen's stomach flopped a little at the sight of her mother. She

198

suddenly, desperately, wanted to see Isolde's face. Years of longing surfaced in an instant, and she gripped Aidan's arm for balance against the maelstrom in her head.

"I see Ellie," Aidan whispered, and Gwen tore her eyes away from the figure under the pavilion to scan the dancers. She spotted Ellie's sky-blue dress without difficulty through the Breenan milling around the central dance. The dancers were dressed today in fresh colors—bright blues, vivid greens, sunny yellows. Many of the women and men had crowns of flowers and leaves on their heads and woven into their hair.

Aidan must have been noticing the same thing, because he leaned down and whispered, "You fit in perfectly."

She smiled up at him as their eyes met. Then she sighed.

"Are you ready?"

"Ready as I'll ever be." They walked forward through the crowd. No one took much notice of them. There were green leaves of tattoos peeking out from underneath dress necklines, and Gwen surreptitiously glanced at her own to reassure herself it was still there. The gesture surprised her. Was she really so accepting and used to the mark already, that its presence comforted her?

They reached the edge of the spectators just as the music finished. The musicians wiped their brows under the warm rays of the sun and flipped sheets of music. Spectators and dancers were moving around, changing places, and Aidan grabbed Gwen's hand.

"Now's our chance," he whispered, and they hurried

into the meadow. Gwen steered Aidan as close to Ellie as she could before the dancers placed themselves in formation. Aidan touched her forehead to put the dancing spell on her, and they parted to take their places in the dance.

Gwen's hands were clammy and cold. The audacity of what they were doing hit her with the full force of the danger they were in. She was totally dependent on this spell that Aidan had made up on his own.

She was so busy fervently hoping that the spell would work that she was taken by surprise when the music started and her body demanded to move. She let it do what it willed, happy to be a passive recipient of the dance. She curtseyed and Aidan bowed, and they walked around each other with their hands just touching.

Gwen breathed a little easier but kept vigilant, trying to figure out how to get to Ellie. She risked a glance at Ellie dancing nearby. Her dress was as clean as before and her hair still miraculously intact, with the addition of fresh flowers laced through her curls. Her face, however, was a mask of indifference overlaid on extensive suffering. She had a gaunt, hollowed look, so bizarre on her normally cheerful visage, and her eyes were sunken with dark circles underneath. Gwen glanced down and her stomach dropped. Ellie's shoes were worn away almost completely and bloodstains edged the holes. Gwen focused again on the dance, tears springing to her eyes.

The music changed slightly and Gwen and Aidan found themselves in a set of four with Ellie and a young Breenan man who wore a crown of laurel leaves on his chestnut-brown hair.

Gwen had hardly made eye contact with Ellie before the Breenan man swept Gwen away in the dance. The two couples whirled around each other, Gwen barely having time to breathe. Her partner's intense eyes were focused on hers as they turned. Gwen concentrated hard on letting her body do what it wanted. After the initial relief of knowing the dance moves, it was difficult for her to let some unseen force control her. She wanted to fight it, and felt very wrong-footed and ill at ease even as she executed perfect footwork. As she twirled past the other two she could hear Aidan murmuring softly to Ellie. Her heart ached at Ellie's nearness and her stomach clenched at their proximity to danger.

Gwen and her partner separated and the two couples faced each other in a square once again. Gwen looked at Ellie's face dripping with tears, spilling out over her cheeks as she fought to keep her eyes open wide enough to see the dance. Her feet never faltered.

Gwen forgot everything in her overwhelming despair. Her body was numb with horror. In her distraction and emotion, Aidan's spell on her diminished. Suddenly she didn't know what to do next. Ellie's eyes widened with terror and Gwen realized she had missed steps of the dance. She tried to listen to her body again but the Breenan man had stopped, watching her curiously. Aidan and Ellie stopped as well.

"You'd better go see the queen," the man said finally. "She'll want to have a word with you. You know she only allows the best in her dances." He jerked his head in the direction of the tent, looking at Aidan. "Go on, take her up."

Gwen's heart sank as she realized she was leaving

201

Ellie yet again. She looked at Ellie as Aidan took her arm. Ellie looked terrified and bereft, but she tried for a watery smile as Gwen walked away. Her heart pounding and her stomach in knots, Gwen walked with Aidan toward the tent. There was no escape. Gwen could feel the eyes of the man burning into her back and the queen had stood up from her carved seat and waited for them.

They approached the tent. The queen stood under its cover with her face obscured in its shadow, dim amidst the dazzling light of the clearing. They stopped a few paces away. Gwen wondered what to do. She bowed her head awkwardly to acknowledge the queen's presence and hoped she wasn't supposed to curtsey or get down on one knee.

"You are very young." Isolde spoke out of the shadows. Her voice was rich and resonant—it was a voice used to being heard. "That might explain your inability to keep to the dance. This particular dance is a very old one indeed, not one of the new ones from my most recent choreographer. Therefore there is little excuse for your misstep, save inexperience and a lack of knowledge of my court."

Gwen glanced at Aidan briefly, wondering what to say. His pale face looked as confused and frightened as her own.

"Well? Have you nothing to say in your own defense?" Isolde said, and stepped forward as if to examine them better. Gwen's breath caught.

It was the face from her father's sketch come to life. The years had aged Isolde, but lines were faint, and only one dramatic stripe of white at her temple lightened the brown-black locks. Age had merely given her beauty an air of gravitas. She was not wearing the smug smile of hidden knowledge as she had for the sketch. Instead, her lips pursed a little and her eyes considered, as if unsure what to do.

Gwen was speechless at the sight of her mother in the flesh. Aidan came to her rescue.

"We're sorry, my lady," he stumbled out. "It won't happen again."

"Missteps are something I cannot allow too frequently. The dance is a kind of magic, you know, beyond its own intrinsic beauty. The magic made by the dance and music powers much of this realm. The enchantments on the forest to keep the realm safe, for example, are born of these beautiful formations." She swept a hand toward the dancers, and then turned back to Gwen and Aidan. "Without the dance, the forests would be overrun with dangerous beasts, our borders would be breached by malevolent enemies, and this court would sink into ruin. Even the food at our table relies on the magic of the dance and without it the people of this realm would go hungry. So you see, I must ask you to leave. Every misstep weakens the magic. When you have mastered the moves, you are more than welcome to return and join again in the pleasures of the dance."

Isolde looked expectantly at them while Gwen gathered her scattered thoughts. She blurted out, "Why do you bring the humans in? Surely they're a source of error. They aren't perfect."

"Too true." Isolde nodded. "But it is a necessary evil. The magic of the dance loses its potency with too much repetition. We would survive for a while without new choreography and creativity from the humans, but eventually the magic would weaken and the realm would be susceptible to war and famine. Besides, my dancers would get very bored doing the same dances over and over again." She glanced out to the dancers. "Speaking of which, my newest acquisition seems almost spent. I'll have to dispose of her shortly, I suppose. Perhaps on the morrow."

Gwen followed her gaze to see Ellie on the other end. Anger started to burn deep in her chest. Anger at her own impotence and failed rescue attempts, anger at the whole crazy Otherworld, and above all anger at Isolde, her cold, cruel, abandoning Breenan mother. Her frustration must have shown on her face, because Aidan surreptitiously snuck his hand into hers and gave it a gentle squeeze. She released the breath she didn't know she had been holding.

Isolde turned back to them.

"Safe travels," she said dismissively. Then she looked more closely at Gwen, searching her face curiously. "You look very familiar, my dear," she said. Gwen tried to make her face as blank as possible. Isolde's eyes travelled up to Gwen's hair, and Gwen glanced down. She noticed a delicate gold chain lying against Isolde's neck. At the end of the chain dangled a large gold locket, the metal face worked with patterns of golden vines and leaves.

Gwen glanced back at Isolde's face, her heart pounding. Everything she wanted was here—Ellie, the locket—they were so close but so unattainable. Isolde's face was puzzled.

"There is a riddle spelled out in the flowers in your hair," she said. "It's very skillful work. Did you do this?"

Gwen frowned in confusion.

"No, I didn't. I had help."

"From whom?"

Gwen couldn't see any reason to lie. She realized that this must be the 'message' Loniel sent to Isolde.

"Loniel did it."

Isolde stared at her for a minute, her hand reaching up to finger the locket absentmindedly. Then she collected herself.

"That will be all. You may go now." She waved them off.

Aidan grabbed Gwen's arm and pulled her away. She stumbled after him and they quickly walked the circumference of the clearing. Gwen glanced back once. Isolde still looked after them, frowning.

They walked into the dim of the forest and promptly bumped into a man.

"Sorry," Gwen gasped.

"Wait," the man replied. "What are you two doing here?"

Gwen squinted into the darkness as her eyes adjusted. Aidan sucked in his breath beside her. Suddenly the man grabbed her shoulder and pushed the edge of her dress down, leaning in to look at her mark. She recognized Corann.

"Oh, no," she breathed. She wrenched away from him, but it was too late. His shocked face and wide eyes filled her vision. Aidan grabbed her hand and they fled, Corann watching them go with an open mouth.

Chapter 16

Corann stared after Gwen and Aidan's frenzied escape, making no move to stop them. His forehead creased in confusion. He stood beneath the trees, thinking, until a change in the music brought him out of his reverie. He turned quickly and exited the relative darkness of the trees into the shimmering light of the meadow.

Isolde stood in the shade of her brocade pavilion. Her face was thoughtful as she surveyed the dancers floating in intricate formations to the pulse of the orchestra. Her fingers stroked the locket around her neck absently.

Corann approached the queen.

"My lady?"

She turned and smiled in welcome.

"Corann. I was wondering where you had

disappeared to." She brought her hand down from the nape of her neck and smoothed her skirts. "I'm pleased with our little excursion today. We all needed a change, I think."

Corann bowed his head in agreement but did not reply. He stared at Isolde's face, his lips tight, as she gazed out over the meadow. She caught his eye and laughed lightly.

"So intense! Is there something you wish to say?" She reached out and gently brushed away an errant lock of hair on his forehead.

Corann did not smile back.

"My lady." He paused. "When I acquired your latest dancer," he waved toward Ellie, dancing dead-eyed nearby, "I also met her friend, a girl about the same age. I would have thought no more about her, except that she must have followed me into our world, along with a male companion. The bartender, if I recall correctly."

Isolde frowned.

"Why have you said nothing until now?"

"I did not know. I only saw the two of them as they left the meadow just now. The girl was dark-haired with a green dress. The male was tall with red hair."

"Yes, I remember. I just spoke to them." Isolde stared at Corann in puzzlement. "The girl wasn't following the dance correctly, and so I asked them to leave." She frowned. "She had a mark, and certainly looked Breenan. But you say they came from the human world?"

Corann looked unhappy.

"Did you read her mark?"

"No, I didn't bother." Isolde looked sharply at

Corann. "Who is she? Why and how was she in the human world?"

Corann looked directly into the queen's eyes.

"She is your daughter. Your half-human daughter."

There was a long pause as Isolde stared at Corann. Her usually calm expression betrayed her, and various emotions flitted across her face. First came blank shock, followed by a widening of the eyes in panic. Finally a hint of longing stole over her features. She turned her face away from Corann. Her voice was a little unsteady as she said, "So that was Gwendolyn. How—how strange to see her. See her as a grown woman, I mean. In my mind she is always so tiny, such a fragile little thing. And so angry. I remember her little fists and her cries as my mother took her away." She exhaled sharply in what might have been a laugh. "My mother was so afraid I would not let the baby go. From the moment she knew I was with child she hounded me, reminding me I had to give the baby up. She hardly let me see her on the birth day." She looked back at Corann, her face controlled once more. "She needn't have worried. I knew what had to be done."

Isolde gazed at the dancers, a faraway look in her eyes.

"I wondered why the girl looked so familiar. I suppose I saw myself in her."

"She does resemble you a little," Corann said begrudgingly. "But there is something strange and other in her features. It is an uncanny meld."

"It's her father," Isolde said softly. "She has a lot of him in her. Alan." She stared into the distance with unseeing eyes, a faint smile playing around her softened

208

mouth.

Corann's face darkened.

"You still have feelings for this human?" He spoke in a light, casual tone, but his eyes were locked on Isolde's face.

Isolde blinked and shook her head.

"Of course not. I never did. He was a means to an end, nothing more." She avoided Corann's searching gaze, keeping her eyes fixed on the dance.

Corann let the subject drop.

"Did the girl say why she was here?"

"No," Isolde said thoughtfully. "But she if is indeed a friend of my most recent human, perhaps that is all the explanation we need."

"Do you suppose she knows? About the portals?" Corann glanced at Isolde's hand, which touched the locket once more.

Isolde frowned.

"If she didn't before, she will now. She's met with Loniel, of all people. He sent me a riddle written in her hair." She sighed. "Not all of it is clear to me, but I think we can conclude that this daughter of mine may be more of a threat than she appears."

"Then we should give chase and hunt her down," Corann said at once. "If she is a danger to you or to the realm she must be stopped. By any means necessary."

Isolde did not immediately reply. Corann pressed on.

"You must not let any feelings you have for the girl blind you to what must be done."

"I know my duty, Corann." Isolde's tone was curt. "The girl will be dealt with. And there is no need to chase after her. She is obviously trying to rescue her friend. Let her come to us. When she appears once again, alert me." Corann nodded. "Inform the orchestra that we will adjourn to the castle presently." She waved him away and he bowed and left silently, his jaw tight.

Isolde gazed at the blue-clad figure of Ellie, endlessly dancing. She touched the locket once more.

***

They burst onto the main path, Gwen holding her skirts up to run.

"Which way?" Aidan gasped.

"Over here." Gwen ran in the direction they had been traveling in, toward the castle. She didn't want to backtrack later when they came to rescue Ellie again. And they would—the fires of anger burned steadily in Gwen's chest. She could picture them licking the walls of the locked box that was her magical core. Gwen and Aidan ran until Gwen's side was in stitches, and still they ran, forcing their way off the main path when Gwen spotted a deer trail cutting a thin line through the undergrowth.

They continued more slowly now, as the path was full of stones and errant roots and tree falls. It seemed that no one had gone this way in many years. Gwen kept looking over her shoulder past Aidan to make sure no one followed them. The forest was still and hot. The only noises Gwen heard were their own.

Gwen finally slowed to a walk, and then stopped.

"How far do we go?" Her voice was rough. She had to push it out past her throat, constricted as it was by their flight and her fears. "I don't want to go too far. I have to go back, before…" She couldn't finish. She gritted her teeth and swallowed hard, the anger and fear threatening to overwhelm her.

"A little farther." Aidan's voice was calm and measured. "I don't think we're being followed, so let's just find somewhere to lie low for the night. Ellie said they were heading back to the castle shortly anyway, so we can try again at first light."

It seemed easier just to nod and carry on. Every step seemed farther and farther away from Ellie, but Gwen knew Aidan was right.

The sun was low in the sky by the time they stopped in front of the mouth of a cave. It lurked in the side of a hill covered in rubble, scrubby bushes, and trees clinging gamely to the slope. The entrance was taller than Aidan by a head, and twice as wide. The setting sun only highlighted the profound darkness within.

Aidan swallowed, then flicked his wrist to produce his usual blue flames.

"I'll check it out, shall I?" he said nervously. "Just in case."

Gwen was reminded of the wolf and lion of their first night. She fervently hoped that they were only the product of Isolde's protection spell.

Aidan stepped forward and raised his palm high above his head. The little flame cast only a small pool of light. Gwen followed Aidan into the cave, straining her eyes to make out anything inside.

The light flickered on dry stone walls, dusty and rough. Jagged protrusions startled Gwen as their shadows moved with life-like animation in the firelight. In the corner of her eye she caught a flash of metal. She looked more closely.

"Whoa," Aidan said softly. "Check out the dragon's hoard."

The back of the cave was piled high with dozens upon dozens of musical instruments. Violins and flutes and guitars were just a few that Gwen could name. Many were completely unfamiliar. The pile reached chest-height, and it glimmered with warm glints of brass and silver.

Aidan threw down his flame where it rolled and bounced against the nearest wall. He started rummaging through the pile, picking up instruments and examining them.

"There are gorgeous. Look, here's a lyre, I'm sure of it. And check out this harp. I've never seen one like it outside of a museum." He gently touched the strings of the harp with delicate hands, his face reverential.

"Why are they just lying in a big pile in a cave?" Gwen said. She didn't really understand Aidan's fascination with the instruments, but the awe in his voice was catching.

Aidan frowned.

"I don't know. It's almost criminal." He patted the golden wood of the lyre as he placed it carefully on the pile. "Maybe they're left over from centuries of musicians that have made their way to the Otherworld. This cave could be a dumping ground for things the Breenan don't want anymore. It doesn't seem like they care too much about creating music for its own sake." He sighed and snapped back to their situation. "Well, this cave seems all right."

"Yeah." Suddenly Gwen was very tired. Tired of

running, tired of fighting, tired of being frightened. Her exhaustion told her to give up. The coals of her anger, however, burned steadily deep inside. Tomorrow, she told herself, tomorrow they would finish this once and for all, even if she had to take on her mother herself.

"Hey, what do you think of a fire tonight?" Aidan said. "No one will see our smoke once it's dark, and the warmth wouldn't hurt."

Gwen considered this.

"I guess if we were being chased, they would have caught up by now." The thought of a campfire pleased her more than she expected. Camping trips with her father always culminated in long evenings by a crackling fire, roasting marshmallows and watching stars twinkle overhead through the smoke. Her heart squeezed as she thought of her father, homesickness grabbing hold. As she pictured his crinkling eyes when he smiled, her magic core lurched deep within her. She gasped and clutched her hands to her chest.

"What's wrong?" Aidan looked at her, concerned.

The feeling subsided quickly.

"My core felt funny, suddenly."

"What happened? What were you feeling? What were you thinking about?"

Gwen stared at him.

"My dad. How much I miss him."

Aidan looked sympathetic.

"Oh Gwen…" He sighed. "We'll get there." He looked out of the cave. "We have to."

Gwen looked at his forlorn face and spontaneously stepped forward to hug him. She wrapped her arms around his middle, resting her head against his chest and

213

neck. He seemed startled at first, then his arms lifted and rested around her shoulders, his face coming to rest tentatively in her hair. She breathed him in, relaxing into his frame. The ache for contact, one she hadn't realized she'd been living with, abated.

They stood there for a while clinging to each other, both unwilling to let go. Finally Gwen lifted her head and stepped back.

"Let's get that fire going," she said. She took his hand and drew him to the mouth of the cave. Aidan's face was an open book, his expression of vulnerability and longing written clearly. Gwen gave him a small smile which he gradually returned. "Come on, there's got to be something to burn around here."

The sun had set by now and the forest was darkening quickly. Gwen let go of Aidan's hand regretfully but was pleased to note that he let her hand only slide away slowly. There were plenty of fallen branches in the undergrowth surrounding the cave.

"Pick up pinecones too," Gwen instructed. "We can use them for a starter, in a pinch."

Once they had a sizeable pile of branches beside the cave, Gwen set to work building the fire. Aidan watched her make a pile of needles and dry leaves and surround it with tiny twigs for kindling.

"I'm glad you know what you're doing," he said finally. "I don't make too many fires, as a rule."

"See, I'm not entirely useless. My dad and I go camping all the time," Gwen replied. "I learned early. Dinner didn't happen until the fire was lit, so I had a major incentive to learn quickly."

Aidan laughed.

"Fair enough. When dinner depends on it…"

"You should come visit. We could go camping and I could take you to my favorite spots."

"And see bears?" Aidan said eagerly. "You boasted that you see them all the time. Now you have to deliver."

Gwen laughed.

"Sure, if we're unlucky we'll come across a bear. Or a bear will come across us."

They smiled at each other, then Aidan's grin faded.

"Yeah, that would be nice," he said, looking down at his hands.

Gwen worked in silence, finishing her fire preparations. The presence of the Otherworld forest was like a physical entity beside them, weighing them down. Bran's ring was warm on her thumb from her exertions.

"Okay, it's ready," she said, leaning back.

"Uh, did you bring matches?" Aidan asked, concerned. "Or are you going to do that wood spinning thing with your hands?"

Gwen stared at him in amusement.

"I was kind of hoping you could bring your skills to the table here."

Aidan's face was blank for a moment, then he looked sheepish.

"Sorry, I must be half-asleep." He held out his hand over the kindling, and a moment later bright flames flared up from the little pile.

"I knew I brought you along for a reason," Gwen joked. She got on her hands and knees and blew air into the fire, fanning the flames.

"It's good to know I'm more than just eye candy," Aidan said. Gwen stuck her tongue out at him. He bent

215

down to join her. "Can I help?"

Together they coaxed the little fire until the larger logs caught. They leaned back and contemplated their handiwork.

A voice behind them said, "Am I missing all the fun?"

Chapter 17

Gwen whirled around, her body tensed and ready for action. The grinning face of Bran made her collapse with relief.

"Oh, you gave me a scare." She sat back in the dirt. "Hi, Bran. It's good to see you again."

Aidan remained tense on one knee.

"Are you alone?"

"So suspicious." Bran chuckled. "Yes, I'm alone. I snuck off from Crevan and followed the ring's pull." He nodded at Gwen's hand. "I said I'd come help get your human back, so here I am." He settled down comfortably across the fire from them, tossing the sack he carried to the ground beside him. "Been having adventures while I've been gone?"

Gwen groaned.

"We tried and failed to get Ellie. And now I think

Isolde knows I'm her daughter."

Bran whistled.

"So, a few, then."

"Isolde's going to get rid of Ellie tomorrow," Aidan said.

"Can we just grab her then?" Gwen asked with sudden hope. "Maybe Isolde will just let her go free. That man we saw at Loniel's bonfire, the one who interrupted the dancing, maybe he was a human from Isolde's collection."

"Mmm, I don't know. By the time Isolde's done with them, the humans tend to go a little crazy. More than the usual human befuddlement, I mean." Bran shook his head. "If you want your human back in one piece, you probably want to get her before she snaps."

"Ellie told me something similar," Aidan said quietly. "She said she was just barely holding on, that she didn't know how much longer she would last. She seemed to have some hope when I told her we were trying to rescue her, but she's in a pretty bad way. She was very confused. I think it must be the Breenan food and drink affecting her."

Gwen swallowed and hugged her knees.

"What else did she say?"

"She said she couldn't leave of her own free will. Early on she tried, and her feet just wouldn't let her go in the direction of the door without someone dancing her that way. She's punished if she doesn't dance. Every night she's forced to create new choreographies while a panel of Breenan watches her and takes notes, and every day she has to dance in the ballroom. I told her the plan, though, and she thought it could work if someone else

218

took control and danced her toward the door."

"Yeah, it's just a compulsion spell," Bran piped up. "As long as someone else leads her, it should be fine."

"Okay, good. We'll try that first thing tomorrow morning." Gwen stared moodily into the fire.

Bran shuffled closer to Gwen and knelt over her. She looked at him, confused, but he said, "Hold still. I'm reading. Did you know there's a message in your hair?"

"What does it say?" Aidan asked. "It certainly puzzled the queen."

"Hold on…" Bran wrinkled his nose in concentration. "Wait—okay, I think I've got it. It says, 'You must give up what is not yours to gain what you've never had.'" He sat back on his feet. "Huh. That's strange."

"That's Loniel's 'message' for Isolde? A cryptic warning?" Aidan looked perplexed.

Gwen sighed.

"So cryptic I don't think even Isolde knew what it meant. Loniel's lived for so long that maybe he forgets we're not all so clever."

"Although it might start making sense once Corann tells her who you are," Aidan said.

"Oh ho, so Corann saw your mark, did he?" Bran said, interested. "I wonder what Isolde will do."

"Don't we all," Gwen muttered.

"So gloomy! Are all humans like this?" Bran grabbed the sack and reached inside. He pulled out a loaf of bread. "I know what will help."

"Oh Bran, you're a lifesaver," Gwen said as she gratefully took a proffered chunk of the loaf.

"Thanks, mate," Aidan said, and they tucked in with

219

gusto.

Gwen felt much better after their supper of bread and a sharp hard cheese that Bran pulled out of his sack.

"I've got apples too," Bran said once they had eaten their fill.

"Mmm, yes. Can we roast them?" Gwen shoved another branch into the fire.

Aidan leaped up and scouted for roasting sticks. He returned with three twisty branches.

"Think these are green enough?"

"Let's try." Bran took the sticks and touched the ends. A brief scraping noise resulted in three sharp points. He speared an apple onto each and passed two to Gwen and Aidan.

The glorious scent of sweet apple tempted Gwen to taste her apple right out of the fire five minutes later.

"Gah!" She spat out the apple and fanned her mouth. "Hot!"

Bran laughed merrily, but scooted over to Gwen. He laid a hand on her forehead, still laughing.

Immediately the burning on Gwen's tongue faded and she could taste the remains of her apple, crisp and sweet.

"Thanks, Bran." She blew on the rest of her apple. She glanced at Aidan who looked at Bran with a strange mixture of frustration and annoyance. He wiped the expression off quickly when he saw Gwen watching and took a bite of his own apple.

After she had eaten the rest of her apple, Gwen leaned back to rest on her hands and contemplated the fire, contentedly full. Bran played with a stick with burning coals at the end, poking it into the dirt.

Aidan spoke into the quiet, his voice drowsy.

"You know, you do look like her, Gwen. Except younger, of course, and prettier."

Gwen stiffened. She didn't know whether to be annoyed that he had compared her to Isolde, who she had managed to not think about for the last ten minutes, or to be flattered that he had called her pretty. She settled on staring harder into the fire.

Bran pitched in.

"Yeah, you know, Aidan's right. Funny no one else has noticed. Although you do have this strange exotic something going on. It must be your human side."

Gwen snorted.

"Exotic?" Then she sighed. "I'd rather not look like her. I don't want anything to do with her. All my life I've wanted my mother, but not like this. Not at this cost."

They fell silent again, until Gwen said, "When I messed up the dance today, I thought I was a goner. But Isolde just scolded us a little and let us go. Why was she so harsh with Ellie's punishment, and not at all with mine?"

"Because she thought you were Breenan," Bran said. "She's not going to hurt you. Who knows who you might be, what tribe might back you? It would be too great a risk, and for what purpose? She can just ask you to leave. But no one would care about a human. She took them and they're her property now."

Gwen was aghast. "They're no one's property! You can't have slaves! It's not right."

Bran looked at her, considering, as if he'd never given it a thought before.

221

"It made more sense before I met you, I guess."

"Yeah, we're people too." Gwen shook her head and looked into the fire. Aidan looked from one to the other.

"Anyone up for a little music?" Without waiting for an answer Aidan sprang up and disappeared into the cave. Gwen and Bran sat in silence as rustlings and clanging floated out. Aidan finally emerged clutching a flute and the instrument he had called a lyre.

"I've always wanted to try one of these," he said, flopping down on the ground and putting the lyre in his lap. He plucked experimentally at the strings. Each note rang out soft but clear over the crackling of the fire. Aidan fiddled with the tuning keys then strummed a few times. Each stroke had a different configuration of fingers on the neck and each drifted on the air, mingling and melding and then floating up to disappear with the smoke.

Aidan looked up at Gwen and grinned with childlike joy. Then he bent over the instrument and began to play.

He played trickling arpeggios first, notes drifting and tumbling over each other. Gwen was reminded of water over stones in a river, flowing and staccato all at once. She watched Aidan's fingers dancing over the strings, deft and sure, pale skin shining against the golden glow of the lyre.

The arpeggios transformed gradually, different notes inserting themselves into the scales like fish jumping in a waterfall. Out of the notes began to emerge a melody. It was tentative at first, almost a hint of a song, but grew in confidence.

Gwen closed her eyes and leaned back on her hands, enthralled. She let the music take over her senses as her

222

imagination travelled on wild, whimsical paths. She recalled the cycle of star births and deaths she had witnessed at the marking ceremony and imagined herself floating in the vast emptiness between stars. The stress and pain of the past few days did not diminish, but the scale of her suffering shrank to nothing compared to the universe. It seemed easier to manage, somehow, after briefly touching eternity.

The music grew softer, quieter, and died away. Gwen let the moment finish before opening her eyes. Aidan smiled contentedly down at the lyre. Bran stared at him open-mouthed.

"That was amazing. How did you remember all that, especially if you've never played a lyre before?"

Aidan shrugged with a shy half-smile. "I just made it up."

Gwen raised her eyebrows.

"That was beautiful, Aidan. Thank you for that."

They smiled at each other.

Bran spluttered, "Seriously? You just made it up? Right now?" Aidan nodded and Bran looked flabbergasted. "Wow, there might be something to being human after all."

"Where did you learn?" Gwen asked.

"I had lessons in piano and flute as a kid," Aidan said, carefully laying the lyre on the ground away from the fire. "I taught the rest to myself, figured it out on my own. We didn't always have money for instruments, but I got good at scrounging and buying used." He made a face. "Mum's not so keen on it. She likes hearing me play well enough, but she doesn't think I can make it a real career. She's a nurse, you see—I don't think music is practical enough for her."

"But you're so good," Gwen said, surprised.

Aidan shrugged.

"Thanks." He picked up the flute and fidgeted with the keys. "I used to imagine my father was into music, like me." He laughed humorlessly. "I guess I was wrong."

Bran pitched in.

"Declan can't make up music like you can, it's true. But he's an excellent player, and always has music in his house. I remember him saying once that he wished he had lived five hundred years ago, when bards still roamed the land and music was fresh and alive."

Aidan stared at Bran, his face unreadable. Then he put the flute down and shoved another log in the fire. Sparks popped out and the wood hissed as sap bubbled within.

Bran said cautiously, "Will you—are you going to play some more? The night is still young, and I haven't heard anything like it before."

Aidan looked surprised, but gratified.

"Well, sure. Gwen?"

"Oh, please," she said, lying down beside the fire and closing her eyes. She let her thoughts drift as Aidan brought the flute to his lips and began to play.

***

The fire was dying by the time Aidan put down his flute. Gwen had long since fallen asleep, her breathing deep and even. Bran was uncharacteristically still. He lay flat on his back, open eyes watching the star-strewn

224

blackness above.

Aidan leaned back on his hands and kicked out his legs, toasting his feet by the fire.

"So what's your game, Bran? Why did you really come to find us?"

Bran turned to look at Aidan with wry amusement.

"I didn't lie. I think it would be the greatest joke ever to steal a human from Queen Isolde. All the ruling families can be so stuffy. Mine included." He turned back to the sky. "And I wasn't kidding when I said I liked Declan. He's not as full of himself as the rest of them."

Aidan swallowed. The fire gave a few weary crackles. Aidan let a few beats pass, and then said, "So it's all just for fun? It's a bit hard to believe."

Bran looked at Aidan, as if measuring him up. He said, "I've always been fascinated with humans, ever since I was a child. My favorite nursery stories were the human tales. It's like finding myth come to life, meeting you two. I guess I couldn't resist knowing you better, learning more about humans, maybe even..." He stopped.

"Maybe what?" Aidan prompted.

"Nothing." Bran laughed lightly. "I'm just always looking for an adventure. You two conveniently gave me one."

Aidan lowered himself to one elbow with a sigh.

"I guess that makes sense. Although you're the myth, you know."

"Ha." Bran rolled over to look at Aidan fully. "While we're asking questions, what's between you and Gwen?"

Aidan picked up an errant pinecone and began fiddling with it.

"I don't know. We were getting pretty friendly before we came to this world, then we were all over each other at Loniel's bonfire, and ever since then she's been off and on. I think she's just been controlling her emotions for so long for fear she'd use magic that she doesn't know how to deal with them anymore. I don't know, she's such a closed book sometimes." He sighed, picking apart the pinecone. "I wish we were back at Loniel's bonfire."

Bran chuckled.

"I bet you do."

Aidan tossed the pinecone at Bran. Bran lazily raised a hand and burst the cone into a silent shower of sparks.

"That's not what I meant." He lay down and gazed upward at the stars. "She just seemed so free. So unburdened by being careful all the time."

They contemplated the stars. Bran yawned.

"She can't hold out forever. No one likes to be caged. She'll stretch her wings eventually."

They lay in companionable silence for a while. Aidan looked at Gwen as she breathed quietly, her face lit by the glowing embers of the dying fire.

"Bran?"

"Mmm?" Bran's eyes glinted with the reflection of the stars above.

"Could you show me how to make that tracker ring thing?"

Bran grinned and sat up quickly.

"Of course. The ring is pretty simple to make in itself. Tracking takes much more effort and

226

concentration. You have to focus all your will on reuniting yourself with the ring you've made. You'll be able to feel the direction it's in, a sort of pull in your gut. It will even come to you, if your will is strong enough. I haven't tried that before, but that's the theory."

Aidan sat up as he listened.

"How do you make it?"

"Get some hairs first." Aidan reached up and yanked a few out of his head, wincing. Bran continued, "Okay, good. Now just do a matter-transformation spell to turn it into metal."

"Oh, of course." Aidan looked at Bran from under raised brows. "The old matter-transformation spell."

Bran laughed.

"It must be terrible to not know anything. Here." He put his fingers to Aidan's temple and closed his eyes. Aidan looked perplexed for a moment, and then his eyes snapped shut and his mouth opened in shock.

Bran removed his hands, beaming.

"There we are. Give it a go."

Aidan opened his eyes, looking astonished. He slowly cracked a smile.

"Wow. I know it now. That was—really easy."

Bran nodded, grinning smugly.

Aidan held out the hairs and stared at them intently. Nothing happened for a moment, until the hairs started to melt together, turning thick and shiny.

"Now twist it into a ring," Bran instructed.

Aidan ignored him. Placing the melting hairs in his hand, he stared at them. Slowly they pooled into the center of his palm. The puddle of molten copper glistened in the firelight until it coalesced into a round,

227

rigid disc with markings across its surface.

"What's that?" Bran asked curiously.

"It's a pence," Aidan said proudly. "I wanted to try a different shape." He passed it to Bran to examine.

"I'm impressed," Bran said. "I'd be more impressed if I knew what a pence was."

"Do you not have money here?" Aidan asked incredulously. "You know, coins and paper you can buy things with?"

"Oh, I've heard of that from the old stories. No, everything is traded here. Goods, labor, spells, secrets."

A sharp crack echoed in the woods beyond Gwen's sleeping form. Aidan leaped up, his face pale.

"Relax, Aidan. It's just the noises of the forest. Are there no forests in the human world?" Bran lay back, his hands behind his head.

Aidan sat down, keeping a wary eye on the darkness beyond Gwen. "Not like this one. Not where I'm from."

***

Gwen awoke with a start at first light. The sky was only just starting to grow pink and the forest was dim and cool. The fire was full of ash, grey and cold. Bran and Aidan lay sprawled on either side of the fire in the mouth of the cave, their matching red hair making them look like brothers. Gwen sat up and pulled Bran's sack toward her, fishing out an apple. She crunched it while she worked out the details of her plan. Today was the day they rescued Ellie. Today was the day they *had* to rescue Ellie. Gwen didn't allow herself to think of failure.

Her apple done, she reached into the sack to grab two more and crawled over to Aidan.

"Wake up," she said, shaking Aidan's shoulder gently. He blinked unfocused eyes at her. "We need to get moving. Here's breakfast." She put an apple in his hand and wrapped his fingers around it.

Aidan sat up slowly as Gwen went to wake Bran. Both were yawning and rubbing their eyes as Gwen sat back down and looked at them.

"Okay, here's the plan." Aidan looked confused, and Bran sleepy. "Eat your apples—you'll need your breakfast." They started chewing obediently. "Okay, Bran, you can go visit Isolde's court, right? Now that you've got your mark?"

"Yeah, she won't refuse a son of Faolan." Bran swallowed a bite of apple. "If I'm visiting properly, though, I'll need to bring a gift."

"Hmmm, we'll have to think about that." Gwen mused a moment. "Do you think if I wear a mask, you can pass me off as your date and Isolde won't recognize me?"

"I reckon so," Bran said. "We can change the color of your dress no problem. I could bring Aidan in a mask as well, but the two of you together might cause her to look too closely…" He considered Aidan for a moment. "What if we made you the gift?"

Aidan raised his eyebrow.

"Umm—in what way, might I ask?"

Bran laughed.

"She's always getting new human dancers and musicians. I could say my father sent you as a goodwill gesture. I could say he received you from Landon's court

229

earlier, but knew Isolde appreciated music. That should get us in and welcomed no problem."

"But everyone thinks Aidan is Breenan," Gwen said. "He's never been mistaken as human."

"People see what they want to see," Bran said. "But we can enchant him to exaggerate his human traits. No one's going to look too closely at a human. No one will care."

"But what if they put that binding spell on me too?" Aidan demanded. "Then both Ellie and I will be trapped."

"The spell is designed for humans, I expect, so it should only hold you half as well," Bran said casually. Aidan looked at Gwen, unappeased. "Besides, you have magic. You'll be able to break free, no problem."

"Well," Aidan said, looking nervous but mollified. "If you think it will work."

"Okay, so we all walk in. I'm masked, Aidan's disguised, and Bran is himself. Bran will 'give' Aidan," here Gwen made exaggerated quotation marks with her fingers, "to Isolde, and Bran and I will start dancing close to Ellie. Bran will cut in and dance her away and Aidan and I will follow when we can. We'll all meet in the forest directly outside the castle door when we're done. Then we'll try to find the stone doorway."

Aidan whistled his misgivings but made no comment. Bran grinned.

"Perfect. Aidan, remember to toss a confusion enchantment at your fellow musicians when you leave, so they don't stop you."

"Umm…" Aidan laughed once. "Don't know that one, sorry."

"Oh!" Bran thought for a moment. He reached out and touched Aidan's forehead. "I'll show you. Close your eyes and feel what I do." Gwen watched as Aidan closed his eyes and Bran narrowed his in concentration, looking at her. Gwen was curious, until it clicked.

"Hey! Are you going to use it on me?"

Bran grinned briefly. A woozy feeling passed over Gwen, and her brain felt fuzzy. She could see things in front of her, but nothing made sense. She blinked a few times, then her mind cleared and Bran sat in front of her laughing delightedly.

"Bran!" She tossed her apple core at him. He dodged it, still laughing. "A little warning next time." She stopped. "Where's Aidan?"

"Right here," said a voice in her left ear. She jumped violently and turned toward Aidan's excited face. She swatted his arm.

"Oh, you made me jump." She laughed. "So, the spell works? You get it now?"

"Oh yeah, no problem." Aidan and Bran grinned at each other.

"Good." Gwen leaped to her feet. "Let's get this show on the road."

***

They hiked to the main path and walked until they were just out of sight of the castle doors. Bran cleaned Gwen's dress with magic while Aidan did his own clothes, then Bran set to work on Aidan's face.

"It's just an illusion spell." Bran's voice was soothing as Aidan looked at him warily. "You won't feel

231

a thing."

"Why don't you do it on yourself too?" Aidan asked. "Then we could all just go in without anyone noticing."

"Illusion spells are pretty easy to see through. I'm counting on your status as a human to make sure no one looks too closely. No one would expect a human to have an illusion spell on them because humans don't have magic, so no one would be looking for it." He turned to Gwen. "So how do I make him look more human?"

Gwen chewed her lips and studied Aidan. He made a silly face back.

"Rounder cheeks and chin, larger rounded nose," she said decisively. "Try that for starters. Oh, and brown eyes and brown hair, because she saw Aidan and his red hair yesterday."

Bran cocked his head sideways and stared at Aidan. Gwen watched, fascinated, as Aidan's face melted into a new shape. It was and it wasn't Aidan. He was still there behind the now-brown eyes, but she wouldn't have recognized him if she passed him on the street.

"That's so weird," she breathed.

"Damn, I want to see," Aidan said. He sighed and tucked his flute under his arm. "Ready?"

"Don't forget my dancing spell. And my dress color. And my mask." Gwen fidgeted with her fingers in her nervousness.

"Yes, my lady." Bran looked around in consideration. Then he whistled a short tune and waited, head upturned. Presently an answering whistle sounded in the trees above, and a small bird with striking orange feathers darted out of the branches of the nearest tree. Bran extended his arm and the bird landed on his wrist.

Bran slowly reached toward the bird, hummed a few notes, and plucked out an orange tail feather. The bird flew away with a trill of indignation and Bran held up the feather in triumph.

"Come on, Gwen, let's make this mask," he said.

She looked at him questioningly. He stepped up to face her and laid the feather between her eyes on the bridge of her nose. He stared intently. A tickling sensation crawled across Gwen's face, over her eyebrows and along her cheekbones. Aidan exhaled loudly in amazement. Bran put his hands on her sleeves, and flicked his head. Her dress shimmered with every color at once like iridescence on an oil slick, and settled on a deep autumnal orange to complement the feather. Bran stepped back, satisfied.

"There, all ready. You can take the mask off and on as you like."

Gwen reached up and felt her face. The area around her eyes and over her nose was soft and nubby. She found the edges of the area along her hairline and pried it away from her face. It came away with a pop as if suctioned on. She turned it over to view the front.

Bran had multiplied the orange feather a hundredfold. The feathers spread in a fiery wave from the nose to the edges, overlapping in layers upon layers. Tiny black feathers outlined the eyes. Overall the mask had the look of a wide-eyed phoenix.

"It's gorgeous," Gwen said, holding it back to admire it. She lifted it to her face again and it latched on with a little whoosh of air. She turned to Aidan. "Can you recognize me?"

He gave her a half smile. "You look just like a

233

Breenan."

"Well, I guess that's the idea," Gwen said, unsettled by the thought. "I just need my dance spell, please."

Aidan came over and touched her forehead gently above the mask. Gwen was a little discomposed to look at him, unrecognizable as he was with his new stubby nose and warm brown eyes. She smiled tentatively.

"All ready then?"

He stroked the feathers of her mask gently, his face serious. Then he nodded and they turned to go. Bran offered his arm to her and gestured to Aidan.

"You should walk behind us, as the gift."

Aidan grimaced but fell into place. They rounded the corner as the castle loomed large above them, and mounted the steps to the sound of the orchestra swelling through the door. Gwen's stomach knotted, and as she looked back at Aidan she saw his knuckles whiten on his flute. Only Bran seemed unfazed, striding forward confidently. Gwen breathed out hard through pursed lips. Then she straightened her shoulders, put her chin up, and walked through the door with Bran.

Chapter 18

Gwen's eyes adjusted to the candlelight quickly. She gripped Bran's arm tightly as he looked around. He waved to an older Breenan in a brown suede jacket with green trim. Gwen thought it might be a sort of uniform, because the man moved smoothly over and bowed to Bran.

"Yes, my lord?"

"I wish to greet the queen and present her with a gift. I am Prince Bran, King Faolan's seventh son of the Wintertree realm."

"Certainly, my lord. Follow me and I will announce you."

The man turned swiftly and walked along the perimeter of the ballroom, skirting groups of Breenan dressed in their finest, chattering and holding crystal goblets glittering with a pinky-orange liquid. Gwen was supremely grateful that many of the crowd sported fantastical masks of feathers and beads and fur. Dancers swirled nearby and Gwen was dazzled by the colors and textures of the clothes floating past. She scanned the dancers for Ellie and was relieved to see her blue dress on the far side of the room.

They approached the dais at the edge of the ballroom. Isolde stood in front of her carved wooden seat, scanning the dancers with a worried expression, her hand fingering the locket around her neck. Gwen found herself clenching her jaw at the sight of Isolde and she forced herself to loosen it.

Their guide stepped up to Isolde and murmured quietly to her. She nodded and he slid away. Isolde turned to Bran and Gwen, smiling graciously.

"Welcome, Prince Bran."

Bran patted Gwen's hand and released her arm. He stepped ahead and bowed to Isolde.

"Thank you, Queen Isolde. May I present my cousin Ava? We have both recently come from the marking rites."

Gwen stepped forward and tried her best to curtsey. Isolde nodded.

"You are most welcome." She glanced to the dancers again, as if distracted. Gwen stepped back toward Bran, weak-kneed with relief that Isolde hadn't recognized her. Isolde's hand went to the locket again. Gwen wondered suddenly if Isolde was looking for her in the crowd. She took a half-step behind Bran.

"My lady, may I present you with a gift? My father always values your generous friendship with our kingdom, and now that I am of age I would like to honor

236

that alliance." Bran turned and beckoned Aidan forward. He stepped toward them, wide-eyed but with a determined jaw. "May I present you with a human musician? I know of your delight in novelty and beautiful music. This human is excellent, I assure you. I hope you like it."

Gwen winced inwardly at Bran's choice of pronoun. His speech had gained the queen's undivided attention at last. She fixed her eyes intently on Aidan, who stared back blank-faced.

"This is a fine gift, Prince Bran. Perhaps a demonstration is in order." She raised a hand and made a closing gesture. The orchestra stopped instantly and the dancers paused mid-stride. All eyes fixed on Isolde. Isolde opened her hand to Aidan.

"Come, human. Play me a song I've never heard. Surprise me."

Aidan glanced at Bran, who smiled and nodded encouragingly. He wiped his palms on the legs of his pants, and raised the flute to his lips.

The haunting notes soared up, floating out across the stillness of the ballroom and resonating between pillars. Aidan played a version of a melody he had created the night before. Gwen guessed it was easier to fall back on something known in the stress of the moment. Isolde had her eyes fixed on Aidan, her expression rapturous.

Aidan cut short his performance, perhaps fearing to break the spell his music had cast by playing a sour note. There were a few moments of pure silence, the quiet of a room holding its breath. Then Isolde snapped upright from her unconscious leaning toward Aidan, and made a gesture to the orchestra. The music started once again, and the dancers swirled into motion.

"This is a generous gift indeed, Prince Bran," Isolde said. She kept her eyes fixed on Aidan. A surge of possessiveness hit Gwen, and she bit the inside of her cheek to control herself. Isolde continued, "He will be a fine addition to my orchestra, and later I will have him create new pieces for me."

"I am pleased that you are pleased," Bran said formally. "May Ava and I join your dance? I adore dancing." Only Gwen noticed the twitch in the corner of Bran's mouth that marked the untruth.

"Of course, my dear prince," Isolde said. "It is a pleasure to share my joys with those who appreciate them." She waved them toward the dance floor. "Please, enjoy yourselves."

Bran took Gwen's arm and led her away. Gwen looked back to share a terrified glance with Aidan before he too was led away by the man in the suede uniform. Isolde returned to her post, scanning the crowd.

"Wait," Isolde said suddenly. Gwen and Bran halted and looked back, Gwen's heart pounding. "Have you perchance seen in your travels two young people? The girl has long dark hair and a green velvet dress, and the boy red hair and a black cape. I wish to find them."

"Unfortunately, many match that description," said Bran smoothly as Gwen nervously patted the skirt of her now-orange dress. "If I see a pair that fit, however, I will inform you at once."

"Yes, thank you, Prince Bran. It was just a wild chance." She waved toward the dance floor. "Please, do not let me detain you any further."

They made their escape in a stately manner, Gwen's

palms sweaty and her breathing shallow.

"We made it," Bran murmured in her ear. He grinned at her. "No problem."

"She's looking for us, though." Gwen didn't return Bran's smile, lost in her worries. "Okay, let's get Ellie and get out of here."

"All business, my lady?" Bran suddenly grabbed her around the waist and swung her into the river of dancers swirling in an endless circle in the center of the ballroom.

Gwen was supremely grateful for the dance spell Aidan had concocted as Bran swept her along, turning and bending in formations she never would have anticipated on her own. She spotted Ellie a few couples away.

"There she is," she hissed to Bran, and then her heart dropped. "Dammit, she's dancing with Corann." Sure enough, Corann's arm snaked around Ellie's waist as he steered her around the ballroom. Ellie's eyes were glazed as she ran through the motions, and her elbows drooped.

"Okay, I'll cut in at the next dance," Bran said, and he steered them closer to Ellie and Corann. A half-minute later, the orchestra finished its piece. Bran gave Gwen a quick bow for appearance's sake, and moved to Ellie's side. Gwen made her way to the edge of the dancers but stayed close enough to overhear Bran's conversation.

"May I have this next dance, my lady?" He bowed to Ellie. She gazed at him without curiosity. "I would love to learn some new steps from you."

The music started again. Corann grabbed Ellie's waist.

239

"Sorry, she's taken for this dance. Perhaps another time." He smiled lazily at Bran and moved away, Ellie at his side.

Bran turned to Gwen with a questioning glance, but Gwen hardly saw it. She was already moving toward Ellie and Corann, who were dancing a slow stationary waltz. She touched Corann's arm.

"Excuse me," she said, doing her level best to appear flirtatious. "I couldn't help notice that you're a wonderful dancer. Would I be too bold to cut in?" She rested her hand on Corann's arm, wrapping her fingers around it one by one. He looked down at her hand, then at her, obviously interested. She tilted her head down and looked through her lashes. She felt ridiculous, that her motives were completely transparent, but Corann looked gratified.

"It would be my pleasure, my lady," he said. "Wait over there," he instructed Ellie, who turned without emotion to walk to the milling crowd. Corann placed a hand on Gwen's waist and they began to waltz.

Gwen was terrified. She worried that the dance spell wouldn't hold, or that Bran wouldn't be able to dance Ellie out. What if Corann's instruction to wait had been a magical command? She worried that Aidan wouldn't find his way out of the orchestra. Above all, she worried that she would give herself away to Corann, the only Breenan here aside from Bran and Isolde who knew who she really was.

So far, Corann seemed to suspect nothing. He smiled at her as they waltzed, and Gwen tried to maintain her seductive façade. She felt like an actress, and a terrible one. Her experience at chatting up the opposite sex was limited to watching movies and Ellie. She looked out of the corner of her eye to Bran dancing with Ellie.

"Are you new to court? I don't recognize you," Corann said as they turned.

Gwen thought quickly.

"Maybe, maybe not. What's the joy of a mask if I can't be mysterious?" She rubbed his shoulder with her fingers. He chuckled softly.

"Keep your secrets, then. I only ask to know who to dance with in the future. You are very graceful."

Gwen spotted Bran moving nearer to the door. She needed to keep Corann distracted for a little longer.

"I have many talents. Dancing is only one of them." She said it only to prolong their conversation, but as Corann smiled wickedly she realized the implications of what she'd said and blushed furiously. She bowed her head, grateful for the mask.

Corann laughed.

"I look forward to getting to know you better."

Gwen tried not to shudder. She stole a glance at Bran and Ellie, who were on the edge of the dance floor nearest the open double doors. Bran had just swirled Ellie off the floor and walked her away from the dance when Corann followed her gaze.

"What interests you?" he asked curiously. He spotted Ellie leaving. His face darkened and his brow furrowed in puzzlement.

Gwen tried to distract him.

"Nothing at all. I'm only admiring all the beautiful dresses here today." She was appalled at herself for jeopardizing the plan so foolishly. She tried to continue dancing, but Corann stopped her. He stared at her for a minute then glanced at her shoulder. Horrified, Gwen remembered that her tattoo remained undisguised. Recognition lit Corann's face, and he swiftly ripped away her mask. She tried to turn and run, but Corann's grip on her was unbreakable. He looked past her toward the dais where Isolde stood, and nodded. Then he pulled Gwen without comment toward the front door.

Chapter 19

Isolde waited for them at the door. She stared hard at Gwen without expression.

"Thank you, Corann. I will take it from here."

"Yes, my lady." He bowed and walked away, moving swiftly to Bran and Ellie who watched nervously nearby. He grabbed Ellie and took her to the dance floor again as Ellie's hopeless face burned into Gwen's eyes. She turned back to Isolde, the living portrait of her father's sketch. Isolde continued to stare at Gwen, searching her face.

"Come," she said at last, and turned to walk out the door. Gwen paused with indecision. Her friends were in the castle, trapped. She couldn't leave them. But the enigma of her mother lured her. She sensed that rescue was futile until she had faced her mother.

Isolde turned.

"Come," she repeated. She walked away. Gwen followed.

Isolde floated down the steps of the castle, her long dress of dark blue silk trailing behind. Gwen followed a few paces back. Her heart pounded. What was Isolde doing? What would she say? What was Gwen going to say? Gwen had been hoping for this moment all her life, and now she didn't know what to do. It was all so different from what she had dreamed of, so disastrously wrong from what it should be. She could read nothing of Isolde's intentions from the set of her shoulders or her steady gait. She wondered suddenly if she walked like Isolde.

"Where are we going?" Gwen asked as they rounded the first bend on the path. Isolde said nothing. They passed another bend and Gwen asked again, her annoyance overriding the ever-present fear and growing anger.

This time Isolde stopped and turned.

"To come where we will not risk being overheard," she answered calmly. She looked at Gwen again, lingering on the features of her face. She let her gaze touch on Gwen's tattoo, clearly visible above her dropped neckline. "I assume you have had your mark read to you."

"Yes," Gwen forced out.

"Good. Then we can dispense with the introductions and expressions of shock and surprise." Gwen raised her eyebrows in disbelief. Isolde said, "I am your mother. You are my daughter by the human Alan."

Gwen just stared at her, wondering at her cool detachment. Isolde continued.

"I suppose you have questions for me. I can spare a few minutes, certainly. But first, I must ask—can you do magic?"

Gwen was silent. Isolde gazed at her, then nodded.

"As I suspected. I detected the dancing spell on you, and it did not match your own signature. Someone has placed the spell on you."

"You can tell that?" Gwen was a little astonished. Had it been that obvious?

"I'm rather talented at magic. Most would not have noticed. The spell was crude, but performed well. I expect it was cast by someone unschooled but talented. Perhaps your half-blood friend you've been traveling with? I believe Corann called him Aidan?"

Gwen's jaw clenched. Isolde was too knowledgeable. Gwen's face must have revealed her confusion because Isolde gave a soft laugh.

"I am correct, then. Let me see if I can piece together the rest of the tale. Corann seduced the human girl to bring back to my court to enliven the dancing there. You and the other half-blood followed them through, which you were able to do because of your half-blood status." She looked at Gwen curiously. "This does not surprise you. Perhaps you have already been informed of the great secret? I noticed the flower message in your hair yesterday. I expect you've been consorting with that imp Loniel." She tossed her head in annoyance. "Meddlesome wild man. No matter. Ever since, you've been trying to steal back my new human."

"She's not yours," Gwen spat out through gritted teeth. The more she listened to Isolde, the greater her anger grew. "You can't just kidnap and enslave her for

245

your own purposes. She's a person too, even if she's not Breenan."

"I admire your courage in coming here and facing the perils of this world, and your tenacity in trying to rescue your friend. It leans on the edge of stubbornness, frankly." Isolde looked at Gwen with half-closed eyes, chin tilted. "It reminds me a little of myself." She smiled.

"I am nothing like you," Gwen snarled. She clenched and unclenched her hands, frustrated and angered beyond what she had ever imagined. A small thud jolted her chest, but she ignored it.

"It's true, you are something else altogether," Isolde replied calmly, unfazed by Gwen's outburst. "I expect you've wondered why I had you, and then gave you up." Gwen bit her lips, holding her breath in anticipation. She wanted to rant and rail at this cold, unfeeling woman, but the answers she had been looking for her whole life were about to be unveiled. She now wondered if she really wanted to know.

"I entered your world, seeking a human man, just as my mother had done before me and her mother before her." Isolde answered the question in Gwen's eyes. "No, I am not myself a half-blood, but somewhere in your world lives a brother of mine. The women in our family have each given birth to a half-human for many years, ever since we discovered the secret of Kiera's curse. You have been told of the half-blood loophole?" Gwen nodded. Isolde continued.

"Let me let you in on a little secret. The loophole works when a half-blood touches one of the old portal ways, and focuses their mind on their anchor in the other world. The anchor is generally their parent, someone that ties the half-blood to the world in a tangible way. Once that is achieved, the portal opens and the half-blood may enter. The anchors must be alive for the magic to work. However, so strong is the magic bridge between the two worlds that even a few hairs from a half-blood will suffice to transport anyone between realms, as long as the half-blood's anchors are invoked."

Isolde grasped the locket around her neck and pried it open. Gwen stared dumbfounded. Inside was a miniature painting of Isolde as Gwen knew her from her sketch. She recognized her father's hand. A small curl of hair, as brown-black as Gwen's own, lay on the other side. Isolde carefully moved the lock of hair to her own picture, and exposed a tiny painting of Gwen's father in his youth on the other side.

"So you see," Isolde said, snapping the locket shut, "I needed to have you to be able to travel between our worlds. The magic I create with music and dance is vital for the defense of this realm. Infusions of creativity are needed for continual protection."

Gwen stared at her in disbelief. She shook her head slowly as if to clear it, but nothing made sense. A lock of her hair, in addition to portraits of her parents, somehow created a magical pathway between worlds. Was that the only reason she had been born, to forge a path to collect humans for the Otherworld?

"But—but why?" She swallowed, needing answers, dreading answers. "Why didn't you keep me? Why did you abandon me?" She hated the way her voice sounded, all weak and pathetic. She clenched her jaw and looked away from Isolde.

Isolde sounded surprised.

"I couldn't keep you. It's just not done. No one keeps a human baby, not since Kiera's curse. They're so rare nowadays, anyway." Isolde paused. "I don't think I ever really considered it. You were a half-blood baby, and there was no place for you here."

Gwen closed her eyes in pain. Isolde's tone was so matter of fact. There was no regret tingeing the words, no wish for things to have gone differently, no desire to know Gwen better. Gwen suddenly wished bitterly that she was still in blissful ignorance of her parentage. Surely not knowing was better than knowing this.

Isolde continued, her voice now crisp and efficient.

"You still have no place here, especially without magical abilities. You must understand that I could never acknowledge you or afford you a place in court. You now know how the portals work. I will allow you safe passage through my forest to get to the stone doorway." She pointed to an overgrown side trail Gwen hadn't noticed that branched off the main path. "Do not attempt to rescue your human friend. She is almost spent, in any event, and would not be of much use to you afterward. I believe I will keep your half-blood friend. His music is divine and will prove very useful. He will be under my protection and supervision. Prince Bran, I will deal with separately. But rest assured he will be of no further help to you."

She turned to go, and then looked back at Gwen.

"Goodbye, Gwendolyn. I wish you well."

She turned and walked up the path to the castle.

Gwen stood still as the numb buzzing in her head drowned out the sound of her mother's vanishing footsteps. There was no room in her body for breath, and she wondered distantly how long someone could last without breathing. Her entire body was tight, as if her insides were expanding taut against her skin. Her fingers clenched and unclenched arhythmically.

Ellie was lost to her, soon to be an empty shell or dead. Aidan was in the clutches of Isolde. Bran had his own troubles to attend to and would be no help. The rescue attempt had failed.

On top of that, her dreams of her mother were shattered. The picture in her mind of a smiling, loving mother torn away from her daughter by cruel external forces was extinguished. The cold, dispassionate reality choked her like a rapidly rising river. She was drowning in it.

She was a pent-up ball of tension. Every muscle in her body clenched. Her mind was a whirling maelstrom of emotion. An image of her father's kind and loving face emerged from the chaos, and she suddenly wanted nothing more than to see him, to be wrapped up in a strong warm hug of comfort and love.

Something broke inside. The airtight box where she kept her emotions burst to reveal a gaping hole. All the hurt and betrayal and promise of love lost and hope dashed came pouring out.

She screamed.

Chapter 20

And screamed, and screamed. Eyes closed, she threw back her head as the screams ripped out of her throat. Waves of heat rippled off her, and pulses of what felt like static charge ran through her body. She screamed until the rage drained away and the heat and electricity subsided. She sank down on her knees, gulping in uncontrollable sobs.

She shook with tears, rocking until her breathing quieted. She felt empty but oddly relieved, as if she'd been carrying something and had only just now put it down for a rest.

A branch snapped and fell to the ground with a solid thud.

Gwen opened her eyes. Before her stood the burned-out shell of a forest. She had been standing in a lush grove of poplars with bluebells carpeting the forest floor.

All that was left were the stumps of trees in a twenty foot radius and a delicate snow of ash drifting in the light breeze.

Gwen stared in open-mouthed shock. A round opening was in front of her. It looked like a window to another place. It was a similar sunny green on the other side, but Gwen could sense it was different, other. The edges of the circle of otherness fluttered a little, as if the Breenan world were woven fabric and a hole had been rent in the middle.

Gwen's mind was blank and numb. Slowly the realization of what she saw became clear. This was a portal, a way into the human world. It was a way back home. Through the fog of the aftermath of her breakdown, she found herself contemplating how the portal had been made. She tentatively reached into herself, toward her magical core. Instead of the usual wall of resistance, her imaginary fingers slid straight to the heart of a warm glow in her chest. She gasped aloud at the strange sensation. It was almost viscous, and it swirled around inside, pulsing with energy.

"I did it," she said aloud. The silent forest did not respond. "I found my core." She gave a little laugh of disbelief, more of an exhalation than a show of humor. She reached out and touched the edges of the portal gingerly. The fabric of this world fluttered and swayed against her fingers. She stretched out a hand through the portal. Nothing happened. Taking a breath as if she were diving underwater, and feeling foolish for doing so, she poked her head through.

Before her spread a green field of swaying grass surrounded by hedge rows. Three cows munched quietly, chewing cud without concern for the gaping hole in their midst. To her left lay a quiet country lane bordered by a low stone wall. No cars drove by, but a road sign read:

London, 50 miles

Gwen's bruised heart gave a flutter of hope.

"England," she breathed. She had done it. She had made a portal back to the human world.

She reached down to touch the swaying blades of grass directly below her to make sure they were real. The blades felt coarse and stiff, supremely physical between her fingers. Her face cracked into an inadvertent smile. Just then a pulse emanated from the ragged edges of the portal. She drew her head back into the Otherworld nervously and watched in astonishment as the edges began to weave themselves together. Quicker and quicker they wove as the fissure leading to the human world shrank to a tiny porthole and vanished. The weaving complete, the fabric of air gave a final shiver, then there was nothing.

Gwen put her hand through the place where the portal had been. Empty air greeted her searching fingers, no different from any other spot.

"No," she said with despair, the hope the portal had kindled fading fast. She frowned. "No," she repeated, more defiantly. She had made the first one, why couldn't she do it again? She felt around for her magical core. It was still there in her chest, pulsing with steady heat. A few edges of hardness had crept back as the box remade itself. She swept them away with her imaginary hand. She would no longer be contained by her fears. That was the old Gwen. Her emotions, extended beyond endurance, beyond her capabilities of quelling them, had broken open the barrier to her core. She reveled in its warmth, amazed that she had never let herself feel this before.

Gwen squared her shoulders and held her head up high. She let out a long, slow breath, and reached into her core. She wasn't quite sure what to do next so she thought of her father again, her anchor to the human world, and held out her hand. As she imagined the empty strangeness and torn edges of a portal, she pushed a small piece of her core up through her chest, through the length of her arm, and out her hand.

Her whole arm pulsed and there was a soft ripping sound in the still of the blasted forest. A portal lay just beyond her outstretched fingertips. It was smaller than the last, perhaps the length of her arm in diameter. The same field of grass and cows swayed in the sunlight of the human world. Gwen stared incredulously, gave a delighted smile, and then laughed out loud.

A few seconds later, the portal mended itself and the rent sealed. Gwen tried again, making an even smaller portal by grabbing an even smaller piece of her core. This portal was only a hand span across and Gwen had to press her face to the tear to properly see the other side. It too sealed itself in a few seconds.

Gwen wandered over to a nearby log and let her legs collapse from under her. She stared into space, thinking hard.

"That's it," she said aloud. She bit her lip then laughed in disbelief at her own daring. She would sneak into Isolde's castle and steal away Ellie and Aidan from under Isolde's very nose using portals. No one would see her coming, if she walked to the castle on the human side.

Gwen got up and dusted off her dress, postponing her plan for a few moments while she gathered her courage. She had to make a portal and go through it, allowing the fabric to close behind her. She was fairly sure she could now open portals at will, but what if it worked differently on the other side? What if she got stuck in the human world with Ellie and Aidan stranded in the Otherworld?

To postpone the moment, Gwen took a few steps back along the path around a corner until the castle was in sight. She eyeballed the distance then took a few deep breaths, pushing them out through pursed lips to embolden herself. She had to trust herself, trust in the power she had from belonging to both worlds.

She reached out a hand toward the castle, straight-elbowed, and concentrated on her father. She envisioned him on his painting stool at home, an expression of happy concentration on his face as he dabbed paint on a canvas. She smiled, and pushed a substantial portion of her core out through her hand.

A portal tore open, tall enough for her to walk through. Gwen set her jaw, took one last look behind her at the decimated forest, and left the Otherworld.

The portal closed behind her with a whisper of cloth sliding over cloth. She stood in the bright field of cows with the lane to her left. She closed her eyes, trying to imagine where the path wound in the Otherworld. When she was sure of her direction, she pointed and opened her eyes. Her finger led across the field toward a small stone cottage with a tiled roof and tidy garden.

Gwen picked up her skirts and waded through the grass. She had just reached the lane when a rumble warned her of an approaching car. It had been so many days since she had heard one that she confused it at first for thunder or faraway drums. She cottoned on quickly and stared down at her dress in dismay. She couldn't be seen by anyone here. How would she explain her clothing and why she stood in the middle of a field by herself? She looked around wildly but there was no cover close by. The car's gears ground with a mechanical scraping from behind a nearby hill. She dropped, lying down beside the low stone wall.

The car crested the hill and zoomed past Gwen's hiding spot without slowing. The engine noise faded away and she sighed in relief. She poked her head up to assess. No one else was in sight.

Gwen crossed the road hurriedly, grazing her knee on the rough stone in her haste. She reached a small stand of trees close to the cottage and paused. She needed to check her bearings. What if she lost the path in the Otherworld?

She held out her hand again and hesitated. Now she needed to concentrate on her mother to get back into the Otherworld. Isolde was her anchor there. Anger and resentment started to build in Gwen. This time, instead of suppressing the emotions as she had always done, she let herself feel them. They coursed through her body like a physical thing. Then, to her surprise, the sensations abated. Her magical core burned hotter than ever, unfettered by containing walls. Gwen closed her eyes and remembered the sketch of Isolde that she had cherished for so long, laughing and confident in her

255

youth and beauty. She focused on the version of her mother she had built in her head, but images of Isolde she had seen in the Otherworld crept in beside the static sketch. Isolde's smile of satisfaction as she tightened Ellie's shoes, her worried face as she searched the ballroom for Gwen, her dispassionate expression as she spoke to Gwen in the forest not a half-hour ago. The images melded together in her mind to create a confusing, complex person that was anything but two-dimensional. Gwen took a small handful of her core and brought it out through her arm.

A tiny portal ripped open at face level. Gwen closed her eyes briefly and gave a tremendous sigh of relief. She could get back through. Rescuing Ellie and Aidan was still possible, if she weren't already too late.

She quickly peeked through the portal at the path only a few paces from her opening. The castle was in view through the trees, its dark grey stones contrasting with the warm brown bark of the surrounding forest. She guessed at the distance to the castle wall as the portal mended itself. She looked past the cottage and picked another group of human-world trees that stood in the place of the Otherworld castle. She checked the windows of the cottage, but could see no movement, nor was there a car parked at the gate. Deciding to risk the trespass, she climbed another low stone wall surrounding the cottage and picked her way carefully through the garden, holding her skirts up to avoid breaking flower heads off of plants.

She climbed over the far wall and entered the copse of trees without incident. Quickly she focused on Isolde, drew on her core, and ripped open another peephole portal. This time there were no green bushes or brown trees. The portal opened to nothing but a blank wall of stone.

"What the..." Gwen breathed, perplexed. She wondered suddenly if she were being thwarted by Isolde. Then she laughed at her paranoia.

She was looking at the interior of the stone wall of the castle. She touched the stone, marveling at the smooth slice of granite that had never been exposed since its creation deep in the earth's mantle. She pulled her hand back as the portal wove itself closed, shaking her head with wonder. Then she walked forward one tiny step, just shy of a sturdy birch tree with papery bark peeling off in strips. She took the tiniest piece of her core, focused on Isolde, and made a pinhole portal no wider than her thumb. She pressed her eye to the gap.

The ballroom lay before her. Swirls of bright dresses took over her vision. She tried to look to the right where sunlight spread over parquet tiles of the gleaming floor, but the doorway was outside the scope of her sight. Isolde and Corann were nowhere to be seen. She looked quickly to her left and was astonished and delighted when she spotted Bran lurking in a corner, doing his best to avoid detection. She noted a large pedestal next to him, topped with a bust of a woman with flowing locks and a sleepy expression carved out of pale wood.

Gwen let the portal close and walked five paces to her left, trusting that she guessed the distance correctly. There was a tree in the exact position she had hoped to open a portal in, so she moved to stand immediately to the side. This time she grabbed a substantial chunk of her core in order to tear a portal large enough to climb through. It was a huge risk, but she felt confident that it would be unnoticed in the dim corner behind the statue.

The portal ripped open with its customary swishing noise of sliding fabrics. Gwen looked through to the wall with the pedestal on her right. She carefully stepped through and slid into the space behind the statue. She looked back at the portal as it closed, and cursed inwardly at the pool of light pouring out over the dim floor from the sunny field of the human world. The portal closed, the light growing less by degrees until the corner settled back into dusty dimness.

Gwen let out her breath when she waited a moment and heard no exclamations of confusion or wonder. She peeked her head out from behind the statue. Bran was directly in front of it, arms folded and head darting side to side as if on the lookout.

"Psst," Gwen whispered. "Bran. Back here."

Bran leapt in place and whirled around. His wide eyes quickly crinkled with delight when he saw Gwen. He looked around swiftly. When sure that no one was watching, he squeezed himself in with Gwen behind the pedestal.

"Gwen," he said with equal parts delight and agitation. "What happened? How did you get here?"

"No time to explain fully. The main thing is that I can create portals to the human world whenever and wherever I want. The glories of being a half-blood, I guess."

Bran's face glowed with excitement.

"Truly? You were just now in the human world?"

"Don't get too excited. It was just a field with some cows." Gwen peeked out to look for Isolde. There was

258

no sign of her, nor of Corann. She spotted Ellie's blue dress as she danced in the arms of a man with a fantastical mask of green moss and mushrooms. The orchestra, however, was disturbingly Aidan-free. Gwen's heart lodged itself in her throat. She bit her lip hard in agitation but decided to focus on one problem at a time.

Bran still looked at her with longing eyes and an open mouth.

"I'd love to see cows."

Gwen started to smile with amusement, then her eyes opened wide with the force of her idea.

"Bran, do you think you could dance Ellie over here, and then we could all escape through a portal?"

Bran looked as if presents couldn't come any better than this.

"Really? Really and truly?" He gulped. "If the queen sees me…"

"Well, you're in luck," Gwen said briskly. "Both she and Corann seem to be otherwise engaged." She grabbed his shoulders and pushed him toward the dance floor. "Go on, your cows await."

Bran gave her one last awestruck look, straightened his shirt, and strode confidently to the dance floor. Gwen watched as he deftly maneuvered himself to Ellie and the Breenan in the moss mask. Somehow he cut in, and the moss man left the dance looking disgruntled.

The dance was a more freeform version of a waltz, and Bran easily steered Ellie toward Gwen's corner. They had a tense moment when it appeared that a young Breenan aimed to cut in to dance with Ellie, but Bran quickly twirled Ellie away and the man gave up and retreated. Bran waited until the man had left the area entirely before sweeping Ellie toward Gwen in fluid, graceful movements. Gwen noticed with horror that Ellie's feet were bleeding, leaving glistening marks on the gleaming floor. As the pair danced only paces away, Gwen focused on her father and opened a large portal behind the statue. She leapt through it and seconds later Bran and Ellie tumbled through, the portal whooshing shut behind them.

Ellie dropped to the ground like a puppet whose strings had been cut. Gwen swooped down and grabbed her shoulders.

"Ellie? Ellie!" she said, looking into Ellie's blood-drained face and half-closed eyes. "Ellie! Are you okay? Can you speak to me?"

Ellie's eyes fluttered open. Her eyes remained unfocused for a moment, then she looked at Gwen.

"Oh Gwennie, I'm so sorry."

Gwen exhaled, tears springing to her eyes. Then she carefully enveloped Ellie in an embrace. Ellie's face buried into Gwen's shoulder as Gwen rocked her.

"Don't be silly," Gwen whispered fiercely in Ellie's ear. "None of this is your fault. None of it."

They rocked for a while longer. Gwen released her grip on Ellie and gently laid her down on the grass. Ellie closed her eyes.

"Just rest for a minute, okay?" Ellie nodded without opening her eyes. Gwen turned to Bran.

He stared around in open-mouthed wonderment at the fields and cottage surrounding them. He wore the expression of a child on his first visit to a candy shop.

"I can't believe I'm actually here," he said with awe.

260

"This is incredible. This is like legend come to life." He turned to Gwen, his eyes shining.

Bran's mood was so infectious that Gwen smiled back. Then she frowned.

"I need to go back for Aidan. Can you take care of Ellie while I'm gone?" They both looked at Ellie's immobile form on the ground beside them. "Please, Bran. I know it's a lot to ask, but I'd be so grateful."

Bran grinned at her.

"Are you kidding? You brought me to the human world! This is amazing. I can look after your human for a bit, of course." Gwen gave an exasperated sigh. Bran said quickly, "Sorry, sorry—Ellie."

"Thanks Bran," Gwen said. She sighed again and looked around. "Now, where would Isolde have taken Aidan?"

"That depends on what she wants from him." Bran smiled widely.

Gwen gave him a stern look.

"She wanted him for a spell, I think."

"Well, then you'll want her room of enchantments," Bran replied. "It's through the door behind her dais, I believe. It's specially constructed for magic. You know, circular, wooden walls…"

"Umm, sure," Gwen said. "The usual." She took a deep breath. "Okay, wish me luck."

"Good luck."

***

Gwen passed through the trees, occasionally side-stepping one or climbing over a fallen branch. Bran and

261

Ellie were out of view by the time she exited the stand of birches and clambered over another stone wall. Five paces past the wall she stopped, knee-deep in barley. Feeling foolish, she quickly made a peephole portal and peered through. Brown hair curled elegantly in a fanciful silver wire cage directly before her eyes.

Gwen froze. She hadn't gone far enough. She was looking at the back of an attendee's head. She stepped back and wondered with a certain queasiness what would happen if she opened the portal a few inches farther. She vowed to take a solid five paces before opening another portal.

Her next opening gave her a view into an entirely different room. It was cylindrically shaped with curved wooden panels on every wall. If there were a door, Gwen couldn't spot it. The panels were set closely together and the joins were nearly invisible due to the intricate designs over every inch of the polished oak surface. Dragons sprawled across multiple panels, stretching clawed feet and letting tendrils of smoke twine between small birds, which playfully swooped near sleeping lions and alert roaring lions, which chased panicked deer. More deer grazed peacefully next to rabbits, which burrowed in and out of the surface of the wood. And above all there were vines, endless vines, covering every surface not inhabited by animals, bursting with leaves of every description and delicate flowers that bloomed and blossomed and drooped.

The ceiling continued the menagerie pattern of the walls but the floor depicted only one design—an enormous open daisy, its petals stretching from wall to wall and its center filling the middle of the room. The whole effect was as if Gwen were buried deep in the heart of an oak, or as if she had been sealed in a tree like the wizard Merlin from Arthurian legend. She wondered suddenly how the Otherworld fit into those legends.

Her interest in the room's décor paled next to what was within it. Aidan stood with his flute in the very center of the daisy, facing Gwen and looking very pale. Isolde stood before him, the train of her dress spread out behind her over the carved daisy. The only light came from a yellow flame in Isolde's hand. It accentuated the angles of Aidan's face and washed out his freckles, making him appear strange and somehow older. Gwen noticed suddenly that his face and hair had lost their disguise. Isolde must have stripped off his human features after leaving Gwen. Aidan's shirt was ripped open to expose the mark on his shoulder. His flute hung loosely in his hand.

Isolde started to speak, but the portal was already mending itself. Gwen panicked. She needed to know what Isolde said. She grabbed the tiny pieces of the portal edge and focused fiercely on Isolde, not a difficult proposition with the object of her concentration in front of her. The portal slowed its weaving, then stopped. Gwen kept her hands on the pieces of fabric. She visibly gripped the edges, but they felt like nothing between her fingers.

Gwen listened intently, holding her breath to hear more clearly. Isolde spoke.

"... Declan's son. Well, we don't have to mention this meeting, do we? Not that he knows you exist. He's forever siring children on random women." She reached out to trace a long finger over his tattoo. Aidan

263

shuddered and turned his head away, but stayed in place.

"Why am I here?" His voice was hoarse. "What do you want with me?"

"That's a good question." Isolde started to walk around Aidan, her dress whispering on the daisy petals. "You could be very useful. The combination of your musical skill and your raw magic is a potent one indeed. Not since the days of Kiera have I heard of such a one. Most half-bloods stay in the human realm.

"You are full of possibilities." Isolde stood back and observed him. He stared back at her. She said, "Play me a tune. Let us see how your music resonates in this room, and then I will have a better sense of how to use you."

"Why would I do anything to help you?" Aidan's voice was low and quiet. "Are you going to torture me like you did Ellie, or do I have too much Breenan in me for you to bear to do that?"

Isolde leaned forward and stroked his cheek.

"There will be no torture here. A better question is, why wouldn't you help me? Gwendolyn has left you to go back to the human world, and I have you in my keeping. If you please me, I may grant you your freedom." Aidan glared at her, but said nothing further. Isolde waved expectantly at the flute dangling in Aidan's hand. Aidan sighed and brought the instrument to his lips.

As the first notes drifted hauntingly through the air, low and somber, the fire in Isolde's hand dimmed to a low glow. The notes resonated soft and mellow against the gleaming wood. Gwen looked at a dragon coiled on the ceiling nearby, and could almost swear that the smoke twining from its nostrils swirled gently out. She blinked and looked at the other two. Isolde had her eyes closed in rapturous contentment. Gwen saw her chance.

Gwen stared hard at Isolde and then summoned her core and ripped the door open wider. She stepped over the edge and felt the ridges of the wooden daisy petal under her flimsy shoes. She let the portal close and it wove shut with a swish behind her. Keeping the peephole open had been tiring—she could feel her arms dangling heavy at her sides. She walked silently toward the center of the room. Isolde was turned away, eyes shut. Aidan's eyes were half-closed as he played. The music swelled around Gwen, rich and full. Within two paces of Isolde, Gwen stopped and waited.

Aidan's eyes opened wider to view the effect his music had on Isolde. Then he saw Gwen. His eyes opened fully and his breath stopped. The music died. The last notes lingered for longer than Gwen expected, but they too eventually faded.

Isolde's eyes popped open. "Why did you stop playing?" she demanded of Aidan. Then she looked in the direction of his gaze.

"Hello, Isolde." Gwen's voice was calm and steady. The fires of anger and fear still burned in her belly, but instead of overwhelming her they mingled with her core and gave her strength. She embraced them, and they ceased to control her.

Gwen jerked her head at Aidan, who took four running steps to land at her side.

"Ready?" she whispered, and then looked at Isolde and opened a portal by spreading out her left arm to her side. Aidan gaped as the fabric of the Otherworld ripped open to reveal the field of barley.

"Go on," Gwen urged him. "It's England. I'll be right behind you."

Aidan looked at her briefly for confirmation then climbed through. A second later, the portal started to weave itself closed. Gwen watched it calmly. Aidan's face appeared in the swiftly diminishing hole, looking panicked. She gave him a half-smile as it shut fully with a final ripple.

Gwen turned to face Isolde.

Chapter 21

Isolde's face expressed shock above all. Another emotion danced underneath. As Gwen looked at her mother's face she realized what it was. Isolde was impressed. Gwen gave an inward sigh. Of course. It *would* take a display of magic to gain the admiration of Isolde.

"Gwendolyn." Isolde finally spoke, her voice unsure at first but quickly gaining a mask of confidence. "That was extraordinary magic. I must admit, I have never seen its like."

"I guess that's because you don't know any half-bloods," Gwen replied. Standing in front of Isolde, Gwen's burning anger subsided somewhat. In its place she was surprised by a spark of pity.

"Let me tell you a story," Gwen said, watching Isolde. "Once upon a time there was a little girl without a mother. The little girl couldn't understand why her mother wasn't there. She made up stories to explain her mother's absence. The mother had died tragically, calling out for her daughter at the end. She had amnesia and didn't know who she was. She—" Gwen swallowed. "She had been kidnapped by the faeries, who wouldn't let her leave." Isolde watched Gwen, her face inscrutable. "How else could the little girl explain it? How could her mother leave her?" Gwen closed her eyes briefly. Then she looked back at Isolde. "Then the little girl grew up and learned more about the world and the people in it. She realized that no one could possibly live up to the pedestal she had placed her mother on. She learned to stand on her own two feet, with help from her friends and father.

"And really," Gwen smiled here, a real, genuine smile as she recalled her father, "Now that I understand more, I'm so grateful you left me with Dad. He's the best father I could ever wish for. And I'm glad to be human."

Isolde raised her hand to her chest when Gwen smiled. She wore a look of loss and longing, so foreign to Gwen's vision of Isolde. Gone were the confident beauty of the sketch and the dispassionate queen.

"Your smile—I could see Alan in you." She stared a moment longer then turned away, still clutching her hand to her heart as if it pained her.

Gwen looked at her with curiosity and more than a little wonder.

"You actually loved him, didn't you?" The words surprised her even as she spoke them aloud. Gwen had finally become used to the notion that Isolde was cold and inhuman. Now her views were being shaken once again. Perhaps her mother was capable of genuine feeling.

Isolde nodded slowly, before turning back to Gwen with her face carefully composed.

"Never before nor since have I met anyone quite like him."

"Did you enchant him? To be with you, I mean?" Gwen was starting to see the woman Isolde had been. Still, the question had to be asked.

"No!" Isolde said with heat. Then she gave a self-conscious laugh. "Perhaps it is difficult to believe, but I was once as young and beautiful as you are now. There was no need for enchantment."

"So why did you leave him? Why did you never come back?"

"How could I?" Isolde sounded half exasperated, half sad. "You don't understand. Humans are seen as inferior. I was the crown princess of one of the most powerful realms in the Western Isles. My mother lent me her bridging locket and told me what I needed to do to continue the link to the human world. She had done the same, a few years before I was born. No one but the women in our family knew the truth."

"Didn't they wonder when you started showing in your pregnancy?"

Isolde looked a little puzzled at the question.

"Being with child is no crime. Everyone had guesses as to the father, of course, but paternity is not the important link in this realm."

"Tell me why. Why did you choose my father? Why did you choose Alan?" Gwen still couldn't picture her father ever loving Isolde.

Isolde gazed at Gwen as if evaluating her. After a long moment she looked away and gave a heartfelt sigh at odds with her façade of detachment.

"I came into the human world not knowing what I was looking for, not really. I wandered the green hills, searching for someone who excited me, who might be worthy. What he might look like, I did not know.

"Then one clear day, when the veil of mist and rain had parted briefly to brighten the world, I came across a young man with an easel before him."

Gwen hardly breathed. This was her father's story. She knew it by heart, but to hear it through another's voice was bizarre.

"He was so different from anyone I knew, yet he seemed as familiar as if I had always known him. His chestnut brown hair gleamed in the sunlight, and his eyes were both dreaming and intent. Occasionally he would stick the tip of his tongue out in concentration." Gwen smiled. She knew exactly what Isolde meant.

"I fell in love then and there," Isolde said simply. "Silly, isn't it? I introduced myself and the rest is history. I performed no enchantments over him, save only the ones every woman casts, human or Breenan. I like to think he loved me too, as much as one can after only a week." She shrugged. "I had to leave him. I never truly entertained any other option. It could never be.

"Just as I could never keep you. My own mother ingrained that in me very early on, and all throughout my pregnancy. I never questioned it. How could a half-blood survive here? What would people say? It would have been cruel both to me and to you to keep you here."

270

Gwen gazed at her. She felt very old suddenly, weary.

"You shouldn't care so much what people think. You miss out on a lot of life that way." She sighed. "Trust me, I speak from experience." She thought of the barrier around her core, protecting her from what others might think of her 'strangeness,' taking away her ability to feel deeply and immerse herself in life fully.

They stared at each other, emotion playing beneath Isolde's mask of composure.

"I've always wanted a daughter," Isolde said quietly.

"You've always had one," Gwen replied. Then she added, "I've always longed for my mother."

Isolde's face worked before she collected herself once again. She said haltingly, "I know—I know nothing can give back time. But if there is anything—anything at all…"

Gwen nodded slowly.

"There is one thing." Her eyes travelled down to Isolde's neck. "The locket. I'd like the locket." She brought her eyes back up to Isolde's face to gauge her reaction. Isolde's eyes widened and she instinctively grasped at the locket. Gwen pressed on. "It's mine, anyway. You made the locket with my hair, and my father's paintings, so that anyone possessing the locket could use it to go through a portal doorway. The purpose of the loophole was so children could see their parents. You've never once used it for that purpose. You have given me nothing, ever."

"Save for your life," Isolde said softly.

"For your own agenda? Please excuse me if I don't express my gratitude on bended knee." Gwen held out

271

her hand. She was pleased that it didn't tremble, and that her voice was strong and sure. "This kidnapping of humans has to stop. It's cruel and wrong. I saved my friend, but I can't leave here knowing that you can do the same thing to other innocent people in the future." Gwen kept her hand out.

Isolde stared at Gwen's outstretched palm. She said, "I must give up what is not mine to gain what I've never had." Gwen recognized her words as those in the flower message Loniel had woven into her hair. Isolde's eyes moved up to Gwen's face. "What will I gain?" Her voice was more curious than greedy.

"The knowledge that you're doing the right thing. And the beginnings of respect from your daughter."

Gwen's arm started to ache, but she kept it outstretched. Isolde looked into Gwen's eyes for a long moment. Finally, she reached up behind her neck to unfasten the clasp of the locket. She placed the locket in Gwen's hand, letting the fine gold chain pour into a pile on top. Isolde stared at the locket and swallowed hard.

"Thank you," Gwen said softly, her fingers closing over the metal warmed by Isolde's skin.

"Wait," Isolde said, and she pulled out a tiny dagger that had been concealed beneath the sash around her middle. It was no longer than a finger, the miniature gilded hilt topped with a blue sapphire on the pommel. Isolde pricked her index finger so a drop of blood beaded on the tip. She held it up, and the two of them watched the red sphere balance precariously. Isolde reached out with her other hand and grasped Gwen's wrist that held the locket. She touched the bead of blood to the locket where it left a wet streak on the polished metal.

"The blood of womanhood, the blood of childbirth, and the blood of death. You are a child of my blood, and I give it all to you."

Gwen looked at her curiously, recognizing the words from the marking ceremony, but Isolde just smiled and stepped back. Gwen turned to the side and stretched out her arm, imagining her father. A wide portal opened with a faint ripping noise, clearly audible in the silent wooden room.

"You are a remarkable woman," Isolde said unexpectedly. Gwen turned to her, surprised, as Isolde continued, "I'm glad to have known you, if only for this short time."

Gwen's heart was full to bursting with a mix of so many feelings, she couldn't identify them. She looked at Isolde's emotion-filled face and felt pity, tinged with a faint longing for a life she had never had. Then she thought of her father, and her life in the human world, and Ellie. This woman she had never known, who had given her up without a second thought, who had only conceived her for opening portals—that woman had made her choices, and Gwen was now fiercely glad she had.

She lifted her chin and smiled at Isolde.

"Goodbye, mother," she said finally.

Isolde's breath caught.

"Farewell, my daughter," she said, her face a tableau of loss and regret, touched with pride.

Gwen turned and walked through the portal. It wove itself shut, closing off the Otherworld.

Chapter 22

Gwen blinked in the brilliant sun. The barley tickled her ankles and a fresh breeze brushed by her face, so different from the close wooden room.

"Gwen!" A strangled voice called to her. She shielded her eyes as red hair and a black cape descended on her. She was enveloped in Aidan's arms. He trembled as he hugged her fiercely. She leaned into him and closed her eyes, relaxing for the first time in what felt like forever.

They swayed together on the spot until Gwen recalled Ellie.

"I need to go see if Ellie's okay," she said, pulling herself away from Aidan regretfully. She was tired, so bone-numbingly exhausted. She had no more adrenaline reserves to draw on.

Aidan cupped her chin and cheek in his hand.

"Are you okay? What happened back there?" His eyes, back to their usual green, were concerned. Gwen noted dark circles under his eyes to rival her own.

"Just a touching mother-daughter moment." She pressed her cheek into his hand slightly, enjoying the feel of his skin on hers. "I promise I'll tell you later, when I've processed it a little." She smiled at Aidan, who still looked concerned. "But hey, on the plus side, I got the locket." She held up the locket by its gold chain. Aidan raised his eyebrows and laughed aloud in triumph.

"Wow," he said, and he picked her up and twirled on the spot. Gwen shrieked in surprise and then started laughing uncontrollably. They clung together, Gwen's face wet from tears of laughter or sadness or relief or regret, she didn't know.

"Gwen?" A small voice questioned tentatively. Gwen looked across the barley at Ellie. She was ghostly pale and clung to the nearest tree, but her bare feet were clean and free of wounds. In the nearby shadows Bran stood, grinning.

Gwen had eyes only for Ellie. She ran over to her friend and squeezed her tightly, her gulping laughter turning to sobs as they rocked.

"I thought I'd never get you back," she choked out.

"But you rescued me," Ellie said, wiping her eyes and smiling through her tears. "You did it. Even though you had to confront your mother to do it." She looked carefully at Gwen. "Are you okay?"

Gwen gave a laugh or a sob.

"Yeah, eventually. Just maybe not today."

Ellie gave a watery chuckle.

"I hear ya."

Gwen dried her face on her sleeve, the sleeve of the beautiful gown Ellie had made a lifetime ago. She turned to Bran.

"Bran. Thank you so much. For taking care of Ellie," she waved at Ellie's healed feet, "for everything. You've been an amazing friend."

Bran grinned at her.

"It's been a grand adventure. The best prank ever, I reckon. I've got a winter's worth of stories for my younger cousins." He blew air out of his mouth so his fringe flew up into the air. "I'm going to have to have a good story for my father, though. Maybe you could let me back into my world a little way from the castle? I don't fancy meeting the queen again anytime soon."

"I think she'd be all right," Gwen said slowly. "But that's probably smart. I only wish we knew where we were. In this world, I mean."

"Oh, I do," Aidan piped up. "We're only a mile out of Amberlaine. That way." He pointed into the afternoon sun.

"Can you walk?" Gwen asked Ellie.

Before she could respond, Bran said, "I'll help," and moved quickly to Ellie's side, lifting her arm to his shoulder. Gwen glanced at Aidan who raised an eyebrow. Gwen gave a smile which she quickly suppressed.

They walked through swaying fields of barley and over stiles. Bran was awestruck, especially by the sheep and cows they passed. Gwen let her mind swirl with everything that had happened in the last few days. A thought occurred to her.

"Bran?"

276

"What's up?"

"Do you know why, when I made a portal in the barrow there was a really bright light, but all the other portals I've made since have been dark?" She recalled the blinding power of the barrow light when she and Aidan first entered the Otherworld.

"Huh. Maybe because the barrows are places of power. They've been used for portals for thousands of years, and they probably have a magic of their own."

Gwen nodded as she digested this, and fell back into her thoughts as they continued down the lane.

When the village came into sight, Gwen stopped.

"I feel bad just sending you back like this. Let's get you some food or something. You'll be in the middle of the forest with nothing. You won't even know where you are."

Bran looked at her, amused.

"Crevan's only a day or two away. I'll catch up to them soon enough. And the forest is my home—I know how to fend for myself. Don't worry about me." He carefully disengaged from Ellie's arm and gave her a sweeping bow. "It was a pleasure, my lady." He kissed her hand. Ellie smiled, the first Gwen had seen since this had all began. It transformed her face, and Gwen could see the start of her journey of recovery.

He turned to Aidan, who held out his hand awkwardly. Bran looked at it, bemused.

"Come, cousin. Say farewell to me properly." He put his hand on either side of Aidan's head. "Do the same to me," he instructed. When Aidan had done so, looking puzzled, Bran brought their foreheads together briefly. "There. That's how it's done in our world." Aidan looked unsure, but pleased.

Bran turned to Gwen. "An embrace from my lady?" he said, eyes twinkling. Gwen laughed and threw her arms around him. A brief moment of vertigo momentarily dazed her. She released him.

"Thanks, Bran, for everything. You ready?"

"Back to the real world, I guess," Bran said. Gwen laughed aloud—it sounded so bizarre. She reached out her arm and thought of Isolde. It was less painful, somehow, to think of her. Gwen's core remained barrier-free. A large portal opened into the Otherworld forest, dark and still.

Bran held up a hand in farewell.

"So long, hermits. Until we meet again." He smiled wickedly, his eyes bright. Then he stepped through the portal and it sealed shut behind him. Gwen gave a heartfelt sigh and turned Bran's ring absentmindedly on her finger. They all began walking toward Amberlaine, Ellie leaning on Gwen's arm. As they reached the first cottage Gwen stopped short.

"What's up?" Aidan asked.

"I don't know where the locket went," Gwen said, patting her dress in vain. The truth hit her and she gasped.

"That little sneak!"

"What?"

"Bran took it! When he hugged me goodbye—he used a spell on me, I could feel it." She shook her head, amazed at Bran's gumption. "I was wondering why he was so accepting of returning to the Otherworld right away. He can come back whenever he wants."

She and Aidan stared at each other. Aidan laughed

incredulously.

"Well, nothing we can do now. Hopefully it's in better hands than before."

Ellie swayed beside Gwen.

"Come on, let's get her back."

***

Gwen fought to keep her eyes open. The echoing hall was dim and cool. The only sounds came from her literature professor, whose words were having difficulty permeating Gwen's brain. Beside her, Ellie gazed at the wall with her eyes unfocused. She was still very pale and frail-looking, although food and sleep had done wonders. Gwen tried to focus as the professor continued her lecture. Today they were discussing *Gawain and the Green Knight*, one of the many pre-readings Gwen hadn't completed over their long weekend. She wondered if the professor would accept her excuse—*I was trapped in a parallel universe and forgot my textbooks*. She had her doubts.

"Let's spend one minute before I let you enjoy this fine Tuesday to discuss the figure of the Green Knight. He's the one who tests Sir Gawain to see if he is a worthy knight. His character is very mysterious, and scholars are unclear as to what or who the Green Knight represents. One theory postulates that he symbolizes the Green Man, a mythological figure epitomizing the wild, the forest, nature—a sort of vegetative deity of pre-Christian cultures in Britain. He is often depicted in art as a face surrounded by dense foliage. Perhaps you have seen the excellent carved sign of our village pub. I

279

imagine you've all visited that establishment thoroughly during your time here."

The class tittered. Gwen almost laughed aloud but for a different reason. She'd met the Green Knight. She shook her head, marveling, and wondered if she should have called him 'Sir Loniel.' The title seemed far too civilized for the green man she'd met.

"How are you feeling? Do you have enough energy to go shopping with me?" Gwen asked as they packed up their backpacks at the end of the class.

"What a silly question." Ellie pushed herself upright with a groan. "I'm always ready to go shopping with you." She looked at Gwen. "Anything in particular?"

"Yes," said Gwen definitely. "I want you to choose me some new shirts. Sexy shirts," she added to clarify.

Ellie's eyes widened.

"Who are you and what have you done to Gwen?" she asked. Her face opened up with a crafty smile. "Do we get to burn your boring tees, then?"

Gwen laughed.

"Well, I'll put them in the very bottom of my drawer, at least." She paused. "I have another errand, too, but I won't tell you yet. I don't want you to get too excited in your present state."

"You're full of surprises, young Gwendolyn," Ellie said as they walked to the door. "I think I like the new you."

"I still don't like dancing," Gwen said warningly. "In case you were getting ideas."

"Ugh, don't remind me," Ellie shuddered. "I'm off dancing for good."

***

The phone rang through the speakers of Gwen's laptop as she waited for her father to pick up. She still wasn't sure what to tell him.

"Hello?"

"Hi Dad." Her father's familiar voice made Gwen's throat constrict almost too tightly to speak.

"Hello, love! It's been a while since you called. Having a good time?"

She answered with a small sob.

"I—uh—I met my mother."

Silence on the line, and then, "Oh, Gwennie. Are you all right?"

Another sob escaped her. Her father always asked the important questions. Not how she met her mother, or what happened, but how Gwen herself was doing.

"I'll be fine. I just really miss you. She's not what I expected. Also, she's—I'm—" Gwen searched for the words to tell her father that she was only half human. "Just keep an open mind as I tell you this, but—Isolde is a faerie. Like, from another world. I swear I'm telling you the truth. That's why I had all those crazy accidents as a kid. I'm not—entirely—human."

Her father released a long sigh.

"Is that so?" He didn't sound incredulous, but rather contemplative. "That would explain a few things, wouldn't it? You've got some pretty special abilities, kiddo, and now I guess we know where they came from. And why there was never any record of Isolde."

"You're taking this awfully calmly." Gwen was a little shocked. Acceptance of a parallel world and a half-

281

human daughter were pretty big facts to swallow.

"I had my suspicions. And besides, you and I both know there's a lot in the world we can't explain. First-hand experience, right?" He chuckled.

Ellie appeared in the doorway of their room and mimed pointing at her watch. Gwen waved at her and said, "Yeah, I guess so. Look, I've got to go, but I'll tell you everything when I get home. I'll see you in a couple of days."

"I'll be waiting at the airport."

Gwen swallowed. "Thanks, Dad. I love you."

"Love you too, Gwennie."

***

"I still can't believe it," Ellie said as she and Gwen strolled down the main street of Amberlaine. They had just exited the bus from nearby Cambridge and Gwen wanted to stop by the pub to see Aidan. Ellie had agreed, seemingly happy to do whatever Gwen wanted, but Gwen could see she was tiring. She promised herself to keep it short.

"You can't believe what? That we were trapped in a parallel universe? That I'm not fully human? That my mother tried to kill you?" Gwen shaded her eyes against the setting sun. The street was quiet at this hour with only a few stragglers heading home.

"No. Well, yeah, that too. But I really can't believe the wardrobe change." Ellie brushed her fingers over Gwen's shoulder, the neckline of Gwen's shirt swooping low to expose her tattoo. It snaked by her collarbone and disappeared into the shirt down her back. She'd already

282

received raised eyebrows from an elderly lady at the bus stop, and admiring glances from some younger girls in the shopping mall. It was much more attention than she'd ever been used to. Gwen thought she might like it. Ellie continued, "The clothes and the new 'do. You look amazing."

Gwen, to Ellie's astonishment and delight, had stopped in at a trendy salon in the town center and asked about their craziest hair dye. An hour later she sported a bright stripe of blue amongst her black waves. She kept fingering the lock unconsciously, admiring the brilliant splash of sky.

"Thanks," she said, pushing her hair back over her shoulder to stop herself touching the blue again. "There's the pub." The wooden sign swung in the slight breeze with its carved likeness of the green man staring intently out of a multitude of leaves. Gwen gave the sign a small smile as they ducked through the pub's doors.

The pub was quiet, with only two tables filled and an empty bar. Aidan stood behind the counter listlessly stacking glasses. He glanced up at the sound of the door. His face lit up when he saw Gwen, and then his eyebrows rose as he took in her hair and the flattering top. He grinned when he caught her eyes again. Gwen blushed, but only a little. It was nice to be noticed. She'd spent her whole life staying under the radar and had never realized what she might have been missing.

"You've been busy," he said when they climbed onto bar stools in front of him.

"Yeah," Ellie groaned in relief as she removed the weight from her feet. "Doesn't she look amazing?"

"Yeah, she does," Aidan said, gazing at Gwen. He

shook his head slightly and turned to grab two glasses.

"What'll it be?" he said. "On me, of course."

"Well, in that case—" Gwen smiled teasingly and scanned the taps. "That one."

Aidan raised his eyebrows.

"You seem sure. Do you even know what it tastes like?"

"Nope," she replied brightly. "I'm willing to take the risk."

Ellie laughed.

"That's my girl. My strange, new girl. Nothing for me, thanks Aidan. I think I'll make it an early night."

"So, how did you manage to pacify your boss for your absence?" Gwen asked as Aidan drew her beer. "He must have been wondering where you were."

"Yeah, that's an understatement," Aidan said, placing the full glass in front of Gwen. "He was royally pissed off. I pled family emergency, but I don't think he bought it. I expect I was only kept on because he doesn't have a replacement yet, and he really didn't fancy taking on all the shifts himself."

"I'm sorry, Aidan," Gwen said.

Aidan shrugged. "Nah, it's fine. I was thinking about moving on anyway." He picked up a beer mat and started fiddling with it, not looking at Gwen. "I was thinking of maybe going back to school. For music, I mean." He ripped the mat in half then looked surprised.

"That's great, Aidan! Good for you. You're so talented, it'd be a shame to let you languish in the shadows." Gwen beamed at him. He smiled shyly back.

"I wish I had heard you play," Ellie said with mock-grumpiness. "When you're rich and famous, send me a

284

ticket to your concert, okay?"

"Will do," he said, grinning.

Ellie pushed herself off the counter.

"I'm going to head out. I'm exhausted, and I should pack a little tonight. Here," she waved at Aidan to come around the counter, "Come give me a hug goodbye."

Aidan looked confused as he made his way around the bar to their stools. Ellie stood waiting for him.

"Packing? Are you leaving already?"

"I know, right? It's been a quick month." She gave him a swift, tight hug. He returned it, his face fading from confusion to loss. Ellie pushed back and held his shoulders. "Thanks for saving me, Aidan. Words can't express. And thanks for looking out for Gwen, especially when I couldn't."

"She didn't need a lot of looking after," Aidan said, still looking bewildered. "But, hey, have a—a good trip home. Take care of yourself, okay? Gwen's on her own if you need saving again."

Ellie laughed and punched his shoulder lightly.

"You take care too." To Gwen she said, "I'll see you later, okay?"

Gwen nodded. Aidan waited until the door had swung shut behind Ellie before asking, "You're leaving tomorrow?"

"The day after," Gwen clarified. "But tomorrow night is full of mandatory dinners and meetings and things. I wanted to come tonight to see you. To say goodbye."

She quickly busied herself in her backpack in a futile attempt to lessen the impact of her words. Aidan's body was frozen next to her. She found a pen and scribbled

285

hastily onto a scrap of paper, the force of her pen leaving dints in the soft wood of the counter. She passed him the slip of paper and he took it mechanically, staring at it in a daze as if the meaning of life had been scrawled there.

"There's my phone number and email," she said. "In case you make it out to Vancouver one day. I could show you around. We could go camping."

Aidan was silent for a moment, staring at the paper. Then he said, "And see bears?"

Gwen let out her breath in a half-chuckle, half-sigh.

"Yeah, and go see bears." She hesitated, and then grabbed his hands in each of her own. The scrap of paper crinkled between them. "Look, I want to thank you, for following me into the woods in the first place, for saving me again and again, for believing in me." She swallowed. Aidan looked into her eyes. His were sad, and full of dread for when she would say goodbye. She continued, "I couldn't have got through it without you. So thank you."

She paused, building herself up for what she wanted to say next. Aidan spoke first.

"The thanks go both ways. I'm so glad I met you."

Gwen took a sharp breath and bit her lip.

"I know—I know this has to be goodbye. I live on the other side of the world. But I didn't want to go without telling you something first."

Aidan looked at her, waiting. She let go of his hands and cupped her own around his face.

"This," she whispered, and leaned forward to place her lips on his.

Her core glowed warm as they kissed, and she reveled in it. Aidan's arms wrapped around her waist and back as he returned her kiss with an intensity that frightened and excited her. She let herself float in the embrace for a minute, and then regretfully pulled away. Aidan's eyes were closed and his face woeful. She stood on tiptoe and pulled his head down to lightly kiss his forehead. He opened his eyes to look at her one last time, their startling greenness so familiar now.

"Goodbye," she whispered, and left quickly, picking up her backpack on the way. She didn't look back. She couldn't look back. She knew she would see his woebegone face and forlorn frame drooping beside the counter, and she would dissolve in tears. She wasn't ready to relinquish all control over her emotions, not entirely.

She walked quickly down the road out of Amberlaine, relishing the cool wind and letting it dry the tears making tracks down her face. Stars twinkled overhead, glittering between her wet lashes. She was reminded of her marking ceremony under the very same stars, Aidan beside her. She smiled through her tears. Despite the changes and upheaval in her own life, the stars remained unaffected and unmoved. Her turmoil shrank under their ancient light, and she was oddly comforted by their constancy.

Ellie appeared around a bend, meandering along the road. Gwen caught up.

"There you are," Ellie said as Gwen reached her. "I didn't think you'd be this quick, honestly." She then noticed Gwen's wet cheeks and put her arm around her shoulder. Gwen did the same and they continued up the road linked together.

"You good?" Ellie asked.

Gwen gave one last big sniff then breathed out deeply, letting it all go. It was easier to do after allowing the emotions to take hold for a time. It was less suppression and control, and more of a release.

"Yeah, I'll be good soon."

"Are you still glad you came on this trip?" Ellie asked as they walked together down the road to the castle, the lights at the gate a beacon in the dim.

Gwen laughed, the sound cutting clearly through the gathering twilight.

"Yes. Yes, I am."

Epilogue

Bzzzt.

Gwen dug her phone out of her pocket as she walked down the busy Vancouver street. A text from Aidan waited for her. She smiled broadly as she checked the message.

Decided on a major in music composition and performance, for flute.

Her thumbs hesitated over the keypad, and then tapped out:

There's a good program for that here in Vancouver.

The reply came almost immediately, as if the Atlantic were merely a puddle and the prairies and Rockies were no more than a molehill beside a garden.

I was hoping you'd say that.

Acknowledgements

I am very grateful to a number of wonderful people who helped make this book a reality. First and foremost to my mother, who was the earliest recipient of my writing, and to this day remains my biggest fan. My father needs a special mention for reading to me every single night while I was growing up, building the foundation for my love of reading. My grandparents also gave their support. Judith Powell was full of helpful comments and encouragement. Larry Brooks of storyfix.com evaluated my original story structure. Michele Holmes at Precision Editing Group gave me tremendous insight into my manuscript. Melissa Bowles designed the mesmerizing front cover. And, of course, my husband deserves thanks for his encouragement and patience while I squeezed writing into every available time slot.

About the Author

Emma Shelford grew up in Victoria, BC under the influence of very British grandparents and a fascination with history and magic. She tried living in the big city of Vancouver while she got her doctorate in oceanography, but ended up on a small farm in rural Victoria with her husband where she teaches oceanography and writes fiction.

Made in the USA
Charleston, SC
18 January 2015